PRAYER FLAG

PRAYER FLAG

PETER PRINSLOO

Published by Sunrise Script

PRAYER FLAG

A Sunrise Script book
First published in South Africa 2019

This book is a work of fiction and except in the case of historical fact, any resemblance to actual persons, living or dead, is entirely coincidental.

Sunrise Script
South Africa

Cover design by Deeper Blue www.wearedeeper.blue
ISBN: 978-1-9160819-3-2

To my dearest wife, Gale. Thank you for your encouragement.

1

Early November 1996

Leaning back on the rickety chair, almost to the point of tipping over, Richard Low combed the fingers of both hands through his thick mop of dark hair and let out a heavy sigh. The portly estate lawyer, Philip Kruger, sat on the opposite side of the huge old-fashioned oak desk. He peered at Richard over the top of his rather pretentious tortoiseshell reading glasses, saying nothing.

Richard's eyes flicked to the door. "Is this it then? Just the two of us?"

"Yes, Richard, I'm afraid so," Philip replied. "The late Martin Simmons had no direct heirs. Shall we begin?"

Philip pushed two documents and a neatly folded piece of material across the desk. "For you, Richard, a copy of Martin's will, a letter from Martin and a Japanese prayer flag."

"I don't understand; why the letter and what's the flag all about?"

"I suggest you read the will before the letter and then you'll understand."

As he read the will, Richard's breathing changed markedly, becoming faster, and he started to perspire lightly. Martin's directions concerning the disposal of his ample wealth and Richard's hoped-for involvement were, on the face of them, intriguing and, for the most part, quite extraordinary. Some while later, Richard became filled with different emotions competing feverishly for dominance. He thought it might be surprise or fear or a bit of each but wasn't sure.

For a moment he thought about Martin's deathbed letter and the prayer flag. Although he had a cursory look at the letter, Richard, unsettled by the will and the many thoughts whirling around in his head, didn't feel like unpacking the detail. Instead, he unfolded the flag, gently and cautiously.

"You know, Philip, it's coming back to me; the flag looks like the one I stumbled across in Martin's office some years back. He didn't want to talk about it then, other than to say it came from the Burma Campaign. He appeared distinctly uncomfortable at the time. I guess I'll now find out why."

Philip remained silent. Richard walked to the window at the far end of the exceptionally large office, loosening his tie and fiddling clumsily with his top button. *Why me, for goodness sake why?* He stared out of the window into the distance. His attention wandered away from the will and Martin's wishes and instead focused on the jacaranda blossoms canopying the streets below. The jacarandas were always at their best in early November, with their mauve flowers starkly contrasted against the blue summer skies of the Highveld. He reminisced silently about November being a special time of the year, not only because the blossoms were a vivid reminder of early summer, but also because the Highveld was well into its thunderstorm season. He loved Johannesburg and he loved thunderstorms—most of the time.

The face of reality loomed large as a pall of sadness descended once again. The high-profile funeral occupied his mind, as did the tributes. How could they not?

Poor Martin, Richard thought. *Nobody should have to suffer like he did, and for so long. Seventy-six isn't bad though. He had a good run. And perhaps the protracted illness had been a blessing in its own way, giving him time to put his affairs in order. Most of them, anyway,* Richard thought. *Except these little favours he's left for me.*

Richard let out a long, drawn-out sigh, dabbing the corner of his eyes with a tissue, knowing he would no longer be able to enjoy Martin's mentorship and friendship and knowing Martin and his only family failed to reconcile. He drew some comfort though from the fact that Martin's death brought with it a merciful release.

Suddenly the jacaranda blossoms seemed less attractive. Their colour faded in his eyes, sapping the spectacular beauty of November. The irritating noise of the traffic outside, the oppressive heat and the incessant humming of the inefficient old-fashioned air conditioner began to annoy him.

He lingered at the window and carried on gazing vacantly at the street below, not seeing the people. His thoughts turned again to Martin. He had been fit and resiliently strong, and careful about his health, almost obsessively so. *He seemed so, so immortal, until the cancer took control.*

Richard turned to Philip. "In the last month before his death, I visited Martin frequently and for long periods, and during those times our conversations ranged from the light-hearted to the deeply philosophical and to the sombre. We revelled in moments of relative joy, but there were also moments of darkness. Martin wanted to, and often did, talk about death and suffering. He dwelled on the hereafter, wondering whether it existed at all and if it did, what it meant."

"What a privilege it must have been for you, Richard, to be there for Martin in those last days," commented Philip.

"It was. He wondered whether he would face judgment for things done and for things left undone. He succumbed to intrusions of anger and bitterness with resulting mood swings. I comforted and reassured him as best as I could, and sometimes simply listened. At times introspection and measured reflection took over and whilst I tried to be a pillar of strength for his sake, my own sense of well-being faltered."

"Excuse me for a moment, Richard, I need to pop down the passage. I'll be back shortly."

Richard remained at the window, still reflecting on Martin's passing. Given their special relationship, he shouldn't have been surprised about Martin's letter. They'd first met professionally, when Richard's career was in its infancy and Martin was entering the last quarter of his working life, yet soon became fast, if unlikely, friends. It wasn't long before their relationship deepened, blossoming into something akin to a father and son. Richard absorbed Martin's business and personal wisdom for more than a decade, honoured to give his friend the companionship he seemed to find nowhere else. Richard sometimes wondered whether Martin saw him as a surrogate for his own son Patrick who died at a relatively young age.

As someone said at the funeral, one couldn't think about Martin without appreciating how far his network extended. Throughout South Africa and even beyond its borders he stood out as a respected captain of industry, but for Richard he was a role model, mentor and friend. Richard knew that Martin also treasured their special relationship.

He returned to his chair and flopped down like a rag doll, with an uncomfortable feeling in the pit of his stomach. Philip was back at his desk, his bulbous nose buried deep in a pile of paper and the blunt end of a pencil buried in his right ear. He didn't look up or offer any further comment. Richard took Martin's letter and placed it carefully into the inside pocket of his jacket and then, unhurriedly and deliberately, folded the prayer flag a few times and prepared to leave.

"Goodbye, Philip, I'll be in touch."

Richard made his way out of the building, in a hurry for outside air, and then he walked swiftly across the road and past his law offices, Jacobs, Smuts and Portman Inc. He spent many hours there, a great deal of them with Martin and the other senior executives of the Sangster Group. *What's it all for?* he asked himself, wondering whether in his later years he would regret having become a slave to the relentless and unforgiving demands of his all-consuming practice. *Why even do it?* He carried on walking, somewhat aimlessly now, along the neat tree-lined street. He felt uneasy and disconnected. Those emotions were back again, still vying for top position. Within him lurked a sense of emptiness and futility.

After twenty minutes his mood began to lift despite the heat, and he noticed the traffic noise becoming a drone in the distance.

2

"That bigot deserves to burn in hell after what he did to us. He ruined your life and mine. The swine humiliated us. I refuse to be seen at his funeral." The ranting outburst from Mel, Martin Simmons' daughter-in-law, followed close on the broadcast of his passing on the evening news.

"He's so damn high and mighty that his death makes national news. They obviously don't have a clue of what he was really like?" she said, snatching her son's near empty plate off his lap, leaving him with a surprised look as well as his knife and fork. Mel's considerable clattering and banging of the dishes was interspersed periodically with her tirade. She didn't let up and her shouting escalated into a crescendo. Simon followed his mother into the kitchen, coming up from behind and enveloping her with his arms. She tried to wriggle free, but to no avail.

"Mum, Mum, don't upset yourself, it's in the past, please calm down, you don't want to disturb the neighbours. He hasn't been part of our lives for a long time. You keep bringing him back to haunt us; it achieves nothing other than to upset you. As far as I am concerned, he died and was buried years ago," Simon said in a quiet voice.

It grieved him that Mel wouldn't let go. He let her free herself from him and when she turned around, her face was flushed, her lower lip quivered and her hands tremored.

"It's all well and good for you, Simon, to be so, so ridiculously laid back. That man all but destroyed us. He was the only family we could turn to after your father died, leaving us almost penniless, and after our lives were thrown into turmoil by my divorce from that pathetic weasel of a second husband, and then… and then he goes and destroys everything. All his crawling afterwards, asking for forgiveness, lacked sincerity. Not an ounce of sincerity, I tell you. And you want me to forget about what he did. I'll never forget, and I'll never, never forgive."

Simon tried in vain to interrupt his mother.

"We've scrimped and saved to get by. We've worked our fingers to the bone just to survive and for you to enjoy a varsity education. I say again, may he burn in hell. What have we got? Nothing, not a damn thing and we're sinking deeper into trouble by the day. I'm too scared to answer the phone in case it's another damn creditor demanding payment."

Life had been exceptionally tough for Simon and his mother over the last four years, since the devastating estrangement from Martin. As much as he pretended otherwise, Simon never recovered from the separation. Before then, things were perfect. They were great, and Martin fulfilled the grandfather role wonderfully. Simon could understand the lingering bitterness his mother continued to harbour but knew nothing good could come of this because of its destructive nature. He had let go as best he could in the circumstances, cutting Martin out of his life.

"Have you forgotten all our sacrifices? No holidays, no decent food on the table, a rundown house, poor quality clothes, etcetera, etcetera. Surely you don't need to be reminded of these hardships?"

Mel's voice started to rise again as she became more distraught. The strain had begun to take its toll on her, not only emotionally but also physically, damaging and blunting her many attractive features.

"No, Mum, I don't need reminding, it's pointless remembering. I don't want this as a millstone around my neck. You must forget, Mum; you must move on."

She hurried through to the lounge, roughly adjusting her dress and then her neatly cropped blonde hair on the way. By choice, she kept her hair short because it cost less and was easier to groom.

"Dammit, Simon, how can I forget after all these years of struggle? And now the stupid car has given up the ghost, again."

It became too much for her and the floodgates opened; she broke down and sobbed uncontrollably. It didn't help that her second marriage had been a calamitous failure. She no longer trusted men. Simon dug deep to remain strong, for his mother's sake. His arms folded around her as she cried.

Holding her, his eyes surveyed the lounge and he noticed, as he had done many times before, the threadbare carpet, the tatty furniture, the cracked and chipped picture frames, the shapeless curtains and the walls and ceiling which, as in the rest of the modest house, were grubby and badly in need of a coat of paint. No wonder his mother could take no more. Despite all the hardship though, she managed somehow to keep herself beautiful and presentable. Her natural good looks obviated the need for artificial and expensive enhancements. Simon knew she could, but for the baggage of the last few years, easily find a suitable partner. She dressed well, although simply, she sported a stunning figure and, in normal circumstances, portrayed an engaging personality. If only they could extricate themselves out of this mess they were in, she might be able to see life differently. She was young enough for a fresh start.

Simon knew he had to make some plan. His mother couldn't carry on with the struggle, burning the candle at both ends, trying to supplement her income. She had taken up employment with Mantis Logistics more than fifteen years ago, working herself into the position of senior back-office manager and taking on the serious responsibility of ensuring the smooth running of all its activities. She knew the logistics business well and could quite easily take on a more senior role with better remuneration. His mum needed a lucky break. And if truth be known, so did he.

Simon's second year of his taxing undergraduate studies at the University of the Witwatersrand in Johannesburg (also referred to as Wits) demanded more time than he gave, particularly as he hoped to read for a postgraduate degree in law. He couldn't afford to give up his night jobs as they paid for his fees. Keeping up presented an ongoing challenge. If he could secure decent employment, he would put his studies on hold for the time being. He knew that without a tertiary education the chances of a secure future were remote. More than once he had contemplated working on an inhospitable oil derrick out in some desolate and unwelcoming ocean. He might have to do that, he reasoned to himself.

3

The bold, colourful display of early summer blooms, the potpourri of nature's fragrances and the gentle twittering of the birds came together to make Richard's garden a haven of peace and tranquillity. Two pressing matters demanded his attention. The first involved an urgent review of some complicated clauses in a draft contract from an opponent who was hounding him. He knew from experience that this place offered him the privacy and seclusion he craved at times like this. The other matter concerned the letter from Martin. He ambled lazily across to the ever-inviting bench in his favourite corner where he had so many times before spent hours working through and solving complex matters.

He took Martin's letter out of his shirt pocket and stared for a moment at the folded paper. He muttered, softly, "Poor Martin." Under the relentless November sun, sweat soon slicked Richard's forehead. He shook his head at the piercingly bright orb. *Damn cancer.* Taking off his shirt and folding it neatly over the back of the bench. he covered himself with copious dollops of sun protection cream.

He put the letter to one side and reviewed the clauses in the draft contract. About half an hour later he breathed a sigh of relief and turned his attention to the letter.

My Dear Richard

Please forgive the untidy scrawl; my hand is no longer as steady as it used to be.

By the time you read this letter, I will have boarded my flight from the departure lounge of life and, hopefully, I will have landed in a good place. Thank you for all your support and encouragement and for your willingness to listen to my ramblings. I'm sure they must have been incoherent at times.

We have said our goodbyes and all the good things that needed to be said, and so I will not dwell on these matters.

It's no secret that my estate is substantial; some would say obscenely so. As you know, I came to South Africa in my early twenties after serving in the British armed forces as an infantry lieutenant during the Burma Campaign. South Africa gave me the opportunities I needed to eventually build my business empire and accumulate the substantial estate I leave behind. My earnest wish is that the Trust I have created will be managed with the necessary passion, wisdom and shrewdness to ensure its objectives are met for generations to come. Sadly (very sadly) I no longer have a family for this legacy of mine.

Richard put the letter down and stared into space, shaking his head and grimacing as he contemplated Martin's sadness. Before long the distinctive call of a turtle dove close by brought him back to the letter.

You will know that you have impressed me enormously, not only in the way you handled the legal work for the Sangster Group, but also in all aspects of your life. You have always shown a maturity ahead of your years. Your ethics are beyond reproach and your integrity is of the highest order. You are tough when toughness is called for and you are gentle when gentleness is required. Not only are you passionate about everything you take on, but you are also shrewd. I trust you absolutely. Over and above all this, you have been like a son to me. I sincerely hope you will accept appointment as the lead trustee of my Trust.

As you would have gathered from my will, your remuneration as trustee will be reasonable, although nowhere close to your current earnings. However, your appointment will afford you a wonderful opportunity to embark on those laudable pursuits you so often spoke about, such as helping to address the racial inequities of colonialism and apartheid. You will also have an opportunity to attain new levels of standing and recognition in the business community and possibly to build for yourself, if you so wish, a business portfolio, especially through the black economic empowerment initiatives. Of course, this will not be without the usual risks that come with investing in businesses.

The authority and power given to you in my will are wide and far-reaching and demonstrate the considerable confidence and trust I place in you.

He interrupted his reading to reflect for a moment on Martin's life, some of which he only learnt about in his many conversations with Martin in the last few weeks before his death.

The raucous call of a hadeda ibis as it crash-landed into the giant silver oak tree jerked Richard's attention back to the present and back to the letter. Before resuming his reading, he detoured to the kitchen to fetch a glass of orange juice.

Besides trying to persuade you to give up your law firm interests, to take up the enormous and demanding trustee challenges and, perhaps, to follow your dream of 'giving back', I also want to contextualise some aspects of my Trust.

Let me begin with the prayer flag. There are two areas in my life where I have been heavily burdened with regret and shame, and one of them relates to the prayer flag incident. In recent years the constant memory of this evil darkness in my life has all but driven me to suicide. It has haunted me day and night. The enormity of my disgrace made it impossible for me to seek counsel from anyone, even from you. I have tried repeatedly to put this behind me as one of those things that can and do happen in war, but to no avail.

I desperately want to make amends to the family of the Japanese soldier who owned this flag. I need to confess my guilt and say sorry. You see, I never did kill this man in the ordinary course of battle; I killed a defenceless man in cold blood. Not only did I brutally murder him, but as in victory I claimed the spoils—his prayer flag and his military notebook.

The battle (one of many) in the jungle was all but over. We had overwhelmed the enemy and mop-up operations were underway. I came across this badly wounded soldier, bleeding profusely. His rifle and grenades were lying a safe distance from him. I couldn't control myself and in a moment of inexplicable madness, I ran up to him aggressively, not hiding my intent. He threw up his arms in obvious surrender; his eyes pleaded with me—and at that moment, instead of reaching out to him, I took my bayonet and butchered him. As if that was not enough, I then shot him many times. As far as I know, no one saw me. I don't know whether the soldier's remains were repatriated home or even capable of being repatriated because air support dropped huge payloads in that area after this incident, resulting in many fires.

Please, please, Richard, I want you to trace the family of this soldier and to confess on my behalf. Return the prayer flag to them and tell them I am sorry. Tell them I carried this burden to my grave. Use whatever financial resources you need from my Trust to provide for them so they will never want for anything. This must seem crass but believe me this is not conscience money or an attempt to buy my way out of perdition. No time remains for the easing of my guilt and this is the only practical thing I can do towards making amends.

I expect it will not be easy to find the family just from the prayer flag. I cannot remember what I did with the military notebook. I last saw it about four years ago in my office in the Rosebank building. If you can find this book it will have the name, address and some other personal details of the soldier. I do remember he served in the 55th Infantry Regiment of the 18th Division of the Japanese Army. This battle took place in the first two weeks of March 1943 while my unit, the Chindits third column, swept through the Burmese jungle from Sinlamaung going southeast to blow the railway line between Wuntho and Indaw. The Japanese intercepted us, and various battles took place over many days, with a series of close quarter engagements erupting in the jungle. Despite our strong air support which constantly strafed enemy positions, we were not able to win in the end. The Chindits lost more than eight hundred men.

The tentacles of the long shadows cast by the trees crept eerily into many parts of the garden and the discordant bird chatter subsided; suddenly an ominous uneasiness hung in the air. Richard slumped down on the bench and his hand, holding the letter, flopped down at his side. *Surely this can't be true. There must be some terrible mistake.*

Almost reluctantly, he carried on reading.

The other area of my life where I have been weighed down and overcome with shame is the sad and painful separation from Mel and Simon. You know we had a falling out. The details don't matter. Suffice it to say that this too was my fault and burdens me with deep regret.

Patrick didn't have much when he died and carried little insurance, leaving Mel and Simon poorly off. In the early days, long before I became wealthy, we helped as best as we could. Mel remarried a few years later to an absolute scoundrel and thug. The marriage couldn't possibly survive and eventually they were divorced. Simon had barely turned fifteen and they were on the proverbial bones because Mel had co-signed for that scoundrel's mountain of debt. She's tried her best to service these debts but with little success.

As I look back on my life, I realise I spent too much time and effort in building material wealth and feeding my ego and too little time on family and 'loving my neighbour'. Regrettably, I made too few good deposits at the Bank of Life.

As you know from my will, my preference is that Mel and Simon should not be informed who their benefactor is. Were they ever to find out, they would, I have no doubt, reject the support with contempt, and probably hate me even more. I know I am asking a lot, but I am sure you will find a way to keep this anonymous.

Richard threw his hands in the air, closed his eyes and bit down hard on his bottom lip. *Damn it, Martin, why me? I'm just not ready to take this on! How on earth did you imagine I would be able to keep things secret. Mel and Simon would quickly put two and two together if they suddenly received a large financial windfall.* Martin's naivety surprised him.

Richard snatched up his shirt and stormed off to the kitchen, forcefully slapping flower heads and muttering to himself along the way, as Martin's comments about confidentiality suddenly contextualised his abortion clinic bequest, which comprised a significant portion of the funds earmarked for Mel and Simon if not used for their benefit. *Oh Martin, did you really think I wouldn't see through your strategy—damn disrespectful.* Back in the kitchen he read the last paragraph of the letter.

Richard, nothing further needs to be said about the remaining terms of the will or of the Trust as they are self-explanatory. I am now exhausted. In my frailty it has taken me a long time to write this letter and I have run out of steam and it's time to let go. I hope you will find it within yourself to take on this responsibility. One caution before you decide—this is, as you will have seen from the detail of my will relating to the black economic empowerment objective particularly, a full-time, long-haul assignment.

Goodbye, my young friend, and God bless you.

Richard walked hurriedly through to the lounge, hurling the crumpled letter across the room before collapsing into the couch.

4

Richard refused to allow the Burma incident in isolation to put him off seriously considering Martin's requests. He anticipated that if he became a trustee he would be able to do an enormous amount of good for others, whilst at the same time honouring Martin's last wishes.

Sitting at his desk, about to tackle the demands of the day, Richard removed the prayer flag from his briefcase. He rubbed the silky fabric softly between his thumb and forefinger; it seemed to tangibly represent something extraordinarily special. Although more than half a century old, the flag was still in relatively good condition. He walked over to the shaft of sunlight filtering into his office and held the flag up. As he looked at it against the light he tried to imagine the scene when the loved ones of the soldier gave him the flag. *Were they scared? Did they put on a brave face? Did he shed a tear? Maybe Japanese soldiers didn't cry.*

The wafting aroma of coffee signalled the arrival of his personal assistant, Olivia.

"Morning, I'm not staying," she said, moving quickly to the door after placing the coffee near him.

"Morning, thanks," he grunted perfunctorily without looking up.

Taken in by the captivating pull of the flag, Richard gazed at the lifeless image of the rising sun, its brightness all but gone. Etched around the sun were Japanese characters embedded in the fabric, still clear enough to read. *Who wrote this and why? Was it the soldier or, perhaps, his wife or a lover, a parent or child? What does it say? Is it a love message? Words of encouragement?*

He was intrigued, being conscious of the tragedies of war. Some survived, others did not, and some went missing in action never to be heard of again. *What happened to this soldier?*

"Olivia, Olivia," he called, "please come through."

She responded immediately, concerned about the apparent anxiety in his tone.

"What's up, Richard, how can I help?"

"Look at this flag, Liv, look at the Japanese script. This meant something to someone at some time and perhaps still does. This flag needs to go back home to Japan."

"But how and to whom?" she enquired.

"I don't know yet, Liv, but there is no question, it must go back."

An unusual calmness hung in the air, and at that moment he knew this could be a dramatic and life-changing time for him as he approached forty. *Do I have the wisdom, the courage or the commitment for this?*

A maelstrom of mixed emotions whirled within him and he wished he could share them with someone.

For one reason or another Richard didn't regard any of his many friends as suitable to meet these needs. Even though his parents were wise and good listeners, they weren't steeped in the issues at play. They wouldn't understand. Regrettably he couldn't discuss these matters with anyone in his family.

Introspection wasn't something he experienced often. He couldn't remember when last he felt this way. He started thinking about family life. His own family, like so many others, had drifted apart over the years. The get-togethers became less frequent with the passing of time. The busyness of life took priority. *Perhaps that's what's wrong with this world,* Richard thought. He believed the value system of the extended family unit had all but disappeared.

* * * * *

Except for the gurgling coffee percolator and the occasional fax coming through, the office remained quiet, everyone else having left for the day. The image of Martin killing the soldier had clung to him all day like a gorging leech, robbing Richard of his usual clarity of thought and efficiency. Thankfully the day gave way to evening and, for a while at least, he stilled himself.

The soft illumination of the streetlights filtered through the darkness to meet him at his window. Draining his umpteenth cup of coffee, Richard looked down to the street below and found nothing to hold his attention. The usual late stayers tended to skedaddle earlier than usual at the first sign of an approaching storm. In the distance he could hear rumbling thunder and see streaks of lightning dancing across an angry night sky. The dark, heavily pregnant clouds warned of the fast approaching storm.

Normally he would have joined the rush home to avoid the downpour and the stop-start traffic, but tonight he didn't feel like rushing; he felt sapped of all energy. Instead, he decided to phone his parents; he missed them and wished he could be with them on the farm.

His mum answered. "I hope you weren't already in bed Mum. I know it's quite late."

"Not yet, my son, I'm waiting for Dad. He's playing obstetrician to one of his prize cows that's in labour. What a lovely surprise. I can't remember when you last called. Are you okay?"

"Sorry for the latish call. Sure, I'm okay," he replied with a flatness in his tone. He remained uncharacteristically subdued, hoping in a way that his mother wouldn't interject with some inane remark. She didn't.

"How are you all?" he asked politely.

"All well, thank you, Son, except your young brother hasn't been well. They think it might be malaria. I do wish he would come back to South Africa. Living and working in that poverty-stricken township with no access to decent medical facilities cannot possibly be good for him."

"He's storing up different treasures, Mother, maybe more of us need to be like Tim. I'll give him a call."

"Thanks, Tim will like that."

"Mum, I want to ask you something and I want you to give me an honest answer. Promise you will?"

"Of course I will. Fire away," she responded hesitatingly.

"Do you think I've done right by my fellowman? More and more I'm beginning to feel guilty, like a privileged taker living off the spoils of colonialism and apartheid. I look back and struggle to see where I've made a difference." Richard's mother didn't reply straight away. "Mum, are you there?"

"Wow, that's rather heavy. I'm not sure how to answer. I don't understand what you're driving at. What has happened that makes you ask this? It's most unlike you. You've always been comfortable in your skin."

"Nothing bad has happened; quite the contrary. I've been given a life-changing opportunity to take on a new challenge and it's made me examine myself and my life."

"Don't you think this calls for more than a discussion over the phone? Why don't you come down and we can talk about it properly?"

This is not the direction he wanted the conversation to go. He didn't really want to seek the counsel of his parents on Martin's wishes, and regretted asking the question.

"That's not why I phoned, Mum. I'm far off making any decision. I don't even know why I asked you. I guess it's the 'approaching forty' thing that's made me take stock." *That wasn't very convincing.*

"Richard, I'm hardly unbiased, but do think you've made a big difference? Take for example your contribution to student politics. Your peers thought highly enough of you to elect you as President of NUSAS."

"Yeh, and I landed in jail for that," he said laughingly.

"All for the cause, my son, all for the cause."

During his time at university, and for some years later, he came face to face with the ugly might of the South African security police. Encouraged by iron fist legislation, designed to eradicate the so-called advancing red tide of communism, the security police targeted the left-wing groups—all and anyone who disagreed with the apartheid regime. Universities not in favour of the apartheid government were fair game. Students and campus staff were spied on, many students and others were detained without trial and most of, if not all, the detainees were subjected to some form of torture. Some, like Biko, Aggett and Timol, died in detention. Those were dark depressing days.

Given his high-profile role in student politics, Richard was fortunate to escape with nothing worse than a few short-term detentions, aggressive interrogations, verbal abuse, being spied on and slapped around a few times.

His parents were proud of the stand all their children had taken against apartheid.

"And now you're a junior partner in a good law firm. It won't be long, surely, before you climb up the ladder to senior partner. I think you need a wife,

Richard, who you can talk to about these things and with whom you can share your concerns and moments of anxiety and who can remind you of your achievements. By the way, what's happening on that front? You're not gay, are you?"

Although tempered with a degree of light-heartedness, he suspected the questions were serious.

"Oh, come on, Mum, give me a break. You know my stand against homosexuality. It's just that the right girl hasn't come along yet."

"Richard, you're nearly forty. At this rate your children's friends will think you're their grandfather. You're letting that job consume you, my son. I'm serious."

He sensed the beginnings of a mummy lecture.

"I hear you, Mum, I hear you. Listen, I'm still at the office and there's a massive storm coming in. I must rush. Love to all. And thanks for making me feel better. I love you. Chat soon."

Before he could put down the phone, a blinding flash of lightning turned night momentarily into day. The light had scarcely faded when a tremendous thunderclap struck, hitting Richard like a blow to the chest and rattling the office windows. His head jerked towards the windows in time to catch the first sheets of torrential rain striking the glass. The rattling was so severe that Richard thought the windows would crack. With the relentless pelting rain, he wasn't going anywhere soon.

No more coffee for me, he admonished himself. *Enough is enough.* He thought about his conversation with his mother and knew the two of them were kidding themselves. He enjoyed all the ample and far-reaching benefits of a privileged upbringing, whilst millions of others suffered, and would continue to suffer, the dehumanising impact of South Africa's sad, sick history. *What have I done and what sacrifices have I made towards changing things for the good? Nothing, I am ashamed to admit, absolutely nothing.* The soft, ample cushions seemed to envelope him as he stretched out on the couch—the one everyone in the office thought grotesque, maybe because it was disproportionately large or its mustard yellow fabric. Richard liked it and tonight it felt cosy and particularly special. He closed his eyes and let his mind drift.

The driving rain lashed harder and harder, smacking against the windows with alarming force. Neither the thunder nor the lightning let up. *It won't be long now,* he figured, *before the lights go out*. He eased off the couch and dragged himself to the kitchen to ferret around for something to eat. The challenges of the day had deprived him of sustenance. If truth be known, he hadn't felt like eating, but now the hunger pangs left him in no doubt.

Grateful for the find of stale crackers and a bottle of still water, Richard made his way back to his office. Periodically he stopped to admire a painting or to look into someone's office. Even though he had not yet broken into the senior partner ranks, he felt enormously proud of his achievements and hoped for promotion soon. He harboured no regrets about choosing a specialist mergers and acquisitions boutique practice over the large firm where he had served his articles.

The predictable happened and suddenly darkness engulfed him. Whilst the storm seemed to be subsiding, there was still enough lightning for him to locate the torch he kept for times like this.

But for the water, he would, in all likelihood, have choked on the mouthful of dry crackers, their staleness not bothering him. He smiled, acknowledging that right then almost anything edible, no matter how unpalatable in other circumstances, would be most welcome.

Nearly an hour slipped by before the thunder and lightning abated. He decided to wait a while longer, hoping the rain would ease. He returned to the couch, lay in the darkness and once again journeyed back to the past. There hadn't been much time for serious romantic relationships, but not because of any lack of interest from others. He was all too aware though, as his dear mother reminded him less than an hour ago, of his age and single status and the consuming nature of his practice.

5

Mid November 1996

Flight 582 cut smoothly through the sky, carrying Richard towards George. Like sentinels at their watch, not moving but quietly observing, the Outeniqua Mountains stood guard on the outskirts of the town. He stared in awe, as he done many times before, at their majesty and splendour. The eastern slopes glistened in the warm morning sun and by contrast the rest of the range slumbered in the dark purple hue of the shadows. The cloudless sky canopied his world in a soothing shade of blue. Richard could never tell whether the colour of the sky around George was either inherently unique or it just seemed so because of the overwhelming beauty of the place.

The plane banked sharply to the left in preparation for landing, treating Richard and the other starboard passengers to an uninterrupted southern view. No more than a few kilometres away, wide, sandy beaches stretched as far as the eye could see to the east and west, parallel to the deep blue waters of the Indian

Ocean. The contrasting colours and shapes of the fields and pastures sandwiched between the ocean and the city gave the surrounding farmland the appearance of a giant patchwork quilt.

He stepped out of the plane, tilted his head back slightly, focusing on the mountains ahead, and sucked in a deep breath of fresh coastal and mountain air.

"Hey, you, young man," screeched a high-pitched voice, as he felt a poke in his ribs from behind. He turned quickly and noticed a middle-aged woman dressed in a revealingly short skirt and a see-through blouse with plunging neckline. Her heavy parrot blue eyeshadow, black grainy mascara and caked, blood red lipstick dominated Richard's private space. Before he could ask what she was on about, she screeched again, trying at the same time to retain her balance on glittering stiletto heels. "You need to be more careful, you silly fool, you bumped me with your backpack nearly making me fall."

"I do apologise, I'll be more careful next time," he replied in a neutral tone.

She responded with a spitting cobra stare, screeching for the third time, "You had better be, I don't know why they allow backpacks on a plane."

It took a concerted effort on Richard's part not to burst out laughing when her bottle blonde coiffed hairdo started collapsing like an imploded soufflé.

He sorely needed the time at his friend's holiday home. Some serious thinking lay ahead. Should he follow through on the trustee appointment or should he carry on practising law? The ongoing nature of the objectives of Martin's trust, particularly with reference to black economic empowerment and the combating of bigotry and prejudice, were long-term goals, making it impractical for Richard to do both.

Feelings of excitement and trepidation had taken hold of his emotions when he boarded the first flight to George that morning. Although enthusiastic about the trip and the chance to avoid clients and their problems for a while, he remained anxious about the looming decision he had to make.

The fifty-minute car journey to Knysna snaked its way through the spectacular Kaaimans Pass and into the heart of the Garden Route—a place of exquisite beauty, showcasing a rare combination of mountains, millennia-old sand dunes covered in coastal vegetation, sandy beaches, pristine lakes ranging from turquoise to azure, and densely wooded forests.

Margaret's Viewpoint came into view as he rounded the bend. He pulled over and alighted from the car. His eyes swept across the Knysna Lagoon, back and forth, taking it all in. From where he stood, the town of Knysna snuggled like a large village between the far side of the estuary and some hills to the north and east of the town.

Immediately beneath him, stretching to the water's edge, rested the immaculately laid out suburb of Belvidere; to its right lay the picturesque and sought-after residential areas of Lake Brenton, Thesen Isle and Leisure Isle. *There can't be many better views than this,* he thought, as he walked hurriedly back to the car, keen to reach the house.

As he approached the entrance of the private eco reserve in which his friend's family home nestled, the strong, salty sea smell of the ocean playfully tickled his nostrils. The architecture of the comfortable home, perched on the edge of a cliff overlooking the sea, captured the tranquillity and privacy of the reserve, without compromising or shutting out the vastness and essence of the ocean.

There was a powerful temptation to succumb to the many leisure activities on offer from the moment of Richard's arrival. He relished the thought of tackling the surf, casting a line for the wily game fish, trying to conquer the challenges of the many golf courses, hiking the diverse surrounding trails and, of course, sleeping, eating and drinking (not for sustenance only, but also to socialise). But necessity demanded he resist, and resist he did by drawing heavily on his strong self-discipline. He filled the days by working through the potentially life-changing decision at hand.

Although the pressure mounted, he managed to keep his stress in check with long evening strolls on the beach and sunrise meditations on the shoreline.

His career so far had been both challenging and rewarding, and the road ahead, if he continued with his law practice, screamed exciting prospects—senior partnership in the short-term, more money, high-profile cases and deals, prestige and a financial foundation to support an enviable lifestyle in his later years.

Anxiety stepped aside for nostalgia; somehow it seemed the perfect evening for that. He poured a glass of red wine and drank a toast to creation, lifting his glass in a salute to the red ball of warmth hovering low over the western horizon. The sea had turned a rich golden crimson as it reflected the shimmering radiance of the setting sun. Richard positioned himself in the south-western corner of the balcony and, leaning against a pillar and sipping his wine, looked out in wonderment, waiting for the sun to lay down its head for the night.

He indulged himself with visits to the past. He didn't have any significant regrets except for the one that gnawed at him constantly. *I've been a taker my whole life, riding the fortunes of a privileged white minority at the expense of others*. His guilt had grown exponentially as he grew older and more successful. His inner voice became louder, at times shouting at him to do something different, to help others and to give back. He began thinking about some of his cases and deals, finding it unsettling to dwell on the guilt.

His reminiscing about the many special moments in his career didn't last long; anxiety fought back as thoughts around the pending decision flooded in. Could he give up these things? *I'm not sure I can, they are who I am, my identity and my security blanket.*

He needed no reminding that his job wasn't all about exciting deals and interesting cases. Unreasonable client demands, fourteen-hour days, multimillion-rand transactions and a heavily regulated business environment made life stressful. On top of this, a large chunk of his working week concerned the humdrum of non-client activities, necessary in the administration and operation of a law firm. *Is this the lifestyle I crave for myself and my future wife and children? Can I give it up?* He had been at it for fifteen years. It left little time for other things. Soon the pace of life's treadmill would be too fast to jump off.

The sun dipped below the horizon, leaving behind its comforting warmth to permeate the balmy evening. He eased across to the barbecue and tested the glowing coals—just right. Soon a generous piece of rump steak sizzled tantalisingly as it seared, sealing in the goodness.

Throughout supper, his thoughts dwelled on his love life or, more accurately, the lack of it. He thought about Karin, his one and only serious love. He blamed his work for their failed relationship. She couldn't take it anymore, the late nights, the working weekends and the after-hours interruptions. Their arguments were mostly about work. She wouldn't, or couldn't, understand that this came with the territory. She branded him weak when it came to his clients; forever admonishing him because he wouldn't take a tougher line with them. She couldn't understand why he had not learnt to say "no" sometimes. *Oh, how little she knew about the cut-throat world out there.*

Despite Richard's hopes of marrying Karin, it was not to be. *Five years down the drain.*

He flirted with a few fleeting relationships since then; nothing serious. Either work got in the way of the relationships or the relationships got in the way of work. *Maybe if I could unshackle myself from the burdens of the law practice I might be able to enjoy a meaningful relationship, and perhaps start a family of my own.* Again, he thought about his age and the fact that most of his friends were already married.

He had no illusions about the responsibilities towards Martin's trust and the workload and pressure it would entail, but it could never, he reasoned, be as relentless and as driven as his clients. If he could learn to delegate and not succumb to everyday operational demands, he believed his life could change dramatically for the good. He realised though that he would have to be hands-on to fulfil the requirements of the will, particularly when it came to the prayer flag and meeting Martin's wishes towards Mel and Simon; he made that clear enough. *But this will be different, the objectives are magnanimous, and this is a golden opportunity to give back.*

As he once again traversed the pros and cons of his options, his heart beat faster and harder. Before long he could feel it pounding in his throat. His mouth became dry and then the butterflies invaded his stomach; first in their tens and then their hundreds.

Just imagine, he thought, *I've been given an opportunity of a lifetime. Enrich a family that will not want to be enriched if they know the identity of their benefactor (and possibly help to heal a deep rift), trace the family of an unknown Japanese soldier and provide financially for them (who will probably be too proud and/or bitter to accept charity), seek forgiveness for Martin, initiate and implement a green fields black economic empowerment program, and devise and put in place practical structures designed to combat bigotry and prejudice. What a challenge. What mountains to climb. That will be giving back. What the hell do I do? I'm so well positioned where I am; maybe I should heed the old cliché of sticking to the knitting.*

Suddenly he felt the urge to clear his head. *A few beers and some good company will do just fine.* He knew just the place.

The dulcet sounds of the laid-back music drifting towards him from Crabs Creek on the shoreline of Knysna Lagoon welcomed him into the convivial atmosphere. The eclectic crowd spilled out of the pub onto the grassy area rolling down to the water's edge. Richard undid a couple of shirt buttons and brushed his hair with his fingers as he watched the partying crowd. He squeezed himself in at the bar, ordered a cold lager and engaged the smiling man standing next to him.

"Hi, I'm Richard, are you from these parts?"

"Hi, I'm Tim, and yes, I live here—used to be in Cape Town and moved here about three years ago to start an outdoor adventure business."

"That's also my brother's name, so I won't forget it."

After a few beers and more than an hour later, Richard knew all about Tim and his business and that, after a near-death experience, Tim escaped the world of structured finance to live out his passion.

"Hey, Richard, I've been selfishly spouting forth about myself, how about you? Where do you live and what are you doing in Knysna?"

"You haven't been selfish, Tim. I've enjoyed hearing about your life and how you plucked up the courage to break out of the mainstream. It's fortuitous because right now I am at a similar crossroads and feeling extremely nervous about making a life-changing switch."

"I'm a great listener and in no rush to go anywhere. Those people over there are leaving, let's grab their table."

Over a few more cold beers and some greasy but tasty pub grub, Richard unpacked his crossroads.

"So, Tim, that's my choice—stay in the secure comfort zone of my law career, which promises much for the future, or venture into something dramatically different, and along the way try to fulfil the dying wishes of my dear friend and mentor and make a difference in our country."

After a protracted silence, Tim asked, "Can't you do both, even if it means taking time out of your practice? I ask because listening to you and watching you, I think you are still captured by a burning passion for your job, despite the negatives, and I think you'll struggle to make the break. I only took my plunge after losing the passion for structured finance."

"I haven't given you all the detail about the trustee responsibilities, Tim. It will be a full-time job for years to come. It would be impossible to conduct any sort of legal practice, even a drastically watered down one, and still discharge the trustee responsibilities."

"Tell me a bit more about Martin; he sounds like an interesting guy."

"A greater mentor and friend you'll not find. He achieved so much in his life. Shortly after coming to South Africa from Britain as a young man he joined one of the large industrial companies and soon started to climb the corporate ladder. His employer rewarded his diligence, commitment and business nous by sending him to Harvard to do an MBA. Some years later he led a management buyout of some of the divisions of this company. Under his leadership, the new Sangster Group (so named in honour of his wife Emily, who was a Sangster) proved to be an enormous success and, in the course of time, Martin's empire successfully listed on the Johannesburg Stock Exchange. For several years before his death, and at the time of his passing, Martin served as chairman. Its growth had been phenomenal—something for which my firm is grateful. We benefitted in many ways as its corporate legal adviser."

"Why are you thinking of taking this on, Richard?"

"My heart tells me to, and I owe it to my friend and mentor. I am worried though about this being an 'all or nothing' appointment because there's no turning back if I accept, it wouldn't be right. Look, Tim, it's not only about fulfilling Martin's deathbed wishes, but also about escaping relentless client demands and being at their beck and call twenty-four hours a day, seven days a week. And on top of this, also hugely important, it's about seizing the opportunity to make a difference, to give back, to contribute towards trying to fix a bit of the inhumane devastation and plundering inflicted on the indigenous people of this country, first by its colonial masters, and then by the perpetrators of apartheid."

"Do you truly believe colonisation was that bad?" asked Tim, seemingly surprised.

"Whoa, Tim, surely you share that view? It was a wicked strategy devised and perpetuated by strong nations aiming to build empires, by ruthlessly stealing more and more from the vulnerable, regardless of the consequences."

"But you can't deny that considerable good also came out of colonisation."

"Listen, Tim, this is a heavy topic and I am more than a little drunk, so I think we should leave things there. You've been very kind to listen to my woes and I have enjoyed your company, but now I need to excuse myself to say hello to someone I think I know. Here's my card, give me a call if you ever need a business lawyer, assuming I haven't given up practice."

Richard manoeuvred himself slowly across the room, holding on to chairs and tables to steady himself. He approached a sensually attractive redhead who had locked eyes with him earlier. Although with a group of people, she seemed more interested in Richard. He winked and she smiled as he headed in her general direction. On reaching them, Richard brushed gently against her. "I'm so sorry," he said mischievously, and then continued on to the grassy bank outside. A few minutes later she drew alongside. "Are you really sorry?" she asked in a polished voice.

"No, not really, how did you guess?" he replied with a charming smile.

* * * * *

Richard sat bolt upright, looking around frantically trying to find the source of the noise which, for a moment, he couldn't identify. He hurriedly squinted at the bedside clock, conscious of a foul taste in his parched mouth, and then scanned the dark room, trying to orientate himself.

"What the hell, I've hardly slept. Damn it, what's that incessant ringing?" he shouted into the dark at nobody.

Then it dawned on him, it was his phone. He almost fell out of bed, still shaky on his legs, searching, first on the bedside tables then the dresser and eventually in the bathroom. He grabbed the ringing phone off the toilet cistern.

"Hello, hello, who is this, do you know it's four o'clock in the morning?" he grumbled in a raspy voice.

"Richard, Richard, it's Dad."

"What's wrong, Dad? You sound terribly stressed, why are you calling at this hour? Please tell me everything's okay," Richard, now wide awake, replied with a clipped cadence.

"Richard, my son, I'm afraid it's terrible news, Tim passed away about an hour ago."

"What, our Tim, my brother Tim?" he replied, not wanting to believe his ears.

"Yes, Richard, our Tim, all of us are shocked and devastated."

Richard didn't respond. His dad waited without cutting into the painful silence.

After what seemed like minutes, Richard spoke again, not masking his brokenness. "Where and how, Dad? He was so young."

"I know, we are at a loss, we just cannot fathom this. We've been told by a doctor at Maputo Hospital that Tim died as a result of malaria. That's as much as we know."

* * * * *

Richard and his parents and sister, guided gently by Santiago, one of Tim's Mozambican friends, walked slowly arm in arm up the dusty gravel road leading into Maputo's main cemetery. They stopped in front of the modest, weather-beaten chapel. The white hearse parked to the side and gleamed in the sun. No one spoke, each holding on to their respective emotions.

A throng of more than 300 mourners followed quietly in their footsteps, coming to pay their respects to their dear, beloved Tim. Most of them were dirt poor who had walked vast distances to bid a final goodbye to their friend, mentor and teacher.

Santiago shepherded the family to the head of the simple coffin that rested on a white embroidered tablecloth that was drawn over a naked brick and mortar platform in the middle of the one-room chapel, immediately below the equally cold cement altar. A melodic harmony permeated the air as the crowd began singing in true African tradition. Despite trying to remain strong for his broken family, Richard lost control of his emotions and soon his quiet weeping gave way to a racking sob. Some of the crowd edged in around him, with one or two patting him softly on his back. An old lady shuffled even closer, taking his hand.

"I did not know Tim," said the visiting priest, "and so I will confine myself to a scripture reading, the prayers and the graveside committal. The eulogist assures me that the scripture selected by some of you is entirely appropriate. The reading is from Matthew Chapter 22, verses 37 to 39.

'Love the Lord your God with all your heart and with all your soul and with all your mind. This is the first and greatest commandment, And the second is like it; Love your neighbour as yourself.'

"I now call on Tim's close friend, Santiago, to honour Tim on behalf of us all."

Except for the sniffing and gentle weeping, a hush descended over the crowd as Santiago began to speak in English, using an interpreter to translate into Portuguese for the benefit of the mourners.

"And the second is like it; Love your neighbour as yourself," he said in a rich, measured tone. He paused, repeated the quote and then continued. "Tim loved his neighbour, he loved us all, more than himself, much, much more."

The touching, warm-hearted eulogy, punctuated frequently with murmuring approvals from the crowd, praised Tim for his caring and loving attributes and his countless selfless efforts in uplifting the poor and the marginalised. After the final blessing, Santiago led the family from the chapel, following the pallbearers as they awkwardly wound their way amongst the numerous graves and broken headstones to Tim's final resting place. The entire crowd joined the procession, once again taking up voice in sweet harmony.

Standing at the edge of the covered grave, close to his parents and sister, Richard watched with awe as members of the crowd approached one by one, planting, instead of laying, beautiful wild flowers on the mound until the brown ugliness of the recently turned soil surrendered to a glorious blanket of vibrant colours.

He shuffled closer to the colourful display and quietly whispered a final prayer for Tim. Then, speaking to himself, he said, "That's it, my mind is made up."

6

Early January 1997

From the newly refurbished offices in the Sandton City Office Towers, Richard's panoramic view covered downtown Johannesburg and most of its surrounding areas, including some of the more prestigious northern suburbs.

The contrast between the affluence of these wealthy suburbs and the abject poverty of the deprived sprawling black township of Alexandra, a few kilometres to the north-east, screamed volumes about the depraved history of the country. More than a million black people had been forced to live in there (just as millions of others had been banished to other less desirable places set aside for black people) because, so the old regime preached, that's what God had intended when he created the different races. Richard wondered whether this same regime thought it was the divine right of white people to reserve to themselves a decent education, all the wealth, all the good fortune, all the decent jobs and, of course, all the cheap migrant labour.

There will come a day, he believed, when those responsible would be held accountable for this gross violation of humanity. No black person could ever be expected to forget the injustices of the past. Richard wondered how it would all play out one day. *Will there be a redistribution of assets and wealth? How will this be achieved? Will we see affirmative action? Will there be benefits for all the people or only for a new black middle class?* He thought about those white people who had nothing to do with apartheid and who, for one reason or another, could not change things. *How will they be treated? Will the sins of their fathers be visited on them?* His guilt returned. *What did I do to make a difference or was I happy to be a hanger-on and a privileged beneficiary?*

The right to vote had been won and the law now protected the rights of every individual, in theory at least, but subject to a correction of certain past inequalities. The way forward for the new so-called rainbow nation would be challenging; they simply had to find a way to give meaningful effect to their new-found freedom.

The offices of Candlewood Investments (the neutral name adopted by the trustees for Martin's Trust) were tastefully designed, furnished and decorated. They made a statement—a statement of success, strength and intent to do business. Richard, as the lead trustee, intended for Candlewood Investments to be taken seriously in the South African business community. It had to be if it wanted to promote and sponsor black economic empowerment in a powerful and tangible way.

He recalled his many conversations with Martin. The release of Nelson Mandela a few years earlier and the recent birth of South Africa's democracy triggered Martin's commitment to black economic empowerment. Martin had hoped that the economic empowerment of those millions of people who were deprived, suppressed and robbed by the apartheid system and, before then, by colonial plundering, would sooner rather than later become a reality. Richard shared the hope that there would be a restoration of their dignity and the acknowledgement of them as equals.

Martin had demonstrated considerable passion for the levelling of the playing fields and embraced Richard as an ally in this endeavour. Both knew that huge challenges lay ahead; the transition wasn't going to be easy. It would take wisdom, tolerance, patience and enormous goodwill. The pendulum of freedom would inevitably swing too far the other way and would, hopefully, over the course of time return to find the level that all good democracies strive for.

The trust's reserves gave it the necessary financial clout. For the first time in his life, bankers and others clamoured to do business with Richard. His withdrawal from his firm some six weeks earlier came as a shock to the other partners, but they soon realised this presented a wonderful new opportunity, not only for Richard, but also for the firm.

The trustees had soon taken up their appointments; Richard was appointed as chief executive officer. Under his operational guidance, the Sandton City offices had been established, support staff had been engaged and all the necessary administrative and infrastructural matters had been attended to. Candlewood Investments was open for business.

Some matters needed urgent attention. The trust had to channel some cash flow to Mel and Simon on a regular basis, as soon as possible. Richard's discreet enquiries confirmed what Martin had told him about their parlous financial circumstances.

The search for the Japanese soldier's military notebook was also a high priority. Without it, the task of tracing his family would, so it seemed to Richard, be most problematic, if not impossible.

Olivia, Richard's PA for more than ten years, joined him in his office for an inaugural briefing.

"Liv, once again, thank you for making this move with me; I derive considerable comfort from the fact that my PA from day one here at Candlewood Investments is someone I trust and respect and who knows me well. It also helps that you are already up to speed on what this is all about."

"Thank you, Richard, that means a lot to me, and thank you also for inviting me to share in this new initiative. I'm sure that exciting and indeed challenging times lie ahead. I'll do my best to support you and Candlewood."

"Great, now let's start working. Please could you set up one-hour meetings for me at the earliest possible dates with Professor Markowitz and John Matthews and try to ascertain the contact details for Martin's former PA, Cheryl Philipson."

"Okay. Where do you want to meet?"

"At the university with the prof and here with John."

"Richard, there are a few things about Martin's wishes which aren't all that clear to me. I'm not sure I fully appreciate the ins and outs of the black economic empowerment aspect, and I don't understand why Mel and Simon won't accept anything from Martin's estate."

"Let me try and explain, Liv. Although the vote in this country is no longer reserved for white people and even though we now have a decent and fair constitution and a Bill of Rights which seeks to treat all of us equally, the reality is that most black South Africans are not free. They continue to suffer the after-effects of a sub-standard education inflicted on them by historical policies, and they have little or no chance of participating in the economy of the country."

"I understand that, but how does black economic empowerment fix this?"

"Black economic empowerment, or BEE as it's known, is a fast-developing strategy aimed at addressing the economic exclusion. One of the many ways of doing this is to employ and train more black people in the workplace; another way, is to create opportunities for black people to become stakeholders in businesses. We're going to use a large chunk of Martin's trust fund to buy suitable businesses and then we'll bring in some broad-based black shareholders. Understand, Liv, this is not a handout, no one wants that, but rather a helping hand to level the playing fields."

"Okay, I see. And I now understand why the work here for you, and me hopefully, is long-term. What's the story with Mel and Simon?"

"There was an almighty fall out amongst Martin, Mel and Simon a few years back and since then Mel and Simon have refused to have anything to do with him. I have no idea what the cause of the rift was, except Martin once told me it concerned 'real deep issues'. He spoke about bigotry and ignorance on his part and said the breakdown was all his fault. The estrangement cut deep, with the result that Mel and Simon even refused to attend Emily's funeral or to send condolences."

"Who is Emily?"

"Martin's wife. She died before he did."

"Of course, silly me. I met her a few times at firm events."

* * * * *

"Hello, Cheryl, Richard Low here, thanks for taking my call."

"Good to hear from you again, Richard. How can I help?"

"I've begun working on various matters that Martin wanted me to attend to and I'm hoping you might be able to assist me as regards one of those matters."

"Of course, if I'm able. What are you after, Richard?"

"Do you by any chance remember seeing a Japanese military notebook in Martin's office or elsewhere? It's rather crucial that I find this book. Martin informed me that he last saw the book in the Rosebank offices about four years ago."

"Gosh, no, Richard. I do however remember Martin asking me to get rid of all sorts of war memorabilia. I can't give you a description of anything specific because the stuff was in a large box."

"What happened to the box, Cheryl?"

"Martin asked me to dispose of it, which I did, to a small war memorabilia shop in the Rosebank shopping mall, I think about three years ago—can't be certain on the date. The shop is about fifty metres down the right-hand side passage as you come off the top of the main escalator."

"Thanks, Cheryl, that's most helpful—I hope. I'll pop into the shop and see what I can find."

Richard stepped off the escalator and turned down the passage, walking briskly, rubbing his hands together. Sure enough, about fifty metres on, just as Cheryl described, he came across the war memorabilia shop. He rushed to the front door and peered in, noticing a frail old man bent over and fidgeting in a drawer behind the counter.

"Hello, I'm Richard. What is your name?"

The collector looked wide-eyed from side to side and then at Richard, before returning to his fidgeting. His ears were covered with a frayed scarf wrapped untidily round his neck and halfway up his head. The weathered patched jacket and threadbare baggy trousers reminded Richard of a wind-blown scarecrow.

"Warwick Pinkstone's the name, can I help you?" he enquired politely, dabbing repeatedly at his dripping, snotty nose with a stained, crumpled handkerchief.

"You have a lovely shop here, Mr Pinkstone—been in the game long?"

"More than thirty years, young man, more than thirty years, and it's brought me untold joy. Now, are you selling or buying?"

"I'm buying Mr Pinkstone, but something very specific, a Japanese military notebook to be exact. In fact, I'm looking for one that a lady brought in here about three years ago together with some other memorabilia her boss wanted to be rid of. Do you remember her popping in?"

"As a matter of fact I do remember her—a very nice lady, and she didn't want any payment either. That doesn't happen too often these days, I can assure you. And yes, I have a clear recollection of the notebook, never having seen one before."

A huge ear to ear smile broke over Richard's face and in a hurried stammer he asked, "You don't by any chance still have that notebook?"

"Oh, no, definitely not. I sold that book a long time ago."

Richard's smile disappeared as dramatically as it had arrived. Through pursed lips, he asked, "Could you please tell me to whom you sold it? I am anxious to retrieve that book so I can fulfil the wishes of a dear old friend who died recently."

"I'm afraid not, because I can't remember," said Pinkstone, exhibiting a blank stare.

"What about your records?" Richard prodded. "Won't they tell us?"

"No, no, definitely not, I don't keep records that long."

"Surely you have an invoice book recording the sale?" replied Richard in a clipped voice.

"It's too long ago, sorry I can't help you," said Pinkstone in a raised voice, turning his back on Richard.

This does not bode well, and it seemed so promising.

"Please, hold on, Mr Pinkstone, I desperately need your help. It's for an old friend, surely you can understand my keenness. What about your bank statements, they would still be in existence, can't we look through those for a clue?"

"Look, young man, I've already told you I can't help, so please leave."

"That's too bad. Perhaps you could think about this more and I'll visit again shortly to see if you can help."

Richard left the shop, biting his tongue. *I can't afford to alienate Mr Pinkstone; his help, however slowly it is given, is fundamentally important.*

* * * * *

"It's good to see you again Professor Markowitz, it's been a while."

It didn't escape Richard's attention that his former law professor still wore the same bow tie and old tweed jacket, with its frayed leather elbow patches that became his trademark during Richard's student days. The badly scuffed patches could do with replacing and the jacket itself needed to be let out somewhat to accommodate the professor's expanding girth.

He vigorously pumped Richard's extended hand with a jovial greeting. "Yes, it's also good to see you, Richard. I've been following your career with some interest. It fills me with pride when our graduates do well. I've heard rumours though that you've given up your law practice. What are you up to?"

Before Richard could answer, the professor pointed to the rickety chair in front of his untidy paper-laden desk and invited him to take a seat. The chair, as well as the clutter on the desk, brought back fond memories from many years ago.

Markowitz manoeuvred himself in behind the desk, almost falling into the same weathered leather chair he sat in for as long as Richard could remember. He wondered which would survive the longest—the prof, the chair or the tweed jacket.

Before attending to the purpose of the meeting, they spoke about many things, including Richard's law career, his new dispensation, the university and some of the old students. Despite Markowitz's advancing years, he hadn't lost any of his mental sharpness or quick wit.

Richard gave him an edited version of recent developments, without canvassing unnecessary detail about the prayer flag objective of the trust or about Mel and Simon. He told him the trust wanted to provide, on an anonymous basis, a bursary to Simon for the completion of his studies. He emphasised that under no circumstances must the source of the funding be capable of being linked to or even suspected of being linked to the late Martin Simmons.

Despite the perplexed look on the professor's face, Richard pressed on hopefully, looking the professor in the eye.

"Prof, I wish I could tell you the reason for secrecy, but unfortunately I can't. Please be assured there's no funny business here. It's all above board. There are personal reasons for the late Martin Simmons not wanting Simon or his mother to find out about the source of the funds."

Richard stood up, walked to the back of his chair and placed both hands on top of the backrest. "I can tell you this much: if the anonymity is compromised, Simon will reject the bursary, a result the trust wants to avoid."

Professor Markowitz continued to look puzzled and started to play with the Rubik's Cube on his desk. Papers, documents and textbooks were strewn all over the place in front of him. They were even in bundles and piles all over the floor. Richard remembered fondly the professor's retort some years back when a brash student suggested that an untidy desk indicated an untidy mind. *"In truth, young man, an empty desk evidences an empty mind!"*

"Are you able to help, prof?"

Markowitz wriggled uncomfortably, causing his chair to creak with every move. "Most unusual, Richard, most unusual. Bursaries aren't simply handed out," he said emphatically. "They're normally applied for by students. It's theoretically possible, I suppose, to single out a student and offer a bursary to him on grounds of need. It's not a route Wits would want to follow because, as you can imagine, every student in need would have a gripe about discrimination. How would one explain the lack of transparency? In any event, even if we could go this route, surely Simon and his mother would put two and two together. After all, Martin Simmons' death, and indeed the wealth he enjoyed, made national news. Don't you think that his grandson and daughter-in-law would figure it out?"

Richard knew his reasoning couldn't be faulted. He pulled back his chair and sat down again. Simon couldn't be singled out; it would be too obvious. Even the claim of an anonymous donation from abroad, specifically earmarked for Simon, would be viewed suspiciously.

"There wouldn't be anything irregular in making bursaries available on a need basis, for example, to Simon's entire class, provided we don't discriminate when adjudicating the applications. You must understand, Richard, there could be as many as thirty to forty needy applicants. That's a lot of money."

Although Richard understood perfectly the stance taken by the professor, he was nevertheless disappointed. He wanted to lighten the financial burden for Mel and Simon, and right now this seemed impossible. As a trustee, he couldn't justify paying out over half a million rand in bursaries to maintain anonymity. The other trustees wouldn't, Richard was certain, support such drastic action. There must be a way around this, he thought, but at that moment a solution evaded him.

He asked the professor whether he had any ideas. Markowitz remained silent as his fingers manipulated the cube faster and faster. After a while, with a well-practiced toss, he consigned his toy to the wastepaper bin at the far end of the office. "I wish I did," said Professor Markowitz, dashing Richard's hopes, "I wish I did."

They spent another twenty minutes chewing the fat about old times and about Richard's new journey before the professor excused himself for another meeting.

Watching his old professor waddle off down the corridor, Richard wondered whether he shouldn't try the direct approach, despite Martin's wish to the contrary. *Why not approach Simon directly and tell him about the availability of funds from the trust to support him through university?*

Richard knew the risks. The cause of the relationship breakdown may be something that makes it impossible for Simon to accept help. The cat would then be out of the bag and he would struggle to find alternative ways of channelling money to Mel and Simon. Mel would soon hear about Richard's approach. The chances of Simon keeping quiet were extremely remote, Richard figured. On the other hand, if Simon reacted positively it could make life easier. Candlewood Investments' challenge would then be limited to financial support for Mel. Once Simon accepted help, there wouldn't be any reason for him to stop doing so. *Do I take the risk?* He needed to think about this carefully, and perhaps chat with his fellow trustees. Taking the risk would mean compromising the anonymity Martin had hoped for.

* * * * *

At his upcoming meeting with John Matthews, Richard wanted to discuss a strategy for Candlewood Investments to acquire indirect ownership of Mantis Logistics, the company Mel worked for, but only if it could serve as a suitable vehicle for black economic empowerment transactions.

John enjoyed a reputation as a shrewd and capable dealmaker. Those in the know thought he ranked amongst the best in the country. Richard came to know him and his firm, Bullrun Equity Services, through Martin and the Sangster Group. John had been the corporate adviser in numerous transactions for the Group and Richard, as corporate lawyer, worked closely with him. Each respected the other highly.

"Howzit, John—it's been a while. Come through."

"Very, very nice, Richie… good to see you're up and running." He touched the furniture repeatedly, as if to test its quality, and then shuffled gradually around the room inspecting closely the artwork. "I love the décor, it's so African."

"Thanks, John. It's great to see you and I'm looking forward to us working together again. The old team, hey? How's the family, and what about you?"

"I tell you what, why don't you show me the rest of the place while I bring you up to speed about the family."

For the next hour the two of them caught up. Richard also gave John some background about the trust and its goals. The prayer flag and other objectives were irrelevant to John's engagement.

The opportunities for Bullrun Equity Services were obvious, particularly to be in on the ground floor when it came to transacting real empowerment deals rather than the smoke and mirror stuff paraded round town. Many so-called sophisticated businessmen thought they could assuage their guilty consciences or gain some sort of credibility through transactions that exhibited the trappings of black empowerment, but which in truth were nothing more than fronting.

"Well, any preliminary info on Mantis Logistics?" enquired Richard.

John opened a leather folder and spread its contents on the table.

"As you know, it's a privately held company. It's been in the De Wet family since its incorporation in the early sixties. As the name implies, it's a logistics business. It specialises in the handling of imports, exports, warehousing and distribution of all sorts of goods for suppliers and manufacturers, both domestically and cross-border. I've been able to establish that it's a credible, medium-sized player. I've put together for you a pack of info relating to financial performance, fleet size, employee headcount, competitors, market share, etcetera, and I have done a SWOT analysis."

Richard took the pack and looked at it cursorily. John carried on. "If the De Wets were sellers, there would be some market gossip about this, but there's not even a hint of such a possibility. Given the fact that the business has been in the same family for more than thirty years I doubt if they would be."

"You should know better, John. Everyone's a seller at the right price and in the right conditions. Right now, people are jumpy about the future of our economy. It might be an opportune moment to persuade the De Wets to exit—if we think the business is solid and we can acquire it for fair value. I'd like you to approach them to see whether they might be interested in exploratory discussions. You can tell them you're representing an offshore trust, looking for opportunities to do black empowerment deals. John, if we do a deal it must be structured in such a way that the ultimate ownership cannot under any circumstances be traced back to Candlewood Investments. It's for this reason I've decided not to engage directly with the De Wets and why the legal work will be handled by Sonny Jacobs, if a deal is done."

They carried on with their discussions for a while longer and then John left, clear on his mandate.

Richard whistled a ditty as he skipped passed Olivia's desk, on the way back to his own office.

"Why so chirpy, Richard?" she asked, looking at him with one brow raised.

"The ship has set sail on its outward bound journey and I'm looking forward to feedback in due course from John Matthews and to a further chat with dear Warwick Pinkstone. He must have a record somewhere to show to whom he sold the military notebook."

And I must decide whether to approach Simon directly, he reminded himself.

7

February 1997

The weeks following his initial meetings with Markowitz and Matthews and the subsequent failed revisits to Pinkstone dragged on frustratingly for Richard. He became impatient, wanting positive results, but he knew his expectations were unrealistic. To make matters worse, he was kept irritatingly busy attending to tedious neglected matters requiring his personal attention.

He thought about Mel and Simon often, wondering how best he could help them. He could see no easy way forward and this stressed him enormously. At best, Mel's position at Mantis Logistics would not be capable of improvement for many months, if at all. For such improvement to happen a successful acquisition of Mantis had to be made, and acquisitions of this kind took time to bed down. Richard feared that unless he could ease Mel and Simon's financial burden in the short-term, Simon would abandon his studies to seek some form of temporary employment—a risk that

Martin would not have wanted to materialise. Something needed to be done and soon.

After brooding on the matter and securing the buy-in of his fellow trustees, Richard decided to take a calculated risk and to initiate contact with Simon. He reasoned it would be better if the first communication to Simon came from someone who did not represent the trust. If Simon could be persuaded to come to a meeting, Richard might be able to persuade him to relent and accept help.

I also need to call on Pinkstone again and try and coax the military notebook information out of him. It must be in his shop somewhere. Either the notebook is buried under all the junk in the shop or he has some record showing when and where it went.

* * * * *

Richard arrived thirty minutes before the scheduled time for the meeting with Simon at the offices of his old firm. Sonny Jacobs, one of the senior partners, kindly agreed to facilitate the meeting and suggested that he and Richard meet first. Sonny had been willing to contact Simon to invite him to talk about a possible financial windfall for him and agreed not to allude to the fact that anyone else, least of all a representative of the late Martin Simmons, would be attending.

"How are you Cindy? It's been a while."

The receptionist's pretty face peeked from behind a courier making a delivery, greeting Richard cheerily with a flashing smile. Clients loved her, often complimenting Cindy on her professionalism and, frequently, commenting on her stunning looks, bubbly personality, fashionable hairstyles, tan, green eyes and many other attributes. She enjoyed the attention and the flirting. Richard and Cindy related well to each other and he had more than once been tempted to ask her on a date. He never did.

"I won't be a moment, Richard, almost done here."

As he waited he flicked through the latest *Financial Mail*. The courier left, and Cindy rushed around to the front of the reception desk to embrace Richard warmly.

"We miss you round here," she said flirtatiously.

He again thought about asking her out at some stage but quickly put the idea on hold, at least for the time being. His thoughts immediately returned to his concerns about the upcoming meeting. The chances were that as soon as Simon discovered the reason for Richard's presence, he would storm out. Richard wished he knew what had caused the rift so that he could have been better prepared to cope with Simon's reaction.

"Is Sonny around?"

"He's expecting you. Come through."

He followed her to one of the meeting rooms where he and Sonny exchanged customary pleasantries before getting down to the business at hand. Sonny disliked wasting time with unnecessary small talk. He required more information because he wanted to avoid anything improper or unethical. Richard proceeded to fill in the gaps. He told Sonny as much as he knew about the situation regarding Mel, Simon and Martin.

"Listen, Sonny, expect an explosive reaction from Simon as soon as he hears why I am here."

"That bad, hey? Like you, I am used to explosive reactions. Let's see what happens. I'm sure we'll manage somehow."

Sonny poured himself a cool drink at the refreshment trolley. His round shoulders, pot belly and unkempt shirt were characteristic, and somewhat of a contrast to all the other meticulous traits of the man. He wasn't the snappiest or tidiest dresser in town, and it didn't bother him. To him, such things were trivial—no matter the audience or occasion.

He asked Richard if he wanted something to drink. "No thanks, Sonny, not now, I'll wait until Simon arrives."

"You do appreciate, Richard, I cannot misrepresent who you are? Simon must be told upfront about your connection to Martin and that the meeting has been arranged at your specific request to discuss the possibility of help from Martin's Trust."

"Absolutely, Sonny. I don't expect you, or anyone else for that matter, to do anything improper." Sonny's admonition irked Richard. For goodness sake, Sonny had known him a long time and knew exactly where Richard stood on ethics. "I'm grateful that you were willing to invite Simon here without telling him that anyone else would be at the meeting. I'm sure he would have declined your invitation if you had mentioned my attendance."

"I also think I should leave the meeting after the introductions have been made, assuming young Simon pitches," said Sonny. "There's no purpose in me hanging around."

Richard agreed. Sonny wanted to know more about Richard's new role and whether the adjustment was a challenge. As if Richard didn't already know, Sonny reminded him of the firm's availability to be of service to Candlewood Investments, assuring Richard that high standards would always be maintained.

"Sonny, Sonny, you should know better than that. You know where my loyalty lies."

Sonny smiled sheepishly and shuffled in his chair, looking slightly embarrassed at even raising the subject.

Cindy knocked on the door and came in. She confirmed that Simon was already ten minutes late, and hadn't phoned. As she turned to leave, a hint of her delicate perfume lingered momentarily in the air. *I must contact her,* Richard thought.

Neither of them felt concerned. Johannesburg almost always suffered from traffic congestion.

"Unfortunately, I don't have a direct number where I can call," said Sonny. "Last time, I contacted him through the law faculty at Wits. Let's give it a little longer."

No sooner had Sonny said that and Cindy was at the door again, this time announcing Simon's arrival. Richard didn't read too much into the fact that Simon pitched up for his appointment for the simple reason that he had no idea the meeting would concern Martin Simmons. The test would come in the next half an hour when Simon was made aware of the source of the potential windfall.

Sonny, with his shirt still hanging out, waddled to reception to greet Simon and bring him into the meeting room.

Richard extended his right hand. "You must be Simon Simmons. I'm pleased to meet you. I'm Richard Low."

Simon hesitated as if uncertain. He acknowledged Richard with a cryptic "Hi," and then sat down in the chair offered by Sonny, who said, "I suggest we wait for refreshments before we start the meeting, otherwise we'll get interrupted. Were my directions clear enough for you, Simon?"

"Yes, yes thank you, Mr Jacobs, I'm sorry for arriving late. Traffic chaos continues to play havoc with us."

Richard made a quick assessment of the young man, observing a close resemblance to his grandfather, particularly in his height, well-built physique, light brown hair, dark brown eyes and the same distinctive bushy eyebrows. He sat bolt upright at the table in the same way Martin used to. It appeared as if Simon's hair hadn't seen a comb or hairbrush in days, perhaps to be expected from a university student. The dark rings under his eyes were prominent, the result no doubt of too little sleep. Professor Markowitz had told Richard about Simon burning the candle at both ends. He needed to work late into the night as a waiter to earn enough cash to sustain himself. Simon's weathered face made him look older than his real age.

Refreshments were served—now the moment of truth.

"Simon, when we arranged this meeting, I told you it concerned a possible windfall for you, without giving you any detail. Were you surprised by what I told you?"

Simon's face radiated a schoolboy innocence. "It came as a surprise to me, Mr Jacobs, and I've been wondering whether it's a hoax of some sort. Luck is a scarce commodity in our family and believe me, we need it. Things are rather desperate now and I'm on the verge of packing in my studies to earn real money on an oil rig somewhere," he said, looking up at the ceiling and wringing his hands.

Sonny and Richard glanced at each other and then back at Simon. Will he accept help from the trust? *Please Lord let him be reasonable, help him to see sense,* Richard prayed under his breath.

"I hope, Simon, this meeting will change things. Promise me one thing though, that you will hear Richard out and you will not over-react to what he has to say. As you will gather from the discussions that follow, this is not going to be an easy meeting for either you or Richard. Tolerance, patience and deep understanding is required for there to be a good outcome. Do you promise?"

The perplexed look on Simon's face spoke volumes. "It's difficult to make promises when I've no idea what's coming at me. I'll try my best but I'm sure you'll appreciate that I'm at a disadvantage here. I'm beginning to feel nervous about all this."

"No need, Simon, no reason to be nervous. Nothing underhand or illegal here. Richard asked me to facilitate this meeting and gave me some background information which has led me to believe that you may not respond well to what follows. As a totally objective party to this matter and as someone who has some grey hair and who happens to be a father of young adults, I feel it's the right thing to counsel you to listen and, if need be, to reflect seriously before you make any decisions. At the end of the day, the final say is yours. Nothing will or can be foisted on you without your approval. Be mature about this, Simon, it could change your life. I think I've said enough. I will leave now and let Richard carry on. Incidentally, until recently, Richard was a partner in this firm. He left to pursue, as you will hear in a moment, some laudable goals. For what it's worth, he is a great lawyer, a wonderfully compassionate person and someone who has values that can only be envied. Listen to his wisdom, Simon."

Sonny left the room. Hands clasped in front of him, Richard looked at Simon for a few moments before he started to speak. Simon leaned forward in anticipation.

"I'm not entirely sure where to start, Simon. Perhaps I should start by telling you what I am now doing with my life. I'm the chief executive officer of Candlewood Investments, a trust set up in terms of your late grandfather's will." Simon's face flushed and he opened his mouth, about to interrupt. "Simon, please, please bear with me before you react. I know you and your mother had a serious fallout with your grandfather, I don't know the cause, but I am aware the repercussions were far-reaching, with the result that the relationship with Martin came to a fracturing end." Simon tried to speak but again Richard retained the initiative. "I do need to finish sketching the background to my involvement and my presence here."

Simon got up. Richard realised that if he left, the initiative would be lost, and Mel would hear all about it within the hour. Richard raised his voice slightly as he fixed Simon with a no-nonsense stare. Slowly and deliberately, he said, "Look, Simon, whatever happened with you and Martin lives or should live in the past and it may never be possible to fix things. However, as a courtesy to me, hear me out. I am an outsider here and as a trustee I'm merely trying to do what the law expects of me. I have no desire to be judgmental or confrontational about what happened. It has nothing to do with me and is none of my business. Please give me a chance to tell you what I feel I'm compelled to tell you. After that, you can do what you like. You need never talk to me again."

Richard knew his firmness posed a risk, but he hoped Simon would respond positively. He believed that if Simon listened he might be able to persuade him to take money from the trust, and that would then be the thin end of the wedge. Thereafter it would be easier to make Simon an ally and to enlist his help to improve his mother's lot in life.

Simon drew himself up to his full height, at the same time giving Richard a prolonged stare, before returning to his chair. "I'll listen, Mr Low," he said, with a quivering top lip, "but you must know, I feel extremely uncomfortable listening to stuff concerning Martin Simmons. That sicko messed up our lives and, by the way, please, don't refer to him as my grandfather. That relationship ended a long time ago."

"Please call me Richard, and thank you for listening. I realise it must be painful."

He then gave Simon some of the background about how he came to know Martin and his involvement in the Sangster Group and how they had spent many hours together as he lay dying. He also told him about the trust, leaving out the detail about the prayer flag incident.

"Simon, Martin didn't disclose the cause of your relationship breakdown other than to say the fault lay squarely with him and that he did something of which he was not proud. I know he felt ashamed and deeply regretted what he had done. He told me his prejudice blinded him and that it had taken him a long time to overcome his bigotry. I saw him in those last days. He showed true contrition and unhesitatingly expressed his deep love for you and your mother. Unfortunately, death robbed him of the reconciliation he so earnestly longed for. You and your mother were his only family after Emily died. He has, through the trust, provided for you and your mother to be taken care of financially for the rest of your lives. I know you're struggling to keep your head above water and that your studies are in jeopardy. I'm here to ask that you give serious thought to accepting his assistance."

"You mean damn conscience money!" came the retort. "Don't you think my mother should have been invited to this meeting?"

Richard was, for a moment, distracted by a pigeon on the balcony feeding her young who were enthusiastically swallowing every morsel offered, almost choking on the sustenance, and here was Simon about to (so Richard guessed) turn away a lifeline—all because of pride. *What a strange old world.*

He refocused on Simon's awkward question, knowing he had to be circumspect with his answer. "My instincts told me that an initial meeting with both you and your mother may have been too difficult to cope with. Out of respect for you and your mum, I decided to meet with one of you only. It could quite easily have been with your mum, but for no particular reason I set it up with you first."

Simon calmed down, responding in a gentler tone. "Mr Low, I mean Richard, I promised to listen and to do my best. You've probably found out we're on the bones of our bums. My mother's second husband left her with huge debts; he's crippled her financially. I can no longer afford my varsity fees, my mother needs to replace her car and there are no savings. The cupboard is bare." Up to this point Simon's reaction filled Richard with hope, but suddenly, to Richard's surprise, Simon's voice rose sharply, "But hell will freeze over before we accept a damn cent from that fucked-up bigot or his trust. You've no idea the humiliation he caused us, and I don't intend sharing the detail. We've managed so far, and we'll make a plan."

Simon's response, although not entirely unexpected, disappointed Richard.

"Can you not forgive and forget? Aren't you better than that? Are there no lessons to be learnt here?"

"It's easy for you to ask that because you were not and are not in our position. Until you experience what that man put us through, you won't begin to understand. Do you think we want to be as poor as church mice? Don't you think we would've reconciled a long time ago if that was possible? You see, we suffered too much pain and humiliation. What's changed? Martin Simmons has died, and he thought he could buy us off. Well, we aren't for sale, not now, not ever, not ever."

"Forgive me if I came across as judgmental or insensitive. That was not my intention. The trust has significant financial reserves. It's my job, within the parameters of Martin's wishes of course, to spend the funds. Martin's most important wish concerned you and your mum, he wanted the two of you to be taken care of. To be clinical about it for the moment, Martin's dead and gone. Why not use the funds and lift the burdens you and, probably more so, your mother continue to suffer? To put it crudely, it will be no skin off your nose if you take the money."

Richard thought he detected tears in Simon's eyes when he mentioned the suffering of his mother.

"Look, Simon, even if you don't want your mother brought directly into the assistance loop, why don't you accept a grant from the trust. It will take away the stress of an after hours job and it will allow you to carry on with your studies. The sooner you qualify the better. You can then earn and help your mother out. It's absolutely crazy to throw away this opportunity." Richard took another risk: "Your mother need not know about this if you're concerned about her reaction."

For a moment it seemed as if Richard had made progress. "This is too much for me. What about the principle? We have principles, you know. Don't you think it would be totally wrong to take the money after refusing to see or listen to the old man? It would be so contradictory of how we felt and how we still feel."

"Do you still feel as angry and as hurt as you felt before? Perhaps the time has come to let go."

"I cannot talk about this anymore now. I feel confused. I need to leave. Please excuse me."

"Can we talk again, Simon, at your convenience?"

"I don't know. I must leave now."

"Here, take my card. Contact me any time. I would appreciate it if you don't discuss this with your mum until we talk again. An ill-timed communication could result in unintended consequences. Please respect the confidentiality of this meeting."

Simon took the card, glanced at it and shook his head, then left.

Richard was by no means certain that Simon would contact him or keep the fact of the meeting from his mother. It all hung in the balance. Richard did however sense a measure of success in triggering a paradigm shift within Simon, when he emphasised the realities of the financial stresses on the one side and the abundance of financial help on the other. He wondered whether issues of principle would muddy the waters. He hoped not, but only time would tell.

8

Just over a week had passed since the meeting with Simon and still no contact. *Damn it, why is he taking so long?* Richard wondered, as he stepped off the escalator to visit Warwick Pinkstone for the fourth time.

"Greetings, Mr Pinkstone, and how are you this fine summer morning?"

The bewildered look which Richard had come to know, washed over the old man's face as he shuffled noisily towards his visitor. "Have we met before?" he asked, showing no sign of recognising Richard.

"Ah, stop pulling my leg, Mr Pinkstone, you know me, Richard, I've visited you quite a few times recently about the Japanese military notebook."

Pinkstone cocked his head to one side, squinting at Richard for a good while and then, suddenly, the bewildered look disappeared as he grabbed hold of Richard's arm and led him into a grubby little office at the back of the shop. "Come, young man, come, of course I remember you. We don't have time to waste."

Richard's heart quickened and his eyes widened. Papers and files were strewn everywhere. Pinkstone brushed a crusty half-eaten sandwich teeming with little black ants off the worn and dilapidated Morris chair, then sat down. Richard followed his lead, sitting down, ever so tentatively, on the equally dilapidated sofa, stinking of cat pee. He leaned towards Pinkstone, anticipating good news.

"Forgive me, my memory's not so good anymore. My advancing years are beginning to affect me and maybe the time has come to call it a day."

"I'm sorry, Mr Pinkstone, aging can, I guess, be frustrating," said Richard, patting Pinkstone on the knee.

"Yes, you were after the military notebook. Now I remember. It's the only one I've ever had in my shop. Now, to whom did I sell it?"

Here we go again, thought Richard, *back to square one*!

"I've looked and looked and can't find any record of my sale." He struggled out of the chair, but only after Richard gave him a helping hand, and then started to scratch amongst bundles of paper stacked in piles on a crooked shelf behind him without really looking.

"Can you remember how you were paid, in cash or by cheque or credit card? Perhaps we could look through your bank statements for clues. At what price did you sell?"

Pinkstone did not reply and again that bewildered expression swept across his face as he stared intently at Richard, wiping his nose with the back of his hand, leaving a streaky mess on his blotchy cheek.

"Relax, Mr Pinkstone, I'm not here to harass you," said Richard, patting the old man's shoulder. "All I'm trying to do is help you so we can together figure out the whereabouts of the notebook. As I mentioned before, if I can find that book it will go a long way to fulfil the dying wishes of a dear old friend. Can you remember anything about the buyer, anything?" The perspiration dribbled down Richard's face, depositing small droplets on the paper pile at his feet.

The collector collapsed back into his chair, burying his hands in his face. Richard returned to the sofa, pinching his nose and looking around for an air conditioner.

Pinkstone thought for a while and then said, "An Englishman, yes he was English. At least I think so, I can't be all that certain now. Quite an elderly chap. I think he came across to visit family. Aah, I also have a vague recollection that he said something about Burma. He either fought in Burma or had an interest in the Burma Campaign or he belonged to some sort of Burma Club. Something like that. Yes, yes, that's it. He was involved in some sort of Burma Campaign interest group."

Again, Richard's face lit up, before asking Pinkstone for the second time if they couldn't together look at the bank records in the hope of finding a clue.

"No, no that won't help. You must leave now; I'm not feeling well," Pinkstone said, trumpeting into the handkerchief as if to emphasise his bad cold. Richard realised it would be futile to persevere at that point but was grateful he had something he could follow up. He thanked Pinkstone for his time and asked him to keep thinking about the matter, and perhaps he would be able to remember more for the next meeting.

"Sorry, Mr Pinkstone, one more small thing on which I hope you can help," said Richard, holding his hands together in a praying posture.

"What is it?" rasped the collector, "I'm not feeling well and need to go home soon."

"Do you know of anyone I might approach for help to repatriate some Japanese war memorabilia to Japan?"

"I most certainly do," replied Pinkstone instantly, with a lightness in his tone.

"You do?" asked Richard with wide eyes and a quizzical look. "I know you're not feeling well, so maybe we can pick up on this next time," he said, considerately.

"Not at all young man," responded a suddenly sprightly Pinkstone. "I can help you now. My housekeeping is perfectly good, you know, so give me a minute to look up some contact details."

How bizarre, thought Richard.

True to his word, the collector returned from his office in less than a minute, brandishing a piece of paper in Richard's direction. "Here we are, it's all there. I must warn you though, repatriation of war stuff to Japan is rarely successful—too much red tape with the Japanese Government, I'm afraid. Anyway, try these people and tell them I sent you."

"Thank you very much, Mr Pinkstone, I certainly will. Goodbye, see you soon to chat more about the military notebook."

* * * * *

"How did you go with Pinkstone?" asked Olivia as Richard stepped into the office.

"Two steps forward, and one step back, I'm afraid. He's trying his best to be helpful but he's very frail and quite obviously suffering from dementia. He furnished me with some apparently useful information which I'll tell you about later."

"Simon called for you, and said he'd call back about now."

"Did he say anything else, Liv?"

"No, that is all he said."

Olivia shouted after Richard, on his way back to his own office, that Simon was on the line. He rushed to his phone and in his excitement and enthusiasm, sent his chair flying.

"Hello, yes, Simon, it's Richard Low here—good to hear from you," he said in a controlled tone, waiting with bated breath for Simon to speak. For a fleeting moment Richard wondered why he wanted to contain his excitement. Probably a case of old habits dying hard—lawyers never liked to play open cards.

"I've thought long and hard about our meeting, and regrettably,"—Richard's heart sank; Simon continued —"regrettably I can't give you an answer yet."

Richard's face lit up.

"Have you discussed this with anyone yet, Simon, including your mother?" Richard looked down at his own hands and noticed that he had bitten one of his fingernails down to the flesh.

"No, but I do need to talk to someone. You know how my mum and I feel about Martin Simmons, but on the other hand I realise our terrible position."

"Simon, I understand what you're saying, and I can't quibble with that, but maintenance of confidentiality remains vitally important. I don't want anything to happen that may jeopardise this initiative. I'm grateful that you have respected confidentiality thus far and I would ask you to continue doing so for the time being. It's imperative that you don't discuss this matter with anyone that may be indiscreet. This means that you can't discuss it with friends or your mum or anyone close to your mum. What about discussing it with your church minister or even a psychologist of your choosing? Candlewood Investments will pay the bill. Perhaps you could discuss it with Professor Markowitz, your dean."

"That sounds like a good idea. I respect Prof Markowitz and he is a wise old owl," said Simon calmly.

Richard sensed that he was winning Simon over.

"I appreciate why you want to keep this away from my mum at this time and I will respect that, but please understand, my mum and I have gone through tough times together and I can't do anything disloyal. I'll call you as soon as I can."

"Thank you, Simon. I can't ask for more than that. It's of considerable comfort to me to know that you're taking this so seriously. Much remains at stake here, and for that reason all of us, and I mean all of us, need to approach all facets of this matter with a great deal of care and foresight."

This isn't going to be nearly as difficult as I first imagined. Hopefully Simon will play ball and hopefully Pinkstone will eventually show the way to the military notebook. I must now be in touch with Pinkstone's contact to find help on the repatriation front.

* * * * *

The irony of the situation did not escape Simon; having cut his late grandfather out of his life for the hurt, humiliation and damage heaped on him and his mother, here he was holding on (more tightly than he would care to admit) to the possibility of bringing him back into their world. *Am I being a hypocrite? Am I being true to myself? Am I now abandoning my principles and values for the sake of money?*

These thoughts and questions swirled on and on for hours, keeping sleep at bay. *Would it be wrong to take money from the trust? Given what that old bigot did, isn't it only right that he should pay? Is this a buy off of some kind? Surely it would be fine to take just enough so that Mum and I can get on our feet, no more? How would Mum react to all this? What about my principles? It would be all too expedient. How in all good conscience could I possibly justify accepting this kind of charity? Is it charity? Doesn't he owe us, whichever way I look at it? Why should we live on the breadline when we've done nothing to deserve this?*

His prolonged restlessness seemed contagious. He could hear his mother next door through the paper-thin walls. Her insomnia played out in much the same worrying way as it had every night for many months. Simon struggled at varsity because of his night jobs and she feared that it wouldn't be too long before he threw in the towel to take up full-time work. She wanted to avoid this if possible, appreciating the foolishness of compromising on his education. No obvious solution presented itself and this, probably more than anything else, compounded her anxiety. Her typical working day stretched from seven in the morning, when she left for her first job at Mantis Logistics, until eleven at night, when she stumbled home after her second job, waiting on tables at a nearby restaurant. She didn't know how much longer she could carry on, given the recent recurring chest pains.

Expenses couldn't be trimmed any more. They were living a frugal existence and things were bound to become even tighter over the next few months as she began repaying a loan she took out for car repairs. But for the kindness and compassion of the company's financial director, she would not have been given the loan, which was against company policy.

Damn you, Patrick, damn you—why didn't you carry more insurance? You've left us in dire straits. Her thoughts about her first husband weren't malicious, nor did she intend any disrespect. *And as for that weasel of a second husband, urghhhhh!*

Simon, still fighting for sleep, could hear her restlessness. She could hear his. She wanted to protect him. She wanted to give him a start in life. She felt a failure.

Her stomach tightened, bringing on nausea. She had no one to turn to. The more she thought about it the more she realised that Simon would not be able to carry on with his studies. He wouldn't be the first young person to resume university studies after some years in the workplace. *Life has dealt us a shit hand and now we simply must do our best to remain in survival mode.* She worried about him entering the big world so soon to make a living. He was an exceptionally sensitive person, a person in touch with his own femininity. He could easily be hurt by the hard knocks of life, particularly in this homophobic world. She needed to talk to her son at the earliest opportunity about him taking up full-time employment. What could he do to earn enough to survive and to save?

Simon looked at his bedside clock and saw he had only two hours left before starting some last-minute cramming for an upcoming test. He always seemed short of time to do all the things requiring his attention. Crunch time loomed; a decision had to be made soon, one way or another. Either he had to quit varsity and take up employment somewhere or he had to accept a grant from the trust. He didn't want to leave university, but what would he tell his mother if he decided to take the grant? How could he disguise the source of the money? He felt uneasy about lying to his mother. He wrestled with his conscience, debating back and forth with himself, whether it wouldn't be better to take his mother into his confidence and tell her about the approach from Richard Low.

* * * * *

A decision continued to evade Simon despite the mounting pressure brought on by his assignments and semester tests and the longer working hours at his night jobs. He knew he had to decide, but his confusion paralysed his thinking ability. His brain told him to accept the grant and to fudge the explanation to his mother, but his heart told him otherwise. He needed to take advice but didn't want to visit a psychologist as suggested by Richard. Although he attended church occasionally, he didn't feel comfortable taking advice from the ministers—he didn't know them well enough. Perhaps he should follow Richard's other suggestion and see Professor Markowitz. He respected his dean and was confident he could discuss these issues with him, but nervous about imposing his personal problems on the professor.

Mel hadn't been able to pluck up enough courage to speak to her son about postponing the completion of his studies. He had almost two years before gaining his undergraduate degree, and then another two years for his postgraduate law degree, assuming he fared reasonably well. How could she ask him to interrupt his studies at this vital stage? It wouldn't be easy for him to resume studying in later years. Mel began to change her mind, desperately wanting Simon to graduate with his law degree sooner rather than later. Perhaps, she thought, she could come up with some sort of plan. Perhaps she could once again prevail on her employer to give her another soft loan.

9

March 1997

"Hey, Liv, have those folks from the UK been in touch yet?"

"Which ones, Richard? I'm waiting to hear from a few different people in the UK."

"Pinkstone's contacts, the repatriation people."

"Not yet. I've followed up a couple of times and they keep promising a return call from their Mr Brigley-Smith, apparently he is the only one who can deal with our query."

"I hope this isn't an indication of how they do business. We initiated contact more than a week ago. Stay on top of it, Liv, I need to get going on my efforts to return the flag to Japan, and without that military notebook I haven't a clue where to start."

"Will do."

Another two days dragged by and still no word from Brigley-Smith. Richard snatched his phone off the cradle, muttered and then keyed in the number for Brigley-Smith's office.

"Good morning, this is Richard Low from Candlewood Investments in South Africa, please may I speak to Mr Brigley-Smith?"

"Good morning, this is Lucy speaking. I'm afraid Mr Brigley-Smith isn't available now," came the polite response. "If you leave your number, I'll ask him to call you back."

Richard's knuckles turned white, as he gripped the phone, resisting the overwhelming temptation to give Lucy an ear bashing.

"Look, Lucy, please don't take this as a personal attack, but I'm becoming thoroughly frustrated and annoyed. My office and I have called several times over the last ten days and each time we are informed that Mr Brigley-Smith is unavailable and will call back shortly, and so far, we haven't heard from him. I'm sure he must be a very busy man, but so am I. My call is about a sensitive and important matter concerning the return of war memorabilia to Japan and, may I say, I was referred to your organisation by Warwick Pinkstone in Johannesburg." *For what that's worth.*

"Oh, Mr Pinkstone, yes we know him well," she said, without letting on what she meant. "I do apologise for this delay, Mr Low. Mr Brigley-Smith is, as you say, a busy man, but I'll try to pin him down in the next day or so."

"Thank you, Lucy, this is a most important matter. Goodbye."

Richard entered Olivia's office, rubbing his temples. "Have you anything strong for a headache, Liv? I was fine until that call. Same old promises. Let's see if Lucy succeeds in 'pinning down' Brigley-Smith. Maybe I shouldn't have taken Pinkstone's recommendation seriously, although he sounded genuine."

Four days later, the long-awaited call came.

"Hello, Mr Low, Brigley-Smith here, I believe you want to speak to me," he said brusquely, with no hint of an apology.

"Morning, Mr Brigley-Smith, thank you for calling back," replied Richard politely. "Warwick Pinkstone, whom I understand is known to you, thinks your organisation might be able to help me to repatriate a prayer flag taken in Burma back to a family in Japan. I have no idea how to trace the family or how to go about this without falling foul of the Japanese authorities. Is this something you are able to assist with?"

Another brusque response. "We deal with Pinkstone occasionally, buying collectible items for clients of ours. He's a little past it; nevertheless, give him my regards. We're approached frequently with requests like yours and no longer take on prayer flag projects, they are labour intensive, costly and rarely succeed. I wish you luck."

"Before you go, Mr Brigley-Smith, I have two questions, if I may."

"Shoot, but be quick, I'm on a tight schedule."

"Thank you. Can you recommend anyone else I could approach for help and, secondly, has your organisation ever acquired a Japanese military notebook from Mr Pinkstone or from South Africa? I have good reason to think he at one point possessed and sold the notebook belonging to the soldier whose prayer flag I want to return to Japan."

"Why not ask him?" he asked impatiently.

"I have and he says he sold the notebook in the last four years, he thinks to an Englishman, but he has no contact details of the buyer."

"I guess it's possible, but will need to check and revert. Try contacting Yoshida Ichiro for help on repatriating stuff. I'll send you his contact details. He's very involved in facilitating the return of World War Two memorabilia to Japan. Bye, I must go."

Richard followed through with the recommendation, initially by online chats with Mr Yoshida, culminating in an arrangement to have a telephone conversation.

"Greetings, Yoshida-san, and thank you for the opportunity to chat over the phone. You would have seen from our online chats what help I'm after and why I need help. I don't know how to take this forward and am deeply concerned about failing my dear old friend and mentor."

"Hello, Mr Low, good to chat live. I'll help wherever I can. Whilst we have met with some success in tracing families, I must warn you that in the case of prayer flags the success has been minimal. It all depends on the uniqueness of information on the flag itself. In most cases the flag writings are too general to be of any help."

"The flag with which I'm concerned definitely shows inscriptions, but unfortunately I can't read

Japanese and so am unable to comment on the uniqueness or otherwise of the information."

"Understood. I would like to introduce you to Miss Nakamura from Nagasaki, being the general area from which soldiers of the 55th Infantry Regiment of the 18th Division came. She is actively involved in the repatriation of war memorabilia to Japan and is exceptionally experienced at this. I can think of no better person to guide you. Miss Nakamura and I work closely together on many projects and I have great confidence in her. But you must keep your expectations in check; without the military notebook, the prospects of a successful trace are close to zero."

'Thank you very much, Yoshida-san, that is kind and helpful of you. I will in the meanwhile persevere in my endeavours to find the notebook."

"Good. I will contact Miss Nakamura in the next two days and then revert to you with her contact details. Please keep in touch and let me know when I can be of any further assistance."

"Goodbye for now, Yoshida-san."

10

The connecting flight from Tokyo banked gently on its approach to Nagasaki, giving Richard a perfect bird's-eye view of the impressive long bay basking in the clear spring day. This trip halfway across the world marked a significant step in his quest to find the family of the soldier. He hadn't been to Japan before and looked forward to the days ahead with excited anticipation.

His mind flitted from one thought to another as he gazed at the bay and its surrounds. *With a little bit of luck the cherry blossoms and azaleas will still be in full bloom; I can't believe how quickly time has flown; it feels like it was only a few weeks ago when I attended Martin's funeral; so much has happened in the last four and a half months, but much remains to be done, including the return of the prayer flag to its rightful place and the bringing about of a reconciliation with Mel and Simon. I hope Miss Nakamura will be able to help me trace the soldier's family. I can't expect her to do the work, but this is a strange country and I will need handholding and direction.*

Richard's stomach lurched uncomfortably as the plane dropped altitude suddenly to prepare for landing and, for a fleeting moment, the reflection of the sun off the shimmering waters below blinded him. He blinked a few times and continued thinking about the purpose of his visit and the upcoming meeting with Miss Nakamura. He wondered what she was like. His interaction with the Japanese had not been extensive, but he knew they subscribed to complicated rules of formal behaviour. He had read somewhere that Japanese generally addressed each other by their last name, followed by a reference to a suitable title. He wondered whether this meant he should address Miss Nakamura as Nakamura-san or even Nakamura-sama. He didn't know.

After an arduous journey from South Africa he was relieved to be checking into Hotel Europe, the flagship hotel of Huis Ten Bosch. He was grateful for the Friday arrival, giving him the weekend free before his meeting with Miss Nakamura on Monday. He didn't bother unpacking when he entered his room; instead he hastily changed into sleeping shorts and a T-shirt before collapsing on the bed.

It took him a while to emerge from his deep slumber, realising that the ringing of the phone wasn't part of his dream. His disorientation lasted for a couple of seconds before he appreciated his whereabouts. He let the phone ring, being tempted to ignore the caller, but then thought better of it. *It could be an emergency.* His watch showed the local time as nine forty-five in the morning, but his body clock suggested otherwise. The eighteen hours of sleep felt inadequate. In a croaky and sleep-laden voice he answered the phone. "Hello, Richard Low speaking."

"Good morning, Mr Low, this is Miss Nakamura," came the cheery voice. "I'm so sorry, it seems I've woken you."

Miss Nakamura's polished English accent threw Richard.

"Good morning, Nakamura-san, and thank you for your well-timed call, I overslept," he said with a chuckle.

She asked whether he needed anything or whether she could make any arrangements for him for the weekend. Her hospitable willingness impressed him. She didn't have to take her private time, particularly over the weekend, to welcome him with such consideration.

"Thank you for your kind offer, Nakamura-san. I'm fine and well taken care of. I'm going to relax around here."

"Excellent. Are we still on for eleven o' clock on Monday morning?"

"Yes, if that works for you. I'll arrange an early working lunch."

"Great, see you on Monday."

Fresh from an invigorating shower, Richard enjoyed a leisurely buffet brunch in the Anchors Lounge before setting out for a bit of sightseeing. Neither his hotel nor Huis Ten Bosch typified a Japanese environment—quite the contrary. Hotel Europe modelled itself on the famous Hotel de l'Europe in Amsterdam and Huis Ten Bosch presented as a Dutch-style theme park, comprising hotels, villas, theatres, museums, shops, restaurants, windmills, canals and a park. He wasn't one for theme parks but given the nature and duration of his visit he accepted his travel agent's recommendation to stay in Little Holland.

The spring morning in all its magnificent glory greeted Richard as he had hoped for: cloudless skies and cherry trees and azaleas in full bloom. He strolled down to Alexander Plein, whistling quietly and feeling peacefully contented, and ended up at the bicycle rental shop, Fiets. He indulged himself, exploring the city, first on his rental bicycle and then on a canal cruiser and finally, using the streetcar system. The real Nagasaki bore little resemblance to his mental picture of the city. He didn't know why he carried such a negative impression. Perhaps, subconsciously, he expected to see the deep ugly scarring from the atomic bomb devastation at the end of World War Two.

The attractive city spread itself around the top end of the historically famous harbour, through two main valleys and up the slopes of the mountains on three sides. The mixed influences on different spheres of city life by the Japanese, Portuguese, Spanish, Dutch, English and Chinese, amongst others, were patently evident and gave the place its eclectic soul.

It had, for the most part, been a fulfilling day for him. He arrived at the famous Spectacles Bridge in the late afternoon, feeling a little worse for wear and somewhat clammy and sweaty because of the humidity. He opened a bottle of cold water and began sipping slowly, marvelling at the image of the spectacles formed by the reflection of the Chinese-style stone bridge which spanned the Nakajima River.

Then, almost as if he felt guilty about being so relaxed, he began to think about Mel and Simon and other trust matters. He wondered about the cause of the rift with Martin and the apparent surrounding secrecy. He reflected on Mel's needs and the difficulties that lay ahead in trying to address Martin's wishes. He felt cautiously optimistic that a solution would be found for Simon, but Mel's situation was a different kettle of fish. *Could I use Simon to make inroads with Mel? I have my doubts.* Richard also suspected that his strategy of trying to secure control of Mantis Logistics had little chance of success. His earlier sense of peace took flight, and he began to question his decision to give up his law practice to steer the ship of Martin's last wishes. The stormy seas and squalls ahead demanded careful navigation. *Would he be a capable captain*? He lingered for nearly an hour before making his way back to his hotel in a sombre mood, hoping the following day would be better.

Richard's mood lifted on Sunday, helped along by the solace he received from early morning mass at one of the Catholic churches close by. He felt a bit like a fish out of water because back home he worshipped in a less formal environment. He preferred the modern packaging of evangelical churches and their adherence to the word of God in its 'true' form. However, the chance to worship on this Sunday afforded him an opportunity to cast his worries aside and insulate himself against the negative thoughts intent on invading his loyalty to Martin.

Richard emerged from the service feeling refreshed, although slightly put out that he wasn't permitted to take communion. His irritation soon disappeared as he carried on from where he left off the day before, but in a better frame of mind.

* * * * *

Whenever an opportunity came Miss Nakamura's way for involvement in the repatriation of war memorabilia to Japan, she embraced it with enthusiasm and conviction. Hearing about Richard from Mr Yoshida created such an opportunity. The bitter disappointments of past failed repatriations hadn't blunted her enthusiasm or diminished her commitment.

This weekend differed from her usual weekends; time seemed to drag, and she lacked enthusiasm for anything, other than thinking about Monday's meeting. She had been told that Richard represented a trust which not only wanted to return a prayer flag to Japan, but also wanted to make a financial contribution to her and Mr Yoshida's war memorabilia repatriation program.

She had been fortunate enough to experience firsthand the indescribable joy of several successful repatriations and the closure this brought for families who, for many years, held onto the hope of one day being united with something belonging to their loved ones.

For some, closure never came. She wondered what lay in store this time around. Somewhere out there a family continued to nurture their flame of hope, waiting for their prayer flag. *Who are they; where are they?*

* * * * *

The pelting rain showed no sign of letting up any time soon. Richard wound his way to the Wellness Centre, feeling out of sorts. He always felt blue on Monday mornings but on this occasion the miserable weather aggravated matters. Perhaps the less than happy memories of Monday mornings from his boarding school days remained embedded in his subconscious. It didn't take too long on the treadmill before his mood lightened, mainly (he surmised) because of his excitement at meeting Miss Nakamura and putting the wheels in motion for the search. He reminded himself to keep his expectations in check.

He started to think about the missing military notebook once again, his efforts up to that point, and how he might be able to find the buyer. He felt uneasy, believing at that moment that without the notebook, failure was inevitable. As these thoughts swirled he ran faster and faster. The increasing pace jerked his attention back to the present and to the realisation that his comfortable jog had escalated almost to a sprint. He breathed heavily and the perspiration poured off him, soaking his training kit.

He jumped off the treadmill and walked around the empty gym, hands on hips. The torrential downpour kept others away, but Richard didn't mind, he was in no mood for small talk. He dried himself and then, without waiting for his breathing to recover, he continued his workout. The place was still empty by the time he slid into the sauna cubicle. He poured water over the heated rocks, causing a welcome eruption of steam with a loud hiss. His body felt satisfyingly sore. He lay down on the bench and closed his eyes. As he did so, he thought again about the day ahead.

* * * * *

Miss Nakamura struggled to sleep. She peeked out of the window into the darkness, and then glanced down at the glow of her bedside clock. Her heart fluttered in anticipation even though the dawning of the new day was still way off. She tossed and turned throughout the night, drifting in and out of confusing dreams about war, loved ones and lost soldiers. She dreamed about the day her family became reunited with her grandfather's flag, but in the dream he returned as an old soldier full of battle scars. She lay awake for what seemed like hours, preoccupied with thoughts about the prayer flag she would soon be holding—a symbol of hope and a means of closure for someone.

At long last, at about four o'clock, drowsiness set in and Miss Nakamura slipped into a deep sleep as she pondered the unique intimacy of each prayer flag. The gentle smile as she slept captured the poignancy of the moment.

Next morning she felt exhausted from the restless night and struggled to get going. By the time she had listened to the news, eaten breakfast, showered, brushed her hair, and made up her mind whether to dress traditionally or not, she realised her time management had gone horribly awry. A glance at her watch confirmed she needed to leave for her meeting. *It's going to take at least forty minutes to reach Mr Low's hotel.* In an impressive display of multitasking, she hurriedly completed her make-up, dressed, applied her perfume, buttoned up the cuffs of her light cotton blouse, slipped on a pair of fashionable black shoes and charged out the front door, grabbing her umbrella on the run.

11

The ill-timed ring caught Richard at an awkward moment as he pulled his shirt over his head. He looked at his watch and assumed it must be the front desk calling to announce Miss Nakamura's arrival. He grabbed at the phone and in his haste dropped it. On the second attempt he managed to retrieve it, hearing the concierge announce her arrival.

"Please tell Miss Nakamura I'll be down shortly."

He tucked in his shirt, brushed his hair and gave himself a final close inspection in the mirror. His navy blue blazer, adorned with gold coloured buttons, looked elegant over the sky blue long-sleeved open-neck shirt. His tan slacks, brown shoes and matching belt complemented the rest of the outfit. On his way out of the room, Richard snatched up the briefcase containing the prayer flag and looked fleetingly heavenward, offering up a rushed prayer of hope.

The concierge pointed out a captivatingly beautiful young woman seated demurely on the far side of the lobby. Richard walked across nervously to introduce himself and she stood up to meet him. He couldn't help noticing her Western or European style attire, expecting to meet someone more traditional.

Miss Nakamura, petite and chic, bowed slightly. He reciprocated. Her dark brown hair had been swept back off her face and secured with an elegant mother-of-pearl fastener at the back. Although Richard took all this in in a split second, he felt embarrassed that he might have given the impression of ogling her.

"Nakamura-san, we finally meet. I'm pleased to meet you."

"Likewise, Mr Low." She exuded an air of confidence, although not arrogantly so. "I trust you've enjoyed your weekend and that you've been comfortable?" She maintained disarming eye contact.

"Oh yes, thank you. I've had a great time, managing to see a little of your beautiful city. I'm sorry about the rain and hope it's not been too inconvenient for you to meet me here at the hotel?"

"Not at all. I'm used to this sort of weather."

"Shall we go?" he asked. "I've arranged for a private meeting room where we won't be disturbed."

Not expecting an answer, he moved towards the lift.

The facilities and furnishings in the meeting room were more than adequate. Richard removed his blazer, hung it on the coat stand, then walked over to the opposite side of the room to a low square coffee table positioned between two large leather lounge chairs.

"I think it'll be more comfortable if we sit here, rather than at the main table," he said.

Miss Nakamura slung her bag over one of the chairs and walked to the window. She folded her arms and took in the view through the abating rain.

"Some refreshment for you, Nakamura-san?" he asked.

"Black coffee, please."

Pouring their refreshments, gave Richard a moment to compose himself. He felt awkward and conspicuous, a little like a schoolboy alone in the presence of a pretty girl for the first time. *There's something very special about this young woman. I've never had this reaction before.*

She asked him about the rest of his weekend, showing more than a polite interest. He told her about some of the things he had done and about his fascination with the strong presence of the Catholic Church in Nagasaki.

"Oh yes, Nagasaki has a mixed and varied spirituality," she said.

"What do you mean?" he asked.

"Diverse faiths and beliefs—religions if you like—exist side by side. How this came about is quite a long story."

"I'm fascinated and interested by this sort of stuff; please tell me more."

"Really? It's not too often that one comes across someone wanting to hear about faiths, beliefs and religions. You needn't be polite," she said with an enquiring smile.

"I'm not asking out of politeness, Nakamura-san. I am genuinely interested."

She responded enthusiastically, telling him about the arrival of Christianity in the middle of the sixteenth century, its subsequent growth and, despite brutal efforts to rid the place of the Catholic missionaries, its survival.

"It might surprise you to know that towards the latter part of the sixteenth century, Nagasaki ended up as a Jesuit colony for a short while."

Her obvious knowledge concerning religion in Nagasaki, as well as her impeccable command of the English language, impressed Richard. His curious nature tempted him to find out more about her, but he didn't want to offend or patronise her in any way. He enquired whether she had a particular interest in the history or religions of Nagasaki or whether her knowledge came from studying something else.

"You seem to speak with such authority on the subject," he said.

She laughed shyly and, cocking her head to one side, said, "Mr Yoshida obviously didn't tell you what my job was." Without waiting for a response, she continued, "I teach comparative religious studies at Nagasaki University."

"I had no idea. Do you enjoy it?" he asked.

"Very much so. You could say I am passionate about all religions in all parts of the world. In fact, I'll be visiting your part of the world later this year or early next year to spend time researching the religion of the San people in Namibia and Botswana."

Although he hadn't known what to expect when he first met her, he certainly hadn't anticipated meeting someone as beautiful and well spoken as Miss Nakamura. *I'm looking forward to this; I think we'll work well together.*

Richard helped himself to more coffee and asked her where she had studied.

"My undergraduate studies were done here at Nagasaki University, but my postgraduate studies were done at Oxford in England."

"Why England and why Oxford?"

"My family has a close association with Britain. My father's diplomatic career took us to London for many years. I attended Oxford because a scholarship paid for all my expenses. Of course, I'm pleased I had the privilege of studying there."

Richard placed her coffee on the table in front of her as he sat down. He took a sip from his replenished cup, looked at her and said, "You're a very talented lady. You must be proud of yourself."

She gave a coy smile, seeming embarrassed.

Before starting their meeting, they placed their lunch orders—a platter of sushi and sashimi with a side dish of tempura prawns and vegetables, followed by some fresh fruit, for him, and a salad for Asami.

Richard opened his brief case and carefully removed the prayer flag. At last, the moment she had been waiting for.

He gave her the flag, and said, "This is what it's all about."

He sat back and allowed Miss Nakamura to inspect it. He noticed her immaculately manicured fingernails as she felt, touched and rubbed the flag softly, seemingly according it respect. She held it to the light and carefully examined each character and marking and then retrieved a large magnifying glass and a small camera from her bag and again inspected the flag, more intently this time.

She examined and photographed the flag for the best part of ten minutes before she folded and placed it tentatively on the table in front of them. The almost unbearable suspense caused Richard to lean forward in anticipation. She offered no comment, but instead asked him to tell her what he knew about the history of the flag. He was tempted to ask her what her thoughts were but decided to be patient.

As he started to tell Miss Nakamura about the prayer flag, she leaned back in her chair, crossed one leg over the other and looked at him attentively. He told her about his relationship with Martin and most of what he knew about the flag and how it had come into Martin's possession. He didn't, however, tell her of the circumstances under which Martin killed the Japanese soldier. In his judgment, he could see no useful purpose, at least for the interim, in anyone besides himself knowing the full facts. He was tempted to keep a permanent silence on these circumstances, notwithstanding Martin's desire for a confession to the soldier's family. In his view, no good could possibly come from such openness. Richard also decided not to talk about the potential financial benefits for the family of the Japanese soldier; that would be dealt with later.

"Mr Simmons' dying wish was that the flag be returned to the soldier's family, and that I extend to them, on his behalf, his deepest and sincerest apologies."

Miss Nakamura again walked to the window and looked out.

"Forgive me for asking this, Mr Low… why would Mr Simmons want to apologise?" she asked with a creased frown. "These things, as sad as they are, happen in war."

He knew that such an apology seemed odd, but he didn't want to risk an immediate rejection. Besides, he couldn't bring himself to dishonour Martin's memory.

"If you knew Mr Simmons as well as I did, you would understand why he wanted to apologise. He disliked intensely the inhumanity of war and other violent conflicts and valued, perhaps more than anything else, the sanctity of human life. I think you ought to see his apology as an apology on behalf of all people for the fact that wars, and World War Two in particular, have taken place, and an apology for the fact that he took the life of this soldier, albeit in a war situation, and an apology for taking his prayer flag and military notebook and then delaying more than fifty years before making any sort of effort to return them."

Although not convinced, Miss Nakamura let Richard's explanation ride for the time being.

"Mr Yoshida didn't say anything to me about a military notebook. May I see it, please?" she asked, returning to her seat.

"I wish I could show it to you but I'm afraid it went missing when Mr Simmons retired and vacated his office. I'm making concerted efforts at tracing it."

A knock at the door interrupted them. "Ah, that must be lunch," he said, walking to the door. Miss Nakamura excused herself and headed towards the bathroom. When she returned, lunch and an assortment of drinks had been set out on the main table. At Richard's invitation, she helped herself.

During lunch, they continued with their business. He could no longer contain himself and asked her what she thought of the flag.

"I'm sure Mr Yoshida mentioned that the chances of tracing a family from a prayer flag are remote, unless there are unique identifying features. That's why it would help immensely to find the military notebook."

"I understand. I'm doing everything I can to find the book. We've made some good progress, but success evades us for the moment. You've looked closely at the flag. What are our chances if we can't find the notebook?" he asked, scratching at his food.

"You don't appear to be eating. Is everything okay?"

"I'm quite fine, thank you for asking. I guess I'm anxious about this whole thing. It's so important to find this family. I have to do it for Martin—err, Mr Simmons."

She told him the flag and the inscriptions were well preserved and reasonably legible. Unfortunately, the Japanese characters were in a form no longer in use, so she couldn't translate them. "However, Mr Low, I know someone at the university who'll be able to translate this for us. Unfortunately, he's out of the country now and will only be back in three weeks' time. There may or may not be clues as to where the soldier came from or about his family."

She sensed his disappointment. "I've noticed what appears to be a shrine stamp on the flag. It might be possible to find the shrine and if we can—and that's a big if—it could be helpful as it's likely to be close to where the soldier lived. We've made a few successful traces this way."

"Nakamura-san, is there anything I could perhaps do to help in trying to find the shrine? Every clue, no matter how small, could point the way. I'm available to follow up any leads, if you could just point me in the right direction."

"That's good of you, Mr Low, and I'm sure there will be occasions where you could do the running or the heavy lifting, but bear in mind, Japan is very different to the Western world and unfortunately there are many areas where you have to be steeped in our ways in order to find what you're after. Searching for a particular shrine is one such area. There is no central registry; shrine information tends to be available by word of mouth.

"From one of my previous traces I came to know someone who has an extensive knowledge of shrines and who also knows others with such knowledge. If it's in order, I'll see if he can help us."

"Of course, Nakamura-san. Every lead must be followed."

"You're right, Mr Low. Our information at this point is sparse. The only relevant facts we know are that the soldier served with the 55th Infantry Regiment of the 18th Division and that he died in a battle which took place in the first two weeks of March 1943 in Burma, somewhere near Sinlamaung, Wuntho and Indaw."

She said it would also be useful to find out from which areas in Nagasaki the soldiers of this regiment were drawn, because that would shorten considerably the number of places to be considered when trying to identify the shrine.

"Nakamura-san, I'll get onto this straight away. Is there a government department in Japan that I could approach?"

"You could, as a starting point, try the Defence Agency of Japan. Their offices are in Tokyo though."

"That's not a problem. I fly home from Tokyo so I can delay my departure by a day or two. Presumably I'll need to take an interpreter with me?"

"Yes, Mr Low. I would have volunteered to contact the agency by phone or email, but going by experience they don't respond well to remote communication and prefer face to face meetings."

"Let me see if I understand your thinking, Nakamura-san," said Richard, pacing up and down. "Once we know where the members of the 55th Infantry Regiment of the 18th Division came from, the search for the shrine will, at least initially, be confined to that area."

"Precisely."

"What happens if and when the whereabouts of the shrine becomes known?"

"Well, by then a translation of the prayer flag writing will be to hand and we'll use whatever useful information can be gathered from that, plus any other relevant facts that come to hand to make enquiries with the priests at the shrine and with local families who visit the shrine. In addition, we'll post the information on some local online services. With a bit of luck we might be successful, but the chances of finding the family this way are slim."

Miss Nakamura finished her salad and stood up to pour herself some fruit juice. *Mr Yoshida had been right when he said she was the best starting point in Nagasaki.* Although Richard realised things weren't looking promising, particularly if the military notebook couldn't be located, he felt a slight degree of optimism.

They took their drinks and returned to the easy chairs at the window. Time had marched on beyond one o'clock and Miss Nakamura still looked as immaculate as she did when she first arrived. Richard would have enjoyed a walk in the inviting gardens of Huis Ten Bosch, now that the rain had stopped and the sun shone brightly. He wondered whether Miss Nakamura would mind carrying on with the meeting on the walk, as it were, but before asking her she spoke.

"Please tell me about your investigations so far into the missing notebook. Finding the book would be first prize. As you no doubt know by now, the soldier's personal details are recorded in the book and with these it should be easier to find his family. At the very least, we'll be able to locate the 1943 family home."

On reflection, he realised her shoes weren't suitable for walking in the gardens, so he dropped the idea. He settled into the comfort of his chair, took a sip of coffee and began to tell her about Martin's personal assistant donating a whole lot of war memorabilia, including the military notebook, to a collector in Johannesburg three or four years ago and about the collector selling off the book.

"Sadly, this collector is old and frail and runs his little business with few or no records. He's certain he received the notebook, but he doesn't know when or to whom he sold it. I'm not sure we can rely on his porous memory."

Richard explained that all angles were being explored, but no steps had been taken to advertise the search.

"You might like to check with the Office of Foreign Affairs, also in Tokyo, whether any military notebooks have been returned, particularly from South Africa, in the last four years. Accurate and detailed records are kept of returned memorabilia. Foreign Affairs isn't always co-operative, especially if they are given vague information to start with. But who knows, maybe details of the regiment and division are enough for them to show some enthusiasm."

"Thank you for that suggestion. I'll also visit Foreign Affairs when I pass through Tokyo."

Richard and Miss Nakamura ordered more refreshments. The meeting went on much longer than either of them had anticipated, but neither minded as they had something to work with. They carried on strategising and discussing related matters well into the afternoon.

"I don't know about you, Nakamura-san, but I've done about as much as I can do for the day. I would still like to talk about some other matters and make arrangements with you for a financial contribution to your repatriation program; presumably Mr Yoshida mentioned this to you?"

"Yes, he did, and of course we're grateful for your generosity."

"I'm scheduled to fly out on Wednesday. Would you by any chance be available to meet tomorrow for a couple of hours?"

"I could, but at awkward times, because I'm running classes for most of the day. How would after five o'clock tomorrow afternoon suit you?"

"Why don't we eat supper near your home, then you won't need to travel out here again after a long day with students?"

"That's so considerate of you, Mr Low, and what a nice idea. How about some traditional Japanese food at an authentic Japanese restaurant frequented by the locals, not tourists?" He accepted the suggestion enthusiastically.

12

The sweet scent of spring blossoms complementing the balminess of the evening became more pronounced as Richard strolled further into the gardens. He arrived early so he could enjoy a pre-dinner walk on such a perfect evening.

He ambled away from the restaurant on the foreshore, leaving behind the sound of lapping water. He followed the dimly lit path at a leisurely pace to nowhere in particular and after ten minutes he came across a wooden bench, set back next to a formally laid out garden. He sat down and admired the little he could see of the handiwork of the gardener.

I couldn't have wished for a better evening, he thought, interlocking his hands behind his head and looking up to the moonless night sky. He became engrossed, staring at the millions upon millions of stars and other extraterrestrial bodies. They twinkled and sparkled and blinked, pulsating rhythmically as they signalled the miracle of their creation. Richard tore himself away from the canopy of the night sky and looked at his watch, realising he couldn't dally any longer.

The petite young woman at the door greeted him with a formal bow. "*Irasshaimase.*"

He smiled and she led him to an area where she asked him to remove and leave his shoes. She then beckoned him to follow, leading him past several small eating rooms filled with patrons seated on the floor around low tables on *tatami* mats, to a dining area at the far side of the restaurant. In this room, about twelve or fourteen guests in traditional dress sat on the floor around their respective tables.

At first, he didn't see her, but when he looked more closely, he observed Miss Nakamura sitting on her own at a table in the corner. As he shuffled towards her, she stood up, radiating elegance and beauty, even more than when he first met her. In traditional dress, Miss Nakamura appeared particularly innocent and fragile. She didn't extend her hand; instead she bowed in a traditional greeting. Richard took his cue and reciprocated.

In keeping with Japanese etiquette, Miss Nakamura invited him to sit on the side of the table furthest away from the entrance and she sat opposite him. Richard sat down, not knowing where to put his legs. He glanced round the room to check how others were seated.

"Mr Low, let me help," she whispered. "You can either sit in the *seiza* position like this, as if you're in a kneeling position with your bottom sitting on your calves—this can be uncomfortable—or you can sit on your bottom and cross your legs in front of you like that man over there. I recommend the second position."

As he settled into the cross-legged position, Miss Nakamura changed from the *seiza* position by shifting both legs to the side. She explained that it wouldn't be the done thing for them to sit similarly.

"Thank you, Nakamura-san, I am rather clueless. This is my first visit to a traditional Japanese restaurant."

"Tonight, you're my guest. I'll order all the food, which we can share, and I'll explain the different foods and the various Japanese traditions, customs and etiquette as we go along. Okay?"

"I tell you what. You order, you teach, and I'll pay."

She agreed, laughing coquettishly.

"I have to say, Nakamura-san, it's so comforting to have your help on this mission. I don't know what I would have done otherwise. It's also a privilege to meet you and to get to know you. I'm excited about us working together."

"I too am excited about being on this worthwhile journey with you. I'll give you as much help as I can, as long as you realise that often the demands of my job will take priority."

"Understood. Would it be rude of me to suggest we drop the strict formality when addressing each other, and that instead we use our first names?"

"Not rude at all—I'm comfortable if we do so in our private interactions."

"Perfect," he said with a smile.

Dinner progressed marvellously. They enjoyed each other's company more and more as the evening slipped by. Richard disposed of the business side of things early on. Asami's surprise at the generosity of his donation wasn't feigned.

"I don't know how to thank you. I knew you were intending to contribute but never, never in my wildest dreams did I expect this much. No one has ever been this generous to our program, not here in Japan or anywhere. Thank you, thank you so much. Your gift will make an enormous difference in our quest to repatriate war memorabilia and to bring closure to many families."

Anyone watching them could be forgiven for believing that Asami and Richard were good friends, or even a couple. They were, quite clearly, enjoying each other's company, with lots of conversation, smiles and laughter. On occasion, they touched each other's hands or arms when making or emphasising a point and more than once their eyes locked fleetingly.

She took pleasure in acting as the host—ordering a variety of Japanese dishes, telling Richard about them, showing him how and what to eat, and getting him used to the idea of pouring each other's drinks. He couldn't recall when last he had such fun at dinner, nor could he think of a more wonderful way to end this leg of his first trip to Japan.

He told her about his life in South Africa, how he came to know Martin and how he agonised about giving up law to take on Candlewood Investments. She probed subtly for a better understanding of why

Martin wanted to apologise to the family of the soldier. Asami sensed that Richard was either not forthcoming, or he didn't know the reason. She couldn't quite work it out. Despite her best effort to be subtle, Richard saw through her probing. Her concern had probably been exacerbated by his generous donation, but he had no intention of providing any better explanation. *Given this concern, imagine her reaction when she hears about the intended financial support for the family of the Japanese soldier.*

In turn she told Richard about her life and her passionate interest in religions. She also told him about her involvement in the repatriation of war memorabilia. Her story was a poignant one but with a happy ending.

"My maternal grandfather was killed in action without any remains returning home. The family, in particular my grandmother, felt the pain of not having closure. As I grew older I came to see this pain and sense of hopelessness my mother and grandmother felt. The joys of family occasions always seemed to be blunted by sadness and I figured this was because there had been no closure for the family. On the anniversary of my grandfather's birthday, the family would come together and visit a shrine close by to say prayers, and spend the rest of the day talking about him, wondering how he died. One day he was there and the next day he was off to war, never to return. Nothing of his came back home, and the lack of closure had taken, and continued to take, its toll on my dear grandmother. And then, suddenly, a few years ago it all happened. Mr Yoshida contacted my mother and told her he had a prayer flag which possibly belonged to my grandfather.

"Mr Yoshida met with the family to show them the flag and my grandmother confirmed, from various writings and markings on the flag, that she had given it to her husband when he departed for war. It also had the stamp of their local shrine with a date. My grandmother remembered clearly giving her husband the flag the day before he left. He, my grandmother and my mother, a child of only a few years old, visited the shrine to say prayers. I cannot even begin to explain to you the sense of relief felt by my grandmother when she received the flag. Thereafter, she became a changed woman.

"When I heard about the efforts and commitments on the part of Mr Yoshida and his associates, and having experienced what this meant for my family, I decided there and then to help where I could, so that others might find similar closure. Now, Richard, you will appreciate why I'm so grateful for your generous donation."

The restaurant emptied out, leaving Richard and Asami lingering with the stragglers.

"I guess we're about to be thrown out," said Richard, struggling to his feet. Stiff from the sitting, he shuffled tentatively towards the door, as if walking on eggshells. Before leaving the dining area, Asami paused and looked at him hesitatingly. She stepped closer and gently placed her hand on his upper arm.

"Richard, this has been special—meeting you, working with you yesterday and spending time with you this evening." She turned towards the door, leaving him wondering what exactly she meant. His heart thumped in his chest, beating faster and faster. He followed her to retrieve their shoes. Her words played over and over in his mind.

The night had been perfect; he didn't want it to end. They reached her waiting taxi and as she approached the rear door, Richard became distracted for a moment by the reflection of the lights off the water a short distance beyond the cab. It looked like a fairyland. He turned his attention back to her. "Asami, wait." He stood close to her, close enough to put his arms around her and to hug her, but he didn't. "It's been a real privilege for me to meet you and I hope that together we'll succeed. I would dearly love to experience the joy of bringing the closure you speak of. And I too am excited about our way forward."

The night sky was still as beautiful as when he first arrived, but the stars seemed much brighter. He extended his right hand to say goodbye and she took his hand in both of hers in a gesture becoming of old friends. She disengaged quickly and climbed into the cab. He watched, with a twinge of sadness, as it drove off, and then he walked to the water's edge and along the shore.

Although close to midnight, Asami avoided bed. All sorts of thoughts and questions, mostly exciting ones, bombarded her. She knew she wouldn't be able to sleep. She put on some light classical music and ran a hot bath. She soaked for more than an hour, trying to relax as she turned over in her mind some of the events of the last two days. Every now and then she topped up her bath with more hot water.

She thought about the exceptionally generous donation of $20,000, knowing Mr Yoshida would be pleased. She could hardly wait until the morning to tell him the good news. Although it was good news for the repatriation program, it bothered her. Why would a trust set up by a former soldier from the Allied forces want to make such a donation in the first place, never mind one so large? Her concern about the intended apology mentioned by Richard, also persisted. His explanation hadn't been convincing. Did he perhaps know something which he hadn't told her, or had Martin Simmons not let on why he wanted to apologise?

* * * * *

Despite ongoing encouragement and support from the unusually talkative Japanese interpreter, Richard's edginess ratcheted up a few notches as the two of them ascended the wide imposing steps sweeping up and into the cold, stark and unwelcoming offices of the Defence Agency. Richard followed the interpreter's lead at the lobby reception area, bowing (probably far too low) at the waist in a respectful greeting to the uniformed official. The stolid official didn't return Richard's out of place smile and refrained from making eye contact when hardly bowing in response.

The interpreter engaged the official in what seemed to be an overelaborate and long-winded explanation, gesticulating frequently and occasionally pointing to Richard and his briefcase. To Richard's unfamiliar ear, the official's staccato style response sounded like a stifled guttural outburst and then, suddenly, it came to an end with him pointing to some rising stairs at the far end of the lobby.

"What was that all about?" asked Richard, as the interpreter led him across the lobby.

"We must go to the war history department on the third floor if we want to know from which parts of Nagasaki soldiers of the 55th Infantry Regiment were drawn."

"But why the long explanation and why the pointing towards me and my briefcase?"

"The official would not have been helpful without cogent reasons being provided for wanting the requested information. Relax, Mr Low, it sounded and looked much worse than it in fact was," said the interpreter, patting Richard reassuringly on the back.

The young officer on the third floor invited them to join him at a small conference table in a private cubicle. He scribbled on a pad, cocking his head towards the interpreter who explained the purpose of their visit. Every now and then he nodded in Richard's direction, even smiling a few times.

After about ten minutes of animated conversation, the young officer left the cubicle giving a pause sign with the index finger of his right hand.

"He says he is going to check their records and will be back with us shortly," said the interpreter.

"He does seem friendly and willing to help," said Richard.

"He is. Your effort in travelling to Japan all the way from South Africa to help a Japanese family impressed him enormously."

Within fifteen minutes the officer returned and both Richard and the interpreter stood up. The officer remained standing, shaking a sheet of paper in his right hand as he spoke very quickly in a raised voice with many interspersed nods of the head. The interpreter also nodded repeatedly, at the same time emitting the staccato-style guttural sounds Richard heard at reception. Suddenly, their interaction halted with the officer handing over the sheet of paper to the interpreter and then bowing to the two of them before leaving.

"We have the information you sought, Mr Low, and now we must leave."

"But I want to ask the officer something else, please call him back," said Richard.

Richard hurriedly followed the interpreter out of the cubicle and ran after the officer. On nearing the officer, Richard bowed politely, saying "Thank you, sir, for your kind help, I'm most grateful, but if you don't mind, I have something else to ask you."

The interpreter translated, whereupon the officer led them back to the cubicle.

"Please ask the officer whether he is able to give me the names and addresses of the soldiers from the 55th

Infantry Regiment who died in Burma in the first few weeks of March 1943."

The interpreter asked and then conveyed the officer's reply. "The officer says there are no longer records of such addresses. He also says he is not permitted to release the names of such soldiers. You will have to make a formal written application, and even then it is unlikely the names will be released."

"But—" said Richard, before being cut-off by the interpreter.

"Mr Low, it's not appropriate to push this, it will cause offence."

"Tell the officer, I am grateful and wish him well."

As the interpreter translated, Richard bowed to the officer who bowed in return.

The formality of their Defence Agency visit repeated itself when they called on the Office of Foreign Affairs in a similarly austere building a little further down the road, except that the attending official was even more officious and abrupt than the earlier receptionist. The exchanges between the interpreter and the official were by now familiar to Richard—animated, staccato-style guttural grunts, interspersed with considerable nodding.

"The official asks why you want to know about the return of military notebooks in the last four years," said the interpreter.

"You know the reason, go ahead and explain to him and please emphasise that I have come all the way from South Africa to help a Japanese family find closure."

The explanation did nothing to soften the apparently unhelpful attitude of the official. He grunted some sort of response, turned sharply on his heels and disappeared.

"I think he's gone to check," said the interpreter, "although I cannot be sure."

They waited, probably for more than thirty minutes, before the official returned, delivering a short response before again disappearing.

"He says they have no record."

As soon as Richard returned to his hotel, he called Asami to share the good news that he had managed to ascertain that the soldiers from the 55th Infantry Regiment were enlisted from the Omura area in the Nagasaki Prefecture.

"That's a concrete step forward, Richard, it will assist considerably in the search for the shrine. Well done. Any luck on the return of the notebook?"

"Thank you, Asami. Unfortunately, no good news on the notebook. The Office of Foreign Affairs has no record of any notebooks from the 55th Infantry Regiment having been returned in the last four years. By the way, I did enquire at the Defence Agency after the names and addresses of the regiment's soldiers killed in Burma, but they refused to release names, saying a formal written application would have to be made and that even then it would be unlikely to succeed. They also told me, for what it is worth, that they no longer have the addresses on record."

"You have been busy, Richard! Not to worry about the names. I'll be able to source those through my network if they become relevant. I'll also check in with the Office of Foreign Affairs periodically about the notebook."

13

March/April 1997

"You wouldn't be here talking to me if you didn't want to take the money, Simon. You must be honest with yourself. Isn't the real reason for your visit that you want me to make you feel better about the decision you've already made? "

Simon winced at the empathy-lacking rhetoric from Professor Markowitz. He wasn't one for beating about the bush, but Simon already knew that when he came to seek counsel.

"No prof, I don't want you to make me feel better," he said, struggling to control his emotions. "I don't know anyone from whom I can take counsel, and right now I need help. I don't know which way to turn."

Markowitz grimaced with shut eyes, scratching his head.

"Of course I need the money, prof, and despite the horrible fallout with Martin Simmons I feel I must take the help, but I am worried. If I take the money and tell my mother, she'll feel betrayed. I'm her only family and she has made many sacrifices, rather than reconciling. If I take the money and not tell her, I'll feel as if I'm betraying her. If I don't take the money, I'll have to leave varsity to earn some sort of living. Whichever way, I'm stuffed. And further, won't it be hypocritical for me to accept the help? We cut him out of our lives because of something he did to me. How can I disown him as family and then take his money?"

Simon cut a lonely, haggard figure.

"I'm sorry, Simon, I didn't mean to make light of your terrible predicament. You must however make the decision yourself because the consequences will inevitably affect you."

His old chair creaked noisily as Markowitz sluggishly and with some difficulty hauled his ample bulk out of it. He eased his way to the front of his desk. He touched Simon gently on the shoulder, continuing to speak to the confused, hurting student.

Professor Markowitz returned to the other side of his desk and sat down heavily with a snort. Simon had never seen this fatherly side of the professor before and felt comforted by the words of encouragement. The touching of his shoulder didn't go unnoticed either. He couldn't remember when last anyone touched him in such a fatherly way. He got up and said, "Yes, prof, I understand exactly what you're saying. Thank you."

* * * * *

Asami's email arrived at the right time. More than three weeks had slipped by since Richard's return from

Japan without hearing anything. She thanked him again for the generous donation, not saying anything about her reservations, and then gave him feedback.

She told him that the writing on the prayer flag had been translated, revealing a message of love and hope: 'From your loving wife and daughter.' Regrettably, the soldier's wife didn't identify him by name. She declared her undying love for him and wrote how proud and privileged she felt to be the mother of his daughter. She prayed he would return home safely, and wanted him to know that he would be in her thoughts every minute of every hour of every day. She wrote also, 'Remember always, as I will, our tree of love.'

'I have since your visit checked again with the Office of Foreign Affairs whether any military notebooks from the regiment had been returned to Japan,' wrote Asami. 'According to their information, the position is as they informed you: no such notebooks have come back. I have also informed my shrine contact that the soldier came from the Omura area.'

Although she thought it unlikely, given the sources of her information, Asami pointed out that possibly there had been some returns, and she would continue making periodical checks about this. She also enquired after progress on Richard's search for the missing military notebook, emphasising again its significance.

Richard hopped and skipped towards Olivia's workstation, delivering an exaggerated air punch. "Oh boy, this is exciting, Liv, we now have a translation of the inscription on the prayer flag and we know it was written by the soldier's wife with love from herself and their daughter. And the man searching for the shrine is confining his search to the Omura area in the Nagasaki Prefecture. Yip, we're making some progress."

"Fantastic, Richard, that is encouraging."

He was even more pleased with the rest of Asami's email. She again told him how special it had been to meet him and that she looked forward to hearing from him and seeing him again. Her intended trip to Southern Africa had been firmed up for three months hence. He replied with enthusiastic immediacy, thanking her for the report and her efforts to date. He informed her that he intended looking into the existence or otherwise of a Burma Campaign society.

His email continued: '*We intend to enquire from the members of the society, assuming one exists, whether any of them recently acquired a Japanese military notebook from South Africa. Unfortunately, all other efforts to obtain more reliable information from the collector have come to nothing at this stage.*

I remain optimistic that we can pull this off. Somewhere from amongst all the leads we're following there must be something concrete. We'll persevere until we find it.

I'm excited about your visit and would like to show you some of my country if you can spare the time. Meeting you was also special for me and our project. Hopefully by the time you come out here we might have something to celebrate.'

Elated at Richard's quick response and charmed by his kind offer, Asami replied without delay. Her keenness to visit South Africa brought Richard immense joy.

His exchanges with Asami over the last two days buoyed his mood.

"What's in the diary for the rest of the week, Olivia, or can I shoot off to Knysna for a few days?"

With the high season tapering off, things would be relatively quiet and this time he could have some fun instead of fretting about major life-changing decisions. There would be few tourists around, and many of the locals would've taken off for their annual travels to the northern hemisphere. It would be a good time to meet up with friends, to play some golf and do a hike or two. He had for some time been meaning to do the hike up to George and Craddock Peaks and this would be as good a time as any to do it. He wondered whether Asami enjoyed hiking.

Olivia's voice brought him back to the present. John Matthews and Simon Simmons had both called earlier in the day, asking for time with Richard before the end of the week.

"Oh heck, so much for my break. Go ahead, Liv, set up the meetings.

"What's happened to 'the new Richard'?" she laughed, remembering his vow to turn over a new leaf. "The Richard that no longer intended being at everyone's beck and call, the Richard that committed to pacing himself?"

"The new Richard hasn't disappeared. I haven't gone back to my old ways. This is different." He knew he didn't sound convincing.

14

Nothing had happened since Richard's trip to Japan to change his mind about the Mantis Logistics initiative being nothing but a long shot with little hope of coming off.

Before their discussions started, John Matthews gave him a file of papers.

"What's this, John?"

"It's something for you to read later—some high-level info about an interesting business looking for a black empowerment partner. I think it's a great opportunity for Candlewood Investments to come in as a funder, possibly with an equity stake or a kicker of some kind to sweeten the return. We could help you find the right black grouping to partner with."

They talked about this for a while and John assured Richard that his company held an exclusive mandate on the transaction and that it wouldn't be shopped around without giving Candlewood Investments first bite. Thus far it hadn't taken any concrete steps towards any black empowerment deal, other than for the Mantis initiative.

"I appreciate you bringing this to me first, John. I've been a bit slow off the mark on the empowerment stuff, so your timing couldn't be better. I've been tied up on other matters for the trust. I'll look at this over the next week and get back to you then."

"I gathered you've been busy since we last met. You've also been to Japan, I understand. Anything I can help you with?" asked Matthews, fishing for a lead.

Richard didn't take the bait. "Thanks for the offer, but these other things have nothing to do with deal-making. One day I'll tell you a bit about it. Well, what's happening on the Mantis front? I guess its bad news, hey?"

John took a sip of coffee before reporting on his meeting with the patriarch of the De Wet family, Piet De Wet. "Knows his game and a seasoned campaigner, and as tough as nails. He's a difficult chap and has the temperament of an old crotchety baboon with itching haemorrhoids. Some of my news is bad, but there's also some that's not so bad."

Matthews stood up and walked around a bit, trying to marshal his thoughts. "Come, come, John, spit it out, what did he say?"

"Well, the bottom line is the De Wets aren't averse to exploring some sort of deal, but there are, so Piet says, some non-negotiables. They're only willing to sell off forty-nine percent, they want top dollar even though they retain control, they want a voting pool agreement which allows them to control seventy-five percent of the voting rights and they're not willing to entertain extensive protections for the minority shareholder."

"Is that all?" enquired Richard, sarcastically.

"No, there's more."

"Oh really, why am I not surprised? I thought you referred to some news that wasn't so bad."

"They're not prepared to give any reps and warranties, and nor will a due diligence investigation be allowed. And, before things proceed any further, De Wet wants to know who he's actually dealing with. He wants to know who ultimately lies behind the offshore trust."

"Oh, give me a break. This guy's crazy, totally damn crazy. What sort of deal is that? No one in his right mind would waste any more time on this. Come on, John, we're wasting our time, let's can it." Richard closed his notepad and moved to stand up, but John interrupted him.

"Hold on, Richard, let's not be hasty. I don't think things are as bad as they look. I've done some ferreting. The De Wet family doesn't need capital; they are stinking rich. Why would the family want to sell off a minority stake only in a private enterprise? It doesn't make sense, and yet everything De Wet said and did during our discussions seemed to indicate a serious intention to negotiate."

"So?"

"I'll tell you what I think. The De Wets are sellers of the whole business and De Wet senior's first salvo has been fired. Remember, we are dealing with an old hand. His opening gambit has been played. He cannot possibly believe he'll make a deal on the basis proposed by him, yet he spent more than two hours with me, over two separate meetings. What does that tell you, hey?"

"I'll tell you what it tells me, John. De Wet's cuckoo if he thinks we'll do a deal on such a basis, stark raving mad."

"That's why you're a lawyer and not a dealmaker, Richard, my son. I've seen this type of approach before. My gut tells me he's trying to lay the ground rules for the negotiations. He wants to show he's tough. I think we must persevere for a while and reassess as the discussions progress."

"Where to from here? What's the next step?"

John asked for more coffee, then gave his battle plan to Richard. They analysed it in depth, dissecting it, turning it on its head and eventually coming up with a modified approach. They had nothing to lose and much to gain.

* * * * *

Richard's facial muscles remained taught as he paced back and forth in the corridor leading from his office, past Olivia's workstation and through the reception area to the main boardroom. Olivia looked on in silence until she could take no more. "Your meeting isn't due to start for another half an hour so why don't you relax in your office?"

He paused, and said, "I know, I know. I'm a little uptight right now. I haven't had any contact with Simon in weeks and I've no idea what to expect."

Richard took her advice but declined the coffee before returning to his office where he collapsed into the chair behind his desk. He leaned back as far as the chair would tilt and closed his eyes. He thought about their previous meeting and their last chat over the phone and tried to remember each little detail—what Simon said and how he said it. Richard tried to work out once again what Simon's likely answer would be.

His anxiety heightened so he got up once again and paced around aimlessly, hesitating periodically at the window to watch people scurrying far below. He wondered if any of them were stress free. He couldn't understand why this whole thing had become so personal and why he allowed himself to become so anxious. As much as he reminded himself that no one could expect him to do better than his best, he still felt personally responsible for Simon's decision. He had experienced the same sense of personal responsibility when he practised law. He always took it personally; he found it impossible to distance himself from the matters at hand. He used to think about his clients' needs and concerns almost every hour when not asleep. At night he struggled to sleep because work-related issues frequently intruded. When he woke up in the course of the night it would be the same. His only consolation, if it could be called that, lay in the fact that many of his colleagues suffered in the same way.

Olivia knocked and came in. "He's here, Richard. I've put him in meeting room one. How about that coffee now?"

"Please."

He hurriedly made his way to meeting room one, a less intimidating environment than the main boardroom.

"Hello, Simon, good to see you again. How have you been?"

Simon stood up, returning the greeting. Richard again noticed the close resemblance between Simon and his grandfather, not only in their physical appearance, especially the strong jaw, but also in their tone of voice. They made small talk for ten minutes or so, each waiting for the other to approach the point of the meeting. Richard watched Simon closely, detecting more fidgeting than usual. He also observed some repeated shoulder shrugging and a rolling of the head from side to side.

"Have you hurt yourself, Simon?" enquired Richard. "You seem to be uncomfortable."

"No, I'm fine, thank you, maybe I slept awkwardly."

Richard doubted Simon's response and became even more concerned.

"Okay, pleased there's no injury. For a moment there you had me worried. Well, let's get on with the meeting. When we last spoke a few weeks back you said you couldn't give me an answer because you wanted to talk to someone about the matter. Where are things now?"

Simon took his time before replying. Richard looked down at his own hands and saw his fists were tightly balled. He consciously unclenched them, waiting for Simon's reply.

"I've thought long and hard about the offer and I've taken advice. I've been told that the estate of the late Martin Simmons owes me a duty of support and that it would be illogical to turn down that support regardless of past events."

Richard started to feel cautiously optimistic but resisted saying anything. He sat quietly and waited for Simon to finish.

Simon shifted uneasily in his chair and scratched his head, ruffling his already untidy hair. He carried on nervously, speaking with a clipped tone.

"It's been very, very difficult for me to accept this advice. You won't understand—you couldn't understand—how my mother and I were hurt by what happened. As hard as we try, we cannot rid ourselves of the spectre that haunts us and that's also why Mum's so terribly bitter about it all. Even though we're desperate, I am pretty certain that she won't look kindly on me accepting support." He stopped and looked at Richard, seemingly expecting him to say something.

"I'm not sure I understand what you're saying, Simon. Are you accepting the support?"

Simon remained silent, fidgeting more and repeating the shoulder shrugging. Richard waited.

"I just can't. It would be an act of painful betrayal and gross disloyalty. I cannot, will not, do that to the woman who has brought me up and sacrificed more than anyone will ever know. I'm sorry, Richard, I wish it could have been different."

"Wait, Simon, don't leave. Let's talk about this more. I know you're between a rock and a hard place and I know it's difficult for you, but surely taking the support will be the lesser of two wrongs. Martin owes you and he owes your mum; don't turn your back on this entitlement. Please, Simon, I beg you, not only for your own sake, but also for the sake of your dear mother, who deserves better."

Simon stood up and hurried to the door, looking over his shoulder. "Sorry, Richard, I can't; this is too stressful. Thanks for all your effort. Goodbye."

What the hell has just happened? asked Richard of himself. *I expected a different outcome; I was so sure.*

* * * * *

Olivia's question startled him. Richard's feet were on the desk and he seemed oblivious of her presence. For the last week, his usual bouncy demeanour gave way to grumpiness and, if truth be told, Richard became downright difficult.

"I'm sorry startling you like that." Without waiting for a response, she added, "I'm concerned about you. You've not been yourself recently."

He didn't stir, seemingly deplete of energy. "I know, I know. I'm sorry. I'm still struggling to come to terms with Simon's disappointing, and may I say, foolish decision. I thought I had won him over and that good sense would prevail. Damn it, this is a devastating setback."

"I'm sorry, Richard, I wish I could do something to help."

"Thanks, Liv. I'm also frustrated by the lack of progress on other fronts. It's weeks now since anything concrete happened on the prayer flag matters, and it doesn't look like the Mantis acquisition will progress any time soon."

"Forgive me if I'm out of line, but I don't think it's all doom and gloom," said Olivia, surprised at his pessimism. "Quite a lot has happened."

"What, Olivia, what? Tell me," he retorted sharply, pulling his feet off the desk. She thought about backing off and then remembered his past admonitions to her that he always expected her to speak her mind. They were a team, he had said.

"Well," she said tentatively, "I can think of a few things. First, the Japanese Office of Foreign Affairs has again confirmed to Asami that, as far as they're concerned, no military notebooks from the 55th Infantry Regiment have been returned to Japan."

"How's that concrete," he snapped, uncharacteristically.

She overcame the temptation to disengage, pushing herself forward. "I remember you telling me that Foreign Affairs keeps a close eye on the return of war memorabilia. Surely then we can assume that the book from the late Mr Simmons isn't in Japan. It's either here in South Africa or Mr Pinkstone's Englishman has it. Don't you think that's a fair assumption?"

Richard grunted a noncommittal response and, for good measure, added, "That's hardly concrete stuff."

She sensed a change in his mood, probably because of her response. He jumped out of his chair and started stretching. She knew that if he wanted her to leave the office he would have said so.

"But," she countered, "you must also look at the other things. Asami's shrine contact has narrowed down the possible areas where the shrine might be. Isn't that good news? I know there's been no response to Asami's posting of the flag on the various Japanese online services, but it's early days yet."

He sat on the edge of his desk, rubbing his chin as if stroking a goatee.

"I guess you're right. I sense though that in the end our success or failure will be dictated by that little book. Unfortunately Pinkstone's deteriorating health causes considerable concern. We've no way of knowing whether his recall about the English buyer is reliable. Did he in fact sell the notebook to an elderly member of some group that has an interest in the Burma Campaign?" he asked, rhetorically.

"Have you heard from Brigley-Smith's office at all?" Richard enquired. "He said he would revert after checking whether they had acquired a Japanese military notebook from South Africa."

"No, I'm afraid not. Would you like me to follow up?"

"It's okay, I'll call him now."

The response was the same as before: *"Mr Brigley-Smith is not available and will call back as soon as possible. He's a very busy man, you know."*

"Of course I know Mr Brigley-Smith is a very busy man—how could I possibly not know this?" Richard muttered to himself.

Olivia left suddenly to take a call. He thought more about her comments and agreed that, perhaps, things weren't as bleak as he imagined. *These things take time,* he reminded himself, *and eventually a solution to help Simon and Mel must materialise. Besides, on the Asami front it couldn't be better*. He again read her meaningful email from the day before and hoped his reading between the lines wasn't misplaced.

'Dear Richard

I find myself becoming impatient about my trip to South Africa. I wish I could bring it forward but unfortunately my commitments here at the university make this impossible.

I'm not sure where all this will end up but am hoping for the best, not only as regards our project, but also in terms of our friendship. After our first dinner in Japan both of us sensed, I believe, a coming together of kindred spirits.

My visit will, I'm sure, allow us to explore this further. I find that rather exciting, don't you?

Richard longed for the days to pass by more quickly. He knew the ten-week wait for her visit would be frustrating.

He would've liked to have shown her the springtime flower spectacle up the west coast, but she was arriving too early for that. He started to think about places to which he would take her. Knysna and the Garden Route would be a priority, notwithstanding the winter. He reminded himself that although the winter evenings could be a bit chilly, the days enjoy relatively pleasant temperatures. He knew she'd also be taken by Cape Town and its surrounding areas. For a moment he thought about some of the wine estates they could explore together. Then, of course, there must be a visit to a game reserve. *You can't come to Africa and not see the big five*. He realised there wouldn't be enough time to take her to the majestic Drakensberg or to the province of KwaZulu-Natal to soak up the sun along some of the finest beaches in the world and experience the warm waters of the Indian Ocean. Much of South Africa would have to wait for another time. It's a large country and its inviting offerings spread far and wide.

He hoped that time wouldn't drag too much. Fortunately he would be kept busy in the next few weeks analysing and considering some interesting black empowerment business opportunities brought to him by John Matthews. *I must also stay close to Simon and try to change his mind*. Richard appreciated the importance of building a strong relationship with Simon, as this would, he figured, help in becoming acquainted with his mother. He wasn't confident the Mantis initiative would succeed and therefore needed some other options.

15

April 1997

Olivia charged into Richard's office, startling him. "Hey, what's up, Liv? I become nervous when you rush in here."

"Richard, it's Simon, I think there's a big problem," she blurted out.

"Liv, calm down, slow down and start again," he said reassuringly.

"Sergeant Olivier, the duty sergeant from Parkview Police Station, is on the line. He wants to speak to you urgently. He says it's about Simon."

"I wonder what that's all about. Put him through."

"Hello, Sergeant Olivier, it's been a while. How are you keeping?"

"I'm well, thank you, Mr Low, it has been more than a while. I hope you're also well. I'm going against protocol calling you, but you've been good to me, so I thought you might want to hear about Simon Simmons."

"Of course, Sergeant, and thank you, but what's wrong and how come you're calling?"

"The night shift arrested Simon in the early hours of this morning for drunken driving and he's not in a good shape. He's still very drunk—must have been on a helluva bender last night. When I inspected the cells at the start of my morning shift, I found him in an incoherent, weepy state, and he kept mumbling the name 'Richard'. I found your business card amongst his personal effects and figured you must be the Richard he's calling for."

"Is he hurt? Has he hurt anyone?"

"No, he was picked up in a routine roadblock check."

"May I come down and arrange for his release, please?"

"Yes, that's why I called. The blood tests have been taken. He didn't want his mother called."

"Thanks again, Sergeant. I'll be with you in about twenty minutes. Do you know whose car he was driving?"

"We've run a check and the car belongs to one Jason Roberts, who says he's a friend of Simon."

"Okay, see you in a jiffy."

Richard snatched the car keys off his desk and flew out of his office and past Olivia, letting her know about Simon's arrest for drunken driving. "I'm going to fetch him and will probably take him to my place to clean up and sleep it off. Chat later."

Sergeant Olivier escorted Richard down the narrow dingy cold cement stairway to the noisy overcrowded police cells. "It looks like it's been a busy night," Richard commented.

"That's for sure. Despite the tougher sentences, the drunken driving incidents are on the increase. Here we go, I moved him into the small cell at the end of the row, so he could be on his own."

A hunched over, forlorn figure huddled in the far corner of the cell, with a rough standard-issue blanket draped over head and shoulders. The place reeked of vomit and urine.

"Simmons," barked the sergeant in a booming voice, "you have a visitor." The pathetic figure remained squashed into the corner without stirring even a little.

"Simmons," came the second bark, but still no movement.

"Please allow me, Sergeant," asked Richard. Not waiting for the go-ahead, he approached, knelt and gently removed the smelly blanket from Simon's head.

"Hello, Simon, it's me, Richard, I've come to get you out."

Simon slowly tilted his face upwards, squinting through shuttered eyes.

"Is that really you, Richard?" he mumbled with a heavy slur.

Richard stood up and took a step back, removing himself from the range of Simon's fetid breath.

"It is, Simon. Come, get up, let's go."

Simon attempted to stand by pushing himself upwards against the wall, but balance evaded him, and he toppled over, seemingly in slow motion.

"Look, Simon, I'm going with the sergeant to take care of the paperwork and then I'll be back for you."

"My mother, my mother, Richard," he croaked.

"What about your mother, Simon?" Richard enquired.

"Please don't tell my mother," he slurred once more in an indistinct voice, before his chin slumped onto his chest.

Richard returned to the front desk and completed the necessary paperwork for Simon's release.

"I can't thank you enough, Sergeant Olivier, for your kindness, I certainly owe you one. If you knew about this young man's background you would realise the enormity of your generous consideration. Do you think I could bring my car into the yard near the cell block where it will be easier to load him onboard?"

"Of course. I'll fetch him from the cells while you bring your car in."

Richard drove quickly to his house, fearing that the sleeping Simon might be sick in the car. He pulled into the driveway, woke Simon with difficulty and then half carried him from the car to the house and into the guest bathroom. He turned on the cold water of the shower and slapped Simon softly on both cheeks.

"Simon, come on now, get a grip and remove those stinking, messy clothes and get into this shower."

Simon moved exceptionally slowly, unsteady on his feet and unsure of his surroundings.

"Simon, you need to sober up because your poor mother must be frantic by now, wondering where you are. Come on, man, get into that shower, I'll go and put the coffee on."

On returning to the bathroom, Richard noticed that Simon had managed to undress and find his way into the shower. *Thank goodness for that, about damn time.*

After thirty minutes, Simon joined Richard, clean shaven, hair brushed, and dressed in the clean, casual clothes provided by Richard. The appetising smell of grilled bacon and sausages welcomed Simon to the sun-bathed patio.

"I figured you would be ravenous, young man, so I've prepared a 'night-after' feast of scrambled eggs and grilled bacon, sausages and tomatoes. You can wash that lot down with some strong coffee."

Simon remained unsteady on his feet, shifting his weight from foot to foot, and avoiding eye contact with Richard.

"Simon, I know you are feeling awkward and embarrassed. Don't, I've been there. Tuck in while I phone Olivia about something."

After chatting to Olivia and making some other urgent calls, Richard returned to the patio to find the breakfast devoured, the coffee drained and Simon missing.

"Simon," he shouted, "where are you?"

Nothing but silence. He rushed to the bathroom and bedroom wing, calling again. Still no response. "Where the hell are you, Simon?" he mumbled to himself, heading for the garden.

"Simon, are you out here?" he yelled. At that moment Simon emerged from the swimming pool area, ambling up the path. "Oh, here I am, Richard, I stretched my legs a bit after that delicious breakfast and coffee, thank you."

Richard smiled, patting Simon on the shoulder. "Feeling a bit better?"

"A bit, just still wobbly. I'm terribly sorry for all the trouble and extremely embarrassed about my stinking drunkenness."

"Apologies aren't necessary. I'm sure there is a perfectly logical explanation for the binge. Right now I'm more concerned about your mother who must be climbing the wall with worry. Hadn't you better call her?"

"I told her I was spending the night at a friend's house to attend his birthday party, so she'll be fine, at least until she discovers my drunken driving charge. I am worried though about my friend's car. I don't know what happened to it after my arrest."

"No need to worry about that. The sergeant told me the police contacted your friend and he has already collected the car. He also knows about your arrest. Why don't I leave you here at my house to catch up on some sleep while I pop back to the office for a few hours? I'll be back at about three."

* * * * *

Richard returned shortly after three to find a refreshed Simon lounging at the pool with his shirt off, soaking up the summer warmth. He stood up and made fleeting eye contact with Richard, asking if he had some time to talk. "I would like to explain about last night."

"Sure, I'm available for the rest of the day. I'm going to have an ice-cold beer—hair of the dog for you?"

Shaking his head vigorously, Simon said "No, definitely not. I'll throw up if I have any more alcohol."

They plonked themselves down at the small wooden table under the deep shade of the magnificent oak tree at the far end of the garden. Richard brought the frosted glass to his lips and waited for Simon to begin.

"Let me start by admitting that I behaved selfishly and recklessly in driving under the influence. My blood test results will confirm, I'm sure, that I was extremely drunk, and I am all too aware of the enormous risk I caused to other users of the road. I am truly sorry and vow this will never happen again. I know there will be consequences because of the impending prosecution."

Simon paused, looked up at Richard, and whispered, "I am very, very sorry!"

Richard continued to sip slowly at his beer without interrupting.

"The celebration of my friend's birthday had little to do with my drunken binge. The time since our last meeting has been a nightmare. My decision to turn down the available support has dunked me into a dark, frightening depression. Trying to sleep or eat has been an exercise in futility, and I've had neither the will nor the energy to attend my classes. Professor Markowitz wants to see me, no doubt because of this. I'm also angry, at myself and at the world, and my patient and loving mother has borne the brunt of the anger. Oh, Richard, I fucked up badly in rejecting your help and at my friend's party I lost self-control. Can you believe it, I even took his car without asking him!"

"Why did you take the car?"

"As if the booze wasn't enough, I went in search of some marijuana. Don't ask me why, I'm not hooked on that stuff. I simply lost it."

"Simon, why did you not contact me sooner to discuss your decision? You know I'm there to help."

"I don't know. I've been so terribly conflicted about wanting to accept the support and yet remaining loyal to Mum. I can't take it anymore. I'm too young and immature for this sort of stuff, it's not fair!"

Simon leaned forward, bringing both hands to his face, and sobbed.

Richard got up and shifted to the other side of the table and put his arm around his shoulders. "Let it out, Simon, let it out."

Simon excused himself after regaining control of his emotions, saying he wanted to wash his face.

"Come through to the family room when you're done, Simon," said Richard.

By the time Simon joined him in the family room, snacks and a selection of drinks were laid out on a table. "Help yourself, Simon, you haven't eaten since the late breakfast."

While Simon busied himself piling snacks on a plate, Richard said, "I think we should revisit support for you Simon, and this time I will not take 'no' for an answer. Listen to me, you cannot possibly carry on as you are, teetering on the edge of the precipice."

"I know you're right, but how will we manage to do this without my mother knowing the source of the money. I'll have to tell her I'm receiving it from somewhere, but I can't say it's coming from Martin Simmons."

"But why not? I could accompany you to tell her. I'm sure I could explain the whole thing convincingly. If you stick to your decision, surely your mum will come around."

Simon's cheeks flushed and his eyes closed momentarily. His knuckles turned white as he grabbed the edge of the table forcefully.

"I cannot and will not tell her," he said emphatically. "If there's no other way, I'd rather not take the money. It will hurt her too much. You must understand her vulnerability, given all that's happened. She's not had it easy. I'm beginning to wonder whether her depression isn't because of some chemical imbalance. She's just not getting better and won't see a doctor."

"I'm sorry. I didn't mean to be insensitive about your mother's feelings. Also, please accept my assurance that I'm not trying to turn you against her. I am merely offering to help to explain things to her."

Richard felt awkward and angry that his explanation might not come across as credible. He reminded himself to be much more alive to their sensitivities. Simon didn't react. This didn't come as a surprise. Richard knew from the moment he first suggested help for Simon that it might become necessary to disguise the source of the funds, at least until he gave permission for his mother to be told the truth. For some time Richard had been mulling over a potential solution which he discarded more than once as it would have required the co-operation of his former firm and a degree of pretence on the part of the partners. Eventually, and as a last resort, he plucked up the courage to approach the partners with his rather unusual suggestion. At first, some of them baulked at the idea, but after some reflection and discussion they all agreed.

He told Simon about his idea. Jacobs, Smuts and Portman Inc would grant Simon an annual bursary for the duration of his studies. The bursary funds would be more than enough to pay for his university fees and study related expenses, such as materials, library membership and transport costs, and on top of that to give him a monthly living allowance. The intention would be for him to give up his part-time jobs and to focus instead on enjoying the benefits of university life and graduating within the normal time.

"I will arrange for a letter of grant from my old firm which you could show to your mother if you wish to. You can pick it up at my office tomorrow after ten."

Simon wanted to know what to say if his mother asked difficult questions about why he, and not someone else, was the lucky one. He was certain she would probe along those lines. She had an enquiring mind.

"You tell her that I, a former partner in the firm, heard of your plight through my association with your law school academic staff and that I punted your cause to the firm and managed to persuade them to put up a bursary on the basis that they could require you to work for them for at least three years after you graduate. You can also tell her that you were interviewed a number of times before the firm agreed to the bursary."

Simon wanted to know how things would work, given the fact that he would supposedly be paid by Jacobs, Smuts and Portman, but that the money would be coming from the trust. Richard told him the trust would provide the necessary funds to the firm.

"By the way, Simon, if there are any queries or difficulties along the way about the monthly support, you must deal directly with me or Olivia and not with my former firm."

The two of them spent the next hour working through practical matters for the arrangement.

"Simon, I'm going to set the monthly payments quite a bit higher than your strict needs. This will allow you to build up a contingency kitty for those sudden unexpected expenses and to help when things become desperate."

"Is that necessary?" he asked, hesitatingly. "I'm so worried Mum finds out."

"She won't if you're smart. And if she does, we'll have to handle the fall-out then," said Richard firmly.

Simon understood all accounts from Wits and suppliers were to be given to Olivia who would ensure they were settled by Richard's former firm.

"So that you can plan your financial life with certainty, the monthly allowance will be paid into your bank account by the twenty-fifth of each month."

Just before wrapping up their meeting, Simon asked whether Richard thought his mother would believe the bursary story. He sounded tentative and uncertain about the plan.

"Look, Simon, whether or not your mother believes our concocted story will to a large extent depend on you. Except for securing your bursary letter, the only other thing I can do is to verify what you tell her about the bursary. It's up to you to be convincing. I'm sure neither of us feels completely comfortable about telling a white lie, but in this case I think the end does justify the means. You need the money. It'll take enormous pressure off you and your mother. You do your bit and we'll take care of the rest. And about the drunken driving charge—leave that with me, I'll see what I can do to avoid her becoming aware of the position."

16

Mel's entire body shivered from the unseasonably plummeting temperature and icy wind which whistled down the corridor of the narrow street, sweeping along leaves, discarded plastic and bits of newspaper. The penetrating cold and her sheer exhaustion hampered the simple task of retrieving the front door key from her bag. The large paper bag of cheap groceries tucked under one arm and the broken porch light didn't help matters. She was too tired to put the bag down. Her back ached and her feet were sore. She had barely managed to see through another long and strenuous day. Her alarm clock had woken her at six o'clock that morning so she could be ready to leave for her day job at Mantis by seven, and then she dragged herself to the restaurant to wait on tables until ten that night.

Simon, waiting for his mother to arrive home, heard a key in the door lock. During the three days since his meeting with Richard events had progressed quickly. He had left his jobs, and his first monthly allowance was already in his bank account. Although anxious about giving her the news, he was also excited. For the first time in many years he felt free. He wanted her also to taste some of that freedom.

Some hot soup simmered on the cooker. He figured she would like that. He tiptoed to the door, ready to surprise her. The door swung open suddenly and she burst in off balance, almost bowling Simon over and screaming at the same time.

"Mum, Mum, it's me, Simon." He quickly put his arms around her in a reassuring way and he could feel her heart thumping against his chest. She pulled away, her face ashen. "Here, let me take that off you." He took the grocery packet and put it on the table. "I'm sorry if I gave you a fright, I didn't mean to."

"What's wrong, Simon, what's happened?" she asked apprehensively. She took hold of the front of his shirt with both hands and looked up at him with grave concern. He could feel her shaking. Again, she asked, "What's wrong? Why are you home so early? Oh no, did you get fired?"

He smiled, and said, "No, I didn't get fired. I quit!"

Gently he prized her hands from his shirt and told her to face away from him. "Don't say a word. I have something for you."

She turned hesitatingly, not knowing what to expect. He walked to the dresser and picked up the large bunch of long-stemmed yellow roses.

"Turn around." As she did so he held out the roses. "I love you, Mum, and thank you for all you've done for me all these years. You're a most special person."

She took the roses and instinctively brought them up to her face. Mel didn't know what to say. Her vision blurred and she could feel herself becoming choked up. She hadn't received flowers in many years, and this was the first time from her son.

She stepped towards the kitchen to fetch a vase but Simon stopped her.

He took the roses, and said, "Mum, I have a surprise for you. Why don't you change into your comfortable old track suit while I sort this out, and then I can tell you all about it?"

For a moment she rose above her exhaustion and her spirits lifted. She wondered about the surprise and where the money came from for the roses. When she returned after changing, she saw the roses arranged in a vase on the small dining table, as well as an opened bottle of red wine and some fresh bread rolls. Two places had been set, each with a crystal wine glass, gifts to her from Simon's father on their first wedding anniversary.

"What's going on, Simon, what's all this about? Come on, tell me your surprise."

With an impish grin he took hold of her elbow and steered her to the table. Instead of answering, Simon fetched the soup and began to serve it. Next, he took the bottle of wine and poured a glass for each of them.

He lifted his glass. "Here's to my freedom, here's to my future, here's to us."

Although overwhelmed and still in the dark, she lifted her glass in the toast. She sat back and looked at him with deep admiration.

"Thank you, my son. What a surprise. I'm touched, and I love you too. Now please tell me what's happening."

Simon told her the bursary story concocted by him and Richard. She sat quietly, listening carefully. She couldn't believe her ears. When he finished telling her how good fortune had come his way, she didn't know what to say. As she calmed down, doubts began to creep in, but she masked them as best she could.

"My son, I'm overcome. It's almost too good to be true," she said, wondering if Simon had become involved in something illegal.

"I'm overwhelmed and confused. Tell me again, but slowly. How did you hear about the bursary?"

"Well, as you know, the university has all along known about my poor financial position and the risk of me leaving." She ate as she listened, taking sips now and again from her wine. "One day, about two or three weeks ago, I'm phoned by someone who tells me he has a close association with the varsity and that he's heard of my plight and that he might be able to help."

"Did he say who he was?"

"He told me his name and that he had graduated from the law school at the university. He said he recently left a reputable law firm where he had been a partner and that he retained close contact with some of the academic staff. He seemed to know Prof Markowitz well."

"Is that the law firm that's given you the bursary?"

"Yes."

"You then obviously met him. Why the willingness to help, and why you and not others?"

Simon knew his mother would question him closely. She was astute and would be suspicious. He needed to remain alert in fielding her questions, of which he was certain there would be many.

"I met him quite a few times. He told me about his former firm and said he still enjoyed a close friendship with the partners there. Apparently he does business with them. He's a helluva nice guy. I like him, your kind of guy."

"But why did he want to help you?" Mel pushed her empty bowl aside and topped up her wine.

"He put it to me this way. He said Wits University informed him about my situation, stating that in their view it would be a pity if my potential wasn't nurtured. According to Richard—"

"Is that the name of this chap who helped you?"

"Yes." Mel didn't ask for the surname and Simon didn't offer it. "Anyway, according to him, Wits asked if he could do anything to help. He also told me that his former firm was always on the lookout for talent and he knew they had recently been discussing the possibility of making a few bursaries available as part of their social responsibility program."

Simon fetched more soup for himself; Mel poured herself another glass of wine.

"What does Richard do now?"

He sidestepped the awkward question. "Although they're helping me, I don't think it's charity. They grilled me at all three interviews. They covered just about everything and they tested my commitment to working for them for three years after qualification if they wanted me."

He felt a little uneasy about lying to his mother but having chosen to go down this road, there was no turning back.

"I'm proud of you, Simon. I always knew you would make it. Our patience, yours and mine, is at last bearing some fruit. Now, tell me, what does Richard do?"

She persevered like the proverbial dog with a bone.

Simon fudged his reply. "Oh, he's involved in all sorts of business things—buying and selling companies, funding them, black economic empowerment and that sort of stuff."

They talked way past midnight until she began to fall asleep in her chair. Although Simon could sleep in the following morning, his mother still had to rise with the sparrows.

* * * * *

"Hello, Lucy, this is Richard Low from South Africa. As you know, I have left numerous messages for Mr Brigley-Smith over the last ten days and despite promises that he would call me back, I've heard nothing. Please, I desperately need to speak to him now, it is rather urgent."

"I do apologise, Mr Low, let me see what I can do. Please hold on."

Brigley-Smith came on the line. "Good day, Mr Low, sorry about the delay, I'm sure you understand how busy things can be. Look, we've checked on our side and I can tell you for certain that we've not acquired a Japanese military notebook from South Africa, or anywhere else for that matter, in the last four years."

Richard doubted that Brigley-Smith's people had even bothered to check. "Thank you for that, Mr Brigley-Smith. While I have you on the line, may I ask whether you know of any group or society that has a specific interest in the Burma Campaign?"

"As a matter of fact, I do. The group, known as 'The Burma Campaign Fellowship Group', was established in 1991 for the purpose of promoting reconciliation amongst British and Japanese veterans. I'll put you back to Lucy so she can provide you with the contact details of the chairman."

Before Richard could respond, Lucy came on the line and asked him to hold on while she looked up the details. *What a rude arrogant shit*, thought Richard.

He wasted no time dispatching an email to the chairman of the group.

Dear Mr Smithies

I write to you in the hope that you might allow me to make an appeal to your Group's members through your next monthly newsletter. I am endeavouring to trace a Japanese family in order to restore to them a prayer flag taken off their loved one, a soldier serving with the 55th Infantry Regiment of the 18th Division of the Japanese Forces in Burma, who died during the Burma Campaign.

The flag, as well as the military notebook of the Japanese soldier, were taken by a British soldier serving with the Chindits, who passed away recently here in South Africa.

The information embedded in the flag is, unfortunately, insufficient to allow identification of the soldier. I know for a fact that about four years ago the soldier's military notebook passed into the possession of a collector, Warwick Pinkstone, who owns a small war memorabilia shop in Rosebank, Johannesburg. Mr Pinkstone has a recollection, although apparently no records, of having sold the notebook to an 'Englishman' whom he thinks is a member of a 'Burma Campaign Interest Group'.

As you can appreciate, if I am able to find the notebook, I will be able to ascertain the name and other personal information of the Japanese soldier and this will go a long way in helping me to trace the soldier's family.

I wish to ask your members if any of them perhaps has or had possession of the notebook with a view to having sight of it.

Please let me know if I may make such an appeal, in which event I will let you have some proposed wording for inclusion in your newsletter.

Yours sincerely

Richard Low.

17

May/June 1997

The lift doors opened smoothly and silently into the plush reception area of the executive suite of Mantis Logistics. John's suggestion to meet for lunch was dismissed out of hand by De Wet, who said, "Business is business and lunch is lunch, let's not confuse the two."

This meeting's going to be interesting, thought John. He intended pushing the boundaries, wanting to test the flexibility or otherwise of De Wet's so-called non-negotiables.

At precisely five to ten the haughty middle-aged receptionist with a coiffed seventies hairstyle showed him to an expensively furnished meeting room. She said rather matter-of-factly, "Mr De Wet will be through at ten," emphasising the word 'Mister'.

John sipped his tea and thought about De Wet. From their dealings so far, he liked him in an odd sort of way. *Intellectually sharp—an old hand at acquisitions and disposals—disciplined—sometimes courteous but generally rude as hell—and tough.* He looked up at the large, ostentatious wall clock and saw he had three minutes left before ten, so he started looking nonchalantly at the original artwork in the room, wondering whether De Wet would be exactly on time as claimed by his receptionist.

Sure enough, at precisely ten o'clock De Wet came through the door. "Hello, John, trust you're well?"

John shook his hand. "Yes, thank you. Yourself?"

"I'm fine. Right, when we last met, I told you where we stood. What's your client's response?"

By now John had come to realise that small talk should be avoided; it would simply irritate De Wet. "As you know, my client is an offshore trust and according to legal advice taken, the trustees would be acting irresponsibly if they did a deal as proposed by you."

John wasn't bluffing. He continued. "Your proposal envisages my client buying a minority stake at a premium price, with no due diligence, no meaningful reps and warranties, no veto rights under any circumstances, diluted voting power and no market for its stake if it ever wanted to exit." John paused to see if this would elicit any sort of response from De Wet.

"Listen, John, let's be accurate. I've not made any proposal. You are the one who came to me, asking whether my family are potential sellers and I told you we would be willing to explore a deal provided certain non-negotiables were met."

He said nothing else, giving John a cold stare as he waited for a reaction. "Piet, you're not going to draw me into an argument about semantics. Call your non-negotiables what you will, my client cannot and will not do a deal on that basis."

John had fired his first salvo. De Wet either had to step back or the meeting would be over. This time, John did the staring and waiting.

De Wet took his time, and then asked, "What precisely does your client find unpalatable?"

First blood to us. "It's the combined effect of your package of non-negotiables. The trustees would be slaughtered for throwing caution to the wind. As you well know, they have a fiduciary duty to act properly. Perhaps we could work through your points, one by one."

They went at it hammer and tongs, back and forth, not letting up for more than two hours. John remained calm throughout, consciously pressing De Wet's buttons at times to reinforce the message that a strong minority shareholder in Mantis would mean nothing but trouble and frustration for someone as controlling as De Wet. On more than one occasion, De Wet threatened to walk out, but he never did; instead, he stomped around the room, huffing and puffing and sometimes even hurling insults. Despite his demeanour, De Wet avoided the final step of rejecting out of hand John's contentions and arguments and suggested solutions on points of concern.

"I want to reflect on today's discussions, but don't for one minute think your client is going to interfere with the way I run my business or that we're going to give any warranties or that your client can come snooping around before a deal is done."

"Well, you go and reflect, Piet, and then let me know your final stance. Perhaps I can leave you with these thoughts: Don't for one minute think my client is going to buy blind or that my client will become a shareholder without reasonable protections."

"By the way, John, you haven't told me who is behind Three Rivers Trust."

Pushing his luck a little, John replied, "What is the relevance of the ultimate founder's identity? It's the trustees you'll be dealing with and no one else."

De Wet pulled himself up to his ample height, grasping the back of the chair with both hands. The muscles in his face tightened. For a moment he said nothing, and then in a cold and measured tone, said, "Don't you ever try to treat me like a fool again. I've been around the block a few times and I happen to know how these trusts work. If you want to do a deal with me, you had bloody well tell me who ultimately calls the shots."

De Wet needed to be placated quickly or John risked him walking away. "It's obvious I've offended you. That wasn't my intention and I apologise. I'm afraid I'm not at liberty to tell you who established Three Rivers Trust or who the beneficiaries are. I can assure you, however, that there's nothing funny or ominous about the trust or its setting up. I'm willing to recommend to my client that if we do a deal with you other than on a one hundred percent buy-out basis, the name of the ultimate founder be disclosed and that details concerning the identity of beneficiaries be told to you, on a confidential basis."

De Wet seemed slightly appeased but wanted to know why he couldn't be given this information much earlier. He couldn't or didn't want to understand the delay, and John couldn't understand why De Wet needed the information so soon. They agreed to leave the issue in abeyance for the time being.

It had, John felt, been a good morning. He believed that a one hundred percent deal remained doable provided De Wet could be accommodated on a few points.

He stepped into the lift and said goodbye to De Wet. He looked at the receptionist, smiled and gave an exaggerated wave as the lift door closed.

* * * * *

The bite of the chilly early morning and the carpet of leaves strewn in the street served as a reminder that autumn had arrived. Richard liked the changing colours of mother nature. He always, whatever the season, tried to start his day in the same way—a strenuous workout either on the road or in the gym. This invigorating autumn morning he felt like a run, which he enjoyed through the wide tree-lined suburbs of Melrose and Lower Houghton. The change in season was marked and it would not be too long before the short winter of the Highveld announced its generally unwelcome arrival.

He powered his way up a long hill, pumping his arms vigorously. As he crested the rise he peeked at his heart monitor and saw he was still well within his exertion range. He barely perspired and his breathing remained easy. The hot summer hadn't curbed his appetite for exercise and now he reaped the benefits.

He thought fondly about Asami, looking forward to seeing her. *Not long now.* Her beauty wasn't easily forgotten. A vivid picture emerged in his mind of that first day they met. She dressed so elegantly, and her swept back hair showed off her pretty looks. He even recalled the mother-of-pearl fastener which clipped back her hair. And how could he not remember their last evening together. Thinking about that and the picture of innocence she portrayed in her traditional dress brought butterflies to his stomach.

He started to fantasise about her upcoming trip and the time they would spend together. He couldn't remember when last he felt as happy and at peace.

He picked up the pace through Killarney and then headed into Parktown towards the war museum. Although still early, the traffic became heavier. He saw three other runners about 100 metres ahead and decided, as he often did on his morning outings, to catch them. He pushed harder and started to close the gap. His monitor reflected an increased heartbeat of 135. He lengthened his stride, maintaining the brisk pace. The gap closed faster now and for a moment he lost himself in the fantasy of a race with the finishing post in sight. His pace reached sprinting speed as he approached the runners, ready to grab victory and then, as quickly as it had started, the fantasy ended. He cut back immediately before passing them, not wanting to make a fool of himself.

His thoughts turned to the circumstances leading to the death of the Japanese soldier. Should he confess on behalf of Martin or not? Was it necessary? Wouldn't it be enough simply to say that he had been killed in battle? Martin had wanted Richard to tell the truth, to confess and to ask for forgiveness. *I can't believe he was thinking clearly when he wrote that; why invite scorn?*

He was about thirty minutes from home, still feeling comfortable physically. Thinking about Martin and the soldier dampened his mood. Suddenly he felt emotionally down and anxious about telling the soldier's family the truth. He wondered how Asami would react to all this. Perhaps he should seek her counsel and tell her what Professor Johnson had said about Martin's self-control snapping because of post-traumatic stress disorder. *Would she believe this? Would the family believe it?*

Of course they should accept the explanation, he reasoned. *After all, Johnson's eminence as a world authority on the subject and unsurpassed experience in the treatment of war veterans could not be doubted.* It took considerable effort on Richard's part to obtain an opinion from Professor Johnson. His opinion came as no surprise to Richard who was convinced there had to be some cogent explanation for Martin's bizarre and barbaric behaviour.

As he neared home, he started having doubts about letting on how the soldier died. He thought it would be the safer option not to say anything, particularly as only he and the psychiatrist knew the truth. Why, he asked himself, should he risk shame and humiliation on Martin's good name?

Reality returned as he reached his driveway. The family of the soldier hadn't yet been found, so no purpose could be served by worrying about the problem.

18

Some would call it British colonial in style. Everything about The Country Club Johannesburg at its Auckland Park venue was grand. It nestled amongst mature oak trees in an out-of-the-way leafy corner of the suburb. Although the facilities were modern, they didn't mask the aura of a bygone era.

Simon looked up into the bare oak tree and tried to guess its age—fifty years, perhaps seventy, maybe more. The leafless branches hung protectively over the lunch tables, letting through the dappled light and autumn warmth of the midday sun. Smartly dressed waiters scurried about their business efficiently and unobtrusively. Simon hadn't eaten at Under The Oaks before. Come to think of it, he hadn't eaten out anywhere much before. He liked the somewhat unimaginative name.

Lunch started off rather stiffly. He wasn't sure what to expect. Richard's P.A. had told him Richard wanted a catch-up lunch and that he shouldn't wear jeans, T-shirt or slops. He felt slightly overawed by the guests dressed in smart business attire and looking frightfully important. Simon wore an old pair of slacks and a short-sleeved open-necked shirt. He wondered why Richard chose to bring him to this place, but he lacked the courage to ask.

After the first beer he began to relax. Richard made a concerted effort to make Simon feel at ease, even dressing down and choosing to drink beer instead of some fancy cocktail or pink gin. They started off with lots of small talk, chatting about all sorts of things in general and about nothing in particular.

"I'm beginning to salivate," said Richard, as the delicious aroma of the food drifted over them. Simon began to understand why they had come to the club. The setting, the food and the weather complemented each other and combined to present something quite unique. "I don't know about you, but I'm starving," said Richard as he readied himself to fetch the first helping. Simon followed, unsure about where to begin at the colourful starters table, tastefully arranged with an array of wonderful food, including a variety of salads, different kinds of fish dishes, oysters, mussels, pink salmon, a large selection of cold meats and breads. "Don't be shy, Simon, take as much as you want—the price is the same."

Richard ordered another beer for each of them, wanting to get to know Simon better and to find out more about Mel.

Simon chatted more freely as they tucked into their first course. He told Richard that things couldn't be better at varsity. With the lifting of the financial burden and all its stresses, his marks had improved exponentially, and he had apparently started to enjoy a social life. His relaxed facial expression testified as much and instead of a dull look in Simon's eyes, they now sparkled.

"Do you still feel guilty about accepting help from the trust?" Richard asked guardedly.

Slowly Simon returned his knife and fork to the plate and just as slowly wiped his mouth with a napkin. He looked at Richard for what seemed a long time.

"No, no, I don't. I've thought about it often and I've come to terms with it. He owes us."

Richard wanted to know more but resisted the temptation to pry.

"Would you like to see around the club before our next course?" Richard didn't wait for Simon's reply. He told the head waiter they would be back in a short while before they walked away in silence towards the front of the main complex, then down to the gardens overlooking the cricket field and bowling green. The rich autumn colours were prolific and the birds were still noisy and busy. Not long now before they start their winter migration. The two men stood and watched them for a while.

By now Richard knew Simon enjoyed his cricket. "There used to be a small river there, where the cricket field is."

Simon asked the question that everyone always asks. "Why are those two trees on the field?"

A large tree could be seen square of the wicket at each end, roughly where square leg would field to a right-handed batsman.

"That's an interesting story. Members just about came to blows when the cricket enthusiasts proposed turning the river into a cricket field. In the end a compromise was reached for the sake of peace. The cricket field could be built but the two trees stayed." They walked and talked, finding their way back, past the generously sized swimming pool. "As you can see, Simon, it's too cool for bathers."

When they arrived back at their table Simon was still smiling at the story about the trees.

Neither of them could resist the lure of the carvery, returning to their seats with their plates piled high. Richard ordered another round of beers and seemed to be settling in for the afternoon. Simon didn't mind. He wasn't under any pressure to leave early and he was enjoying himself. He so wished his mother could share in this.

Richard seemed to read his thoughts. "How's your mum doing?"

"Much better, thank you. She's still working far too hard though, trying to make ends meet."

"You know her financial woes could be gone in an instant. It's entirely up to her."

"She won't accept help from the trust. She hated Martin Simmons. If I dare mention him, she explodes."

"Don't you think it might help if I speak to her?"

"She won't change. I know my mother. If you speak to her, she'll put two and two together."

"What do you mean?"

"She wanted to know why I applied to your former firm for a bursary and I told her you introduced me. If you speak to her about the trust, she'll get to the truth."

"Are you concerned about that? Surely once she calms down, she'll accept what you've done."

"Please, Richard, I beg of you, don't. You'll damage things between Mum and me. Please."

"Don't worry, I will never speak to her without first clearing it with you."

For a while the two of them sat quietly, engrossed in their own thoughts. Occasionally Richard greeted someone he knew. The few people left at the tables weren't in any hurry to leave. They could stay all afternoon and they'd still be welcome. His thoughts turned to Mel and the possibility of getting to know her, and the chances of winning her over.

"How long has she been in her job?"

"I assume you mean at Mantis? She also waits on tables after hours to make a little extra."

"Yes, at Mantis."

"More years than I can remember. She's in quite a senior position. I think it's about fifteen years."

"Does she ever talk about her work?"

"Why do you ask?"

"No particular reason. I'm interested, that's all. We seem to be getting to know each other better, so, I guess it's natural to ask. I didn't mean to be nosy."

"You're not being nosy. She talks about her job often. She loves it. Sometimes I think she's too involved in the company. She has no other interests."

"That might off course be because of her financial predicament. How old is your mum?"

"I suppose so. She's thirty-six, she had me at a young age."

"Simon, that's still very young indeed. That's younger than me. She has a whole lifetime ahead of her. We must find a way to get her on her feet. She needs to live, to enjoy life and what it has to offer." Richard felt a deep empathy towards Mel, even though they had never met. "What is the total of your mum's liabilities and how can I help to make things easier for her? The trust is, as you know, ready, able and more than willing to help."

"Her liabilities are huge, I don't know the full amount. She earns well at Mantis and even with her night job she can't make a dent in what she owes. I just don't know what anyone can do to help her. Maybe we need to be patient. A direct approach now won't work. I know my mother better than anyone else and I can tell you the bitterness and hate are too entrenched. She won't accept anything that comes from Martin. She hasn't got over the humiliation and hurt."

"What did he do to you and your mum that brought all this about?" Richard asked, believing Simon's confidence had been won over.

Simon hesitated. He looked everywhere except at Richard, seemingly weighing up whether to tell. He started to screw up the paper napkin in his hand, looking distinctly ill at ease.

Richard intervened. "Don't tell me if it's too painful Simon. I don't need to know."

"I can't talk about it. Not yet, anyway." Simon's earlier confidence disappeared, and his demeanour changed in an instant.

"If ever you want to talk about what happened I'm always willing to listen. If you'd prefer to speak to someone professional and independent, I can arrange that."

"Thank you."

* * * * *

The email from the chairman of the Burma Campaign Fellowship Group informing Richard that there had been no response to his appeal came as a bitter disappointment. The chairman encouraged him to persevere a while longer, pointing out the possibility that some members may not yet have seen the latest newsletter.

"Why would that be?" Olivia asked, not attempting to hide her shared disappointment.

"I've spoken to Mr Smithies, the chairman. Apparently many of their members travel abroad for months at a time, visiting family or friends or enjoying their retirement years."

"Could be months then before some of these guys know what you're looking for?"

"It seems that way. I could try to track them down. Maybe I could persuade Mr Smithies to give me their contact details. It could become expensive though."

"I think that's a good idea," said Olivia, intent on encouraging him to maintain his resolve.

"I agree. There isn't a hope in hell of trying to prise more information from Pinkstone. That became apparent in my last two meetings where I learnt nothing new."

19

June/July 1997

Richard and Olivia's tireless efforts in contacting every member of the Burma Campaign Fellowship Group eventually bore some fruit and now, clutching in his shaking hands, the long-awaited fax from a member. Richard read the handwritten covering note.

'So sorry about the delay, Mr Low, but I have spent the last twelve days in hospital after some emergency surgery to repair a hernia. I trust you haven't been too inconvenienced.

Accompanying this scrawled note is a copy of each page of the military notebook. As mentioned to you when we spoke on the phone, I purchased the book about eighteen months ago from a fellow collector here in the UK, who told me that he bought the book in South Africa six months earlier. He didn't say from whom or in which town. Sadly, he passed away a few months back. I have enquired from his widow as to where or from whom he made the purchase, but she has no idea as she didn't travel with him. She informed me though that he visited Cape Town, Pretoria and

Johannesburg. I hope this helps, and all the best in trying to trace the family.'

Even though all the writing appeared in Japanese script, Richard used a large magnifying glass to examine the pages sent to him.

"Liv, I wonder if this is it. Surely it must be. It would be too much of a coincidence for there to be two Japanese military notebooks from World War Two in South Africa. What do you think?" he asked, holding the pages out to her. "Here, look at them through this magnifying glass."

"I hope you're right, Richard," she said, commencing with her examination. "Judging from these faxed copies, the book seems to be in good condition except for the blotch over a bit of the text halfway down the second page."

"I'm tempted to get on a plane tonight for Japan to follow through on this information. Maybe I can find the 1943 family home of the soldier and see where that leads."

"That's crazy, Richard, you know Asami arrived in Namibia or Botswana two weeks ago and she's due in Johannesburg in five days' time."

"So what, Liv?"

"Richard, you're not thinking clearly. It will take you at least two days of travelling each way and you need to have the pages of the notebook translated into English and you then need to find an interpreter in Japan who can take you to the address. What if the soldier's family no longer resides at that address? You'll need time to follow up clues from there. And if the right family is at the address, you'll surely need some preparation time for the meetings with them. You know any face-to-face meeting with the family will require diplomacy, empathy and sensitivity, we've talked about this often, Richard. Besides, you can't run the risk of not meeting Asami at the airport."

"Dammit, Liv, I want to get there, sooner rather than later. I want to find the address mentioned in the notebook and I want to visit that address with the notebook and the prayer flag. Who knows, I might just find the right family there."

"But what's the rush? More than fifty years have passed since the Burma incident, another month or so won't matter, other than to increase your anxiety levels," she said with a slight smile. "Also, and just by the way, don't you think Asami would like to share in the joy when you return the flag?"

"You're right, Liv. Isn't this exciting? At last, it seems we're making progress. When I last spoke to Asami on her arrival in Windhoek, she said things were getting exciting on the shrine front, but she wouldn't elaborate for fear of creating false expectations. I so wish she was contactable."

Richard looked at his calendar to confirm Asami's arrival date. He hoped she would enjoy the destinations he had chosen for her. Their time together would be an ideal opportunity to get to know each other. He wondered whether he would still find her captivating. *Was the last time perhaps a momentary deviation brought on by the occasion of his visit to Nagasaki in springtime?*

John Matthews and Piet De Wet were due to meet for the fifth time. All the other meetings tended to follow the same pattern: each time they would meet at the offices of Mantis Logistics, on Piet's insistence, and each time the haughty receptionist with the coiffed seventies hairstyle would announce arrogantly that "*Mr* De Wet" would be through at a specific time, and each time De Wet was exactly on time. His approach remained consistently tough and uncompromising, giving away only a little at a time.

John's patience had paid off. Slowly but surely he chipped away, making progress with a quiet confidence. De Wet had agreed that Three Rivers Trust could have some veto rights, as well as first bite if the De Wet family wanted to sell their remaining shareholding, and a measure of board representation. He had also softened his stance on warranties, agreeing to give limited warranties for a short period.

John knew much work lay ahead as the devil lurked in the detail. De Wet showed a reluctance to traverse the detail until, as he put it, all the points of principle were out of the way. The idea of a due diligence investigation continued to meet with vociferous resistance—De Wet didn't want anyone ferreting around his company unless a deal had been done. Even some creative suggestions by John for a limited and well controlled due diligence with extensive built-in protections for De Wet fell on deaf ears.

John expected the fifth meeting to be difficult. They intended to discuss, so John thought, some of the detail around the veto rights, board representation and warranties.

"Good morning, Dorothy, so nice to see you again. I'm sure you know I'm here to see Mr De Wet."

The receptionist glared down her spectacle-mounted nose before leading John through to the same meeting room and announcing, with her trademark haughtiness, the intended arrival of her boss at the appointed time. Not a second early and not a second late, Piet De Wet walked in and greeted John with uncharacteristic courtesy. But, as always, he quickly focused on the purpose of the meeting.

"Trust you're well, John. Let's see if we can pick up the pace a bit. I don't like matters dragging on."

John smiled in amusement, given De Wet's pedestrian approach to the negotiations.

"I agree. I'm all for picking up the pace." John started to summarise the outstanding issues when De Wet cut across him with a surprise announcement.

"Look, John, based on our discussions to this point, I think a co-ownership deal is not going to happen. I don't like others looking over my shoulder and your client will, as you've already told me, want to become involved."

John wondered nervously where this was heading. He waited worriedly.

"One hundred percent of Mantis is now available subject to certain conditions."

John smiled inwardly because from the start he suspected De Wet in truth wanted an out-and-out sale but was playing hardball for strategic reasons.

They spent the next few hours debating Piet's conditions: he wanted a premium price calculated on a higher than normal PE factor; he wanted to limit the warranties considerably as per his lawyer's wording, which he handed John; and he was only willing to agree to a due diligence investigation as a mechanism for a downward price adjustment. In other words, John's client couldn't walk away from the deal, regardless of what the due diligence investigation revealed. De Wet again insisted on knowing the identity of the person or persons behind Three Rivers Trust.

With some considerable effort John managed to extract some key concessions on matters such as the locking-in of key executives, non-compete undertakings and a smooth and constructive transition of control over the business.

As John left, De Wet said, "John, the take it or leave it stage has been reached. You need to get back to me before the end of the week."

Cheeky blighter, John mumbled to himself as he entered the lift and waved goodbye to De Wet and to the ever-officious Dorothy.

* * * * *

Asami's research project with the San people in Namibia and Botswana exceeded her expectations, the shrine whose stamp appeared on the prayer flag had at last been found, and her plane commenced its descent for its scheduled landing in Johannesburg in twenty minutes. Right now, her life felt perfect. She missed Richard and longed to see him again. Their many emails and telephone calls had brought them closer. In the beginning their contact focussed on the prayer flag project, but since then it had become flirtatious.

She stared out of the window at the countryside, wondering about the future of her relationship with Richard. She was excited, very excited, not only to see Richard again, but also to enjoy the apparent expansive beauty of this vast country. His many vivid and passionate descriptions of the diversity of South Africa in all its facets and dimensions had whetted her appetite.

Richard paced the crowded arrivals hall like an expectant father in the corridors of a bustling maternity ward. Most of the people waited patiently, but a few, like him, couldn't be still. He checked his watch repeatedly. *She should be through any time now.* Although not hot, he wiped his clammy hands on his trousers and took a sip of water for his dry throat. All morning, doubts invaded his thoughts and now those doubts were heightened. Had he read too much into her emails and their many long-distance conversations? Had he perhaps misinterpreted her many endearments and other apparent intimacies? *Surely, she wouldn't have agreed to join me for three weeks if her feelings were merely platonic.* The excitement within him began to soar once again. *How will she be dressed?*

Asami appeared, pushing her trolley through the opening doors into the hall. At that instant their eyes locked and time seemed to stand still. She looked radiantly beautiful dressed in neat-fitting khaki slacks, white long-sleeved top and sneakers. Her shiny hair was stylishly swept off her face and tied back with a mother-of-pearl fastener, as it had been on the first day they met. She wasn't disappointed either. Richard sported a dark tan, despite the winter, and he looked ruggedly handsome. They ran towards each other, arms open, shouting and laughing with joy; then they hugged.

During the journey from the airport to Richard's home they talked, sometimes loudly and at other times quietly. They laughed and giggled, gesticulating with excitement, and every now and then they touched. She told him hurriedly about her trip and he told her briefly more about the arrangements for their time together.

With her two hands she took hold of his left hand, squeezing it gently as she leaned towards him. "Promise me that for the next few days there'll be no talk about the prayer flag. Let this time be only about us."

Richard called on every ounce of self-discipline to quell his burning desire to tell her about the notebook and to follow up on their last conversation about the shrine.

"I promise, only you and me and nothing else."

He lived up to his word. For the next few days they lazed around the heated pool, went shopping and ate at some of the best restaurants in town. He took her on a tour around the greater Johannesburg area, showing her places of interest, including the ugly contrast between the plush northern suburbs and the deprived, poverty-stricken areas of Soweto and Alexandra. They also dipped into some self-indulgence at the luxurious Palace Hotel at Sun City. She was amazed at the country's first world capacity in so many respects, but also saddened by the evident poverty of millions of people.

* * * * *

The dulcet sounds of a saxophone drifted towards them and grew louder as they approached The Ferns. Several food stations, many self-service, enticingly displayed the usual mouth-watering brunch fare. They chose to sit at a table discreetly positioned out of the way and obscured from the main body of patrons by a large pillar.

"How about champagne and orange juice to celebrate us, you and me, and our time together?" asked Richard.

A waiter hovered in anticipation, smiling knowingly.

"Good idea," she replied, her face beaming.

The first five days overflowed with fun, joy and laughter and confirmed for Asami that Richard was everything she imagined he would be. They planned to leave the following day for Kruger National Park, then onto Umhlanga Rocks on the north coast of KwaZulu-Natal and from there to Cape Town and finally to Richard's beloved Knysna. She couldn't remember when last, if ever, she had been so happy. With her elbows on the table and her fists supporting her chin, she gazed at him as he ordered the champagne. Out of the corner of his eye he saw her looking at him and he smiled back with a boyish grin.

A pianist took over from the jazz saxophonist as Richard and Asami moved slowly around the buffet, inspecting the gastronomic offerings. Asami shook her head; she wasn't sure what to go for.

"Listen, Asami, look on this as an eating fest. Take your time—at least three hours."

"You've got to be kidding, even three days would be too little. This calls for careful choice."

They both started off with oysters, with his plate piled considerably higher than hers.

She proposed the toast. "Here's to the rest of our holiday." As they clinked glasses his attention was suddenly drawn to a couple on the far side of the restaurant. The young man seemed to be whispering in his girlfriend's ear as his hand gently stroked her hair. Richard thought he recognised Simon. A closer look confirmed his initial thought.

"I'm sorry, Asami, I've seen someone across the other side whom I know. I had no idea he had a girlfriend." Before Asami could say anything, Richard let out a gasp. "Oh no, oh no, I can't believe what I'm seeing."

Asami's eyes followed his, and she could see the two young people were both men. Her focus returned hurriedly to Richard who appeared visibly shaken. He buried his head in his hands, saying: "This just can't be, there must be a mistake."

She touched his shoulder and frowned.

"Give me a moment, Asami."

He slugged down his orange and champagne and immediately poured himself another glass, shaking his head. He pushed his oysters away. She let him be. The two men across the room remained engrossed in each other, seemingly unconcerned about the world around them.

Now I know what caused the rift between Martin and Simon—he's gay. Richard's breathing quickened as he peered at Simon. He slapped the table. "Damn it, what the hell is wrong with him?"

After a few minutes he managed to compose himself. "I'm sorry Asami, do you mind if we leave? I'm very, very upset right now. I'll explain later."

"Of course. I'm sorry you've been upset." She didn't understand why he felt this way. She hadn't noticed anything offensive.

As hard as he tried to be his usual happy self for the remainder of the day, Asami saw through Richard's contrived demeanour. She invited him, more than once, to share his upset with her but without success.

"I do not want to talk about this now," he snapped. *Perhaps,* she thought, *he needs to sleep on it. I'll ask him about it tomorrow.*

20

July 1997

Asami had hoped for a much better start to their journey, imagining they would delve further into each other's lives and perhaps share their hopes and aspirations, and that Richard might reveal more about the places they would be visiting and about the game they were likely to see. Richard's grumpiness rode roughshod over her anticipated excitement.

"Asami, please won't you pass my sunglasses from the glove compartment?" Richard asked rather coolly, driving directly into the glare of the early morning sun peeping over the eastern horizon. She wiped the glasses before giving them to him. As their hands brushed, she gave a little squeeze.

"Would you like to hear the good news about the shrine we've been looking for?" she asked tentatively.

"Only if you're happy to talk about it. Remember, you said you didn't want to talk about the prayer flag," came the petulant retort.

She replied calmly and measuredly, resisting the strong temptation to respond sharply. "Only for the first few days, if you remember. I'm happy for us to talk about the flag. You seem so damn miserable that maybe, just maybe, my good news will bring back the real Richard I've come to know over these last few months. I don't like to see you like this."

"I'm sorry. I know I've been otherwise since yesterday, with you unfairly bearing the brunt of my upset. I'll tell you all about it after you tell me your good news and I tell you mine," he said, giving her arm a placating rub.

"You have good news?" she asked.

"I think so, but you go first."

"Well, Mr Low, we have …" She let her unfinished response hang in the air as she nuzzled into him, bringing her mouth close to his ear. She started again, but in a whisper. "We've found ..." She paused again.

Richard cocked his head to the left to guard against the tickling. "Oh please, Asami, don't do this to me. Tell me what you've found?"

She nibbled his ear softly, and said teasingly, "Only if you relax and say something nice."

Richard could feel himself succumbing to her charming gentleness. "You're beautiful."

"No, that's not nice enough." This time she kissed his ear, and said, "You have to do better than that, mister."

Richard responded with a few playful replies only to be told each time that they fell far short. "You are the most beautiful, the most intelligent and the sexiest woman in the world."

She giggled. "That's better. Now I'll tell you … we've found the shrine."

"That's brilliant news! Thank you so much, my dear Asami, that's fantastic. Your commitment and hard work is paying off. Where to from here?"

"Now, now, handsome, I told you, you must relax."

"I'm getting there, Asami, bear with me."

"Of course, but only if you behave." She continued with a smile. "I've arranged for someone to talk to the priests at the shrine. There are bound to have been increased visits before soldiers from the area left for war. We might get lucky and pick up some names and addresses and perhaps some other clues. If it becomes necessary, we'll also start making enquiries with the people who pray at the shrine."

Richard asked about the shrine's location.

"It's in Seihi, a small town on the west side of Omura Bay. I'll take you there when you visit next time. Now, your turn. Out with the good news."

"Only after you say something nice," he replied with a naughty smile.

"You're one of the most handsome men I know."

"Not good enough."

"You are the most handsome man I have ever met."

"Better, but you need to do better than that, much better."

"You're just copying me, Richard. Come on, out with it," she said with a chuckle.

"Okay, you win. I only discovered my news after your arrival in Namibia. If you don't mind, please reach into my briefcase on the back seat and pull out the red folder."

"I have no idea what to expect, may I have a look?"

"Of course, go ahead."

She withdrew the copies of the notebook and gasped aloud, bringing her cupped hands to her mouth. She looked fleetingly at Richard and then attentively at each page.

"Is this a copy of the military notebook, Richard, the one you've been hunting for?"

Before he could answer, she said, "I can't believe this. This is a game changer. How did you find it? Quickly, tell all, and don't leave out any detail."

"I can't be one hundred percent certain it is our notebook, at least not yet, but I'm holding thumbs." Richard conveyed the circumstances surrounding the discovery, not sparing any detail. "But more importantly, dear Asami, what information is in the book about its owner? Is there enough?" he asked, chewing on a fingernail.

She scrutinised the pages again. "We have the name of the soldier and a residential address," she said, swallowing repeatedly, "and there is also what seems to be a regiment number."

"What about his unit, Asami, surely that's identified?"

She looked again. "There is some smudging below the number, blocking out, it appears, the name of the unit."

"Damn it, I was so hoping for confirmation that he served with the 55th Infantry Regiment."

"That would have been great, but don't be disheartened, the rest of the information is substantial—a name, a regiment number, which will be invaluable in dealing with the Defence Agency, and a physical address. I think it's most significant that this soldier, Hashimoto Katsu, came from Oseto, a small town bordering Seihi on the west. That's so exciting!"

"You've lost me," he responded, furrowing his brow.

"Richard!" she exclaimed. "I've just told you the stamp on the prayer flag is from a shrine in Seihi and now we also know that Hashimoto Katsu came from an area very near to the shrine. The inference is irresistible."

"Okay, understood. This then gives us some useful pointers, as I see it," he said. "First, we must try to ascertain whether the soldier died in Burma. If he didn't, then this is the wrong notebook and he is not our man. If he succumbed in Burma while serving with the 55th Infantry Regiment, we need to visit his address in Oseto. Do you agree?"

"I do. I will be able to use my network to check these points. I'll fire off some emails as soon as we have decent connectivity. You must be patient, Richard, this could take a week or two."

"It's so gratifying to have your help, Asami. Without you I'd be totally lost. Although I'm keen, as no doubt you are, to find out the answers, I know these things take time. Besides, you and I have a holiday ahead of us, so we can focus on the fun things for the next few weeks."

Richard's demeanour changed dramatically for the good and he became more talkative, even smiling a few times.

She allowed him to go on for quite some time about the Sabi Sands Game Reserve and the Jock of the Bushveld Lodge at which they would be staying, before interrupting him. Asami wanted him to talk about yesterday, hoping for a better understanding of him. "You said you would tell me why you became so upset. I'm listening."

"It's a long story." He told her about the family ties between Martin, Simon and his mother, the traumatic breakdown in their relationship because, so it now seemed, Martin discovered Simon was gay, and about his wish to leave Mel and Simon well provided for. "Because of the breakdown, Martin knew that Simon and his mother wouldn't accept any inheritance, so Martin wanted me to find a way around this."

"But why a breakdown simply because Martin found out Simon was gay? I don't understand. And why did you get so upset yesterday?"

"I would guess there must have been some sort of confrontation. I can understand Martin losing it."

"But surely not to the extent of causing a breakdown in the relationship with his daughter-in-law and only grandson. I can understand his initial upset and disappointment, but for things to implode the way they apparently did, his anger must have got out of control."

"You speak as if his anger lacked justification," he said, raising his eyebrows. "For goodness sake, to discover this about his grandson must have rocked his world."

She could hear the tension in his voice and, for a moment, thought about steering the conversation in another direction. She decided not to; her conscience wouldn't allow her to avoid the issue. "Do you really think you can justify Martin's behaviour?"

"Yes, of course," he replied dogmatically. "What Simon was doing... is doing... is wrong. It's unnatural and against God's law. Martin had no choice but to deal with the situation firmly."

She sat quietly for what seemed like a long time and then, shaking her head and bringing her hand to her mouth, she asked, "Is that really, and I mean really, how you feel, Richard?"

"No question about it. The Bible is clear about this."

She turned away, staring out of the passenger window, still shaking her head. She was on the verge of taking him to task but decided it would be counter-productive. "Why did this upset you, Richard, I don't understand?"

"No one bothered telling me Simon was gay."

"But why did that upset you?" she asked, with a more furrowed brow.

"I felt betrayed. Martin knew my stand on homosexuality and yet he chose to hide it from me. As for Simon, I've gone out of my way to help him and he has said nothing to me about being gay."

"So what? Would you have refused to help if you had known?"

"I don't feel comfortable helping a gay person. It cuts right across my religious convictions."

Richard's prejudice stunned Asami into further silence; she couldn't believe that anyone with a modicum of intelligence could be so bigoted.

"I think you're hypocritical and quite unprofessional," she said. "Surely it's not for you to judge. If you are unwilling to help gay people because of their so-called sinful self-indulgence, then you must feel the same way about all sinners. Have you never helped someone who has committed adultery or who has stolen something or who has coveted his neighbour's possessions or who has told lies etcetera, etcetera?"

He knew that Asami's challenge was logical, but that's not how he felt emotionally. Of course he had many times in the past, and would no doubt again in the future, come to the assistance of others who offended God's laws.

"It's hard to explain. I don't want to be judgmental, but it feels wrong. How can I change the way I feel? It's the way I am. It's my value system."

In a strange way she felt sorry for Richard as he floundered. She guessed he had never been challenged to face his own bigotry.

"Confronting one's own prejudices, whatever they are, can never be easy. You've lived through a period of apartheid, Richard, and will therefore know what I'm talking about."

She wanted to say so much more, not as a criticism, but rather to help him, but her instinct was to leave him be for the moment.

They travelled in silence for a while, simply staring at the road ahead. Asami leaned across and softly massaged the back of his neck. He shifted his head from side to side, acknowledging her touch. Thankfully their fuel stop at the small town of Machadodorp, in the heart of trout fishing country, brought an end to the awkwardness of the last half hour. Asami needed a break and a cup of coffee. Richard's prolonged silence kept her wondering whether he was sulking because she challenged him about his prejudice, or whether he was thinking about it with even a slightly open mind.

In the station cafe, he moved his cup, as well as hers, out of the way, taking both her hands in his. Richard looked at Asami and she held his gaze; then he spoke, quietly and sincerely. "Both of us have been looking forward to this time together and we shouldn't let Simon's sexual orientation spoil it for us. I'm sorry about my reaction these last two days, but hopefully you can understand this is the first time that my feelings on the matter have been tested. It's also the first time, thanks to you, that I've been challenged to think honestly about whether I'm a bigot. I need time to work through my feelings and attitude, if that's okay. Will you forgive me?"

"It's not about forgiveness, Richard, but rather about bigotry and prejudice. I know what it's like to be the victim and can only hope that you will get through this and come to realise that your views do not justify any form of discrimination."

"What do you mean you know what it's like?" he asked.

"My brother's gay."

* * * * *

As they pulled into the reception area of the Jock of The Bushveld Lodge, Richard turned to Asami, and said, "Please, let's put the gay issue on hold for the moment and enjoy the magic of the African bushveld."

"It's a serious difference between us, Richard," she replied, "and one that sooner or later needs to be resolved, but I agree that for the time being we should try not to let this spoil the trip."

The prelunch gin and tonics hit the spot as they relaxed under the shade of a large ebony tree in the open eating area in front of the lodge. Andrew, their assigned waiter, waited on them with a constant smile. They were more than a little overwhelmed by all the activity around them.

The multitasking Andrew attended to their every need, whilst at the same time engaging in a running battle with some mischievous monkeys. Using the ebony tree as their base from which to launch food raids, they were resolute in their efforts to breach Andrew's defences, which included skilful handling of a homemade catapult. Their persistence paid off occasionally as they succeeded in snaffling some juicy fruit from the tables.

The lodge and its ultracomfortable thatched suites were ideally situated to offer the guests to this small, intimate safari camp unspoilt views up and down the Sands River. Asami squealed suddenly, grabbing Richard by the arm and forgetting for a moment about the distracting monkeys. She pointed to a large shimmering pool of water in the riverbed not more than a hundred metres from the lodge. "Look, Richard, look, do you see them?"

There, emerging slowly from the bush towards the pool, he saw a line of elephants, large and small, some not more than a few weeks old. It didn't take too long for the splashing and cavorting to commence, with the nurturing parents using their enormous bodies to shield their young from being knocked over or trampled upon. Richard had seen this before, but for Asami it was a novel and mesmerising experience. No sooner had the elephant spectacle unfolded before their eyes when Asami noticed several other pleasant surprises served up by the wilds of Africa. The Jungle Book came alive before their eyes, with kudu, impala, hippo, zebra, crocodile and warthog entering the picture in or on the banks of the riverbed. Even though Richard promised her a feast of game viewing, Asami never expected so much in such a short time and so close to their lodgings.

After devouring their appetisingly sumptuous lunch, they retired to their adjacent suites on the riverbank to settle in and take a nap before the afternoon game drive.

After their rest, Andrew served some refreshments and snacks in the lounge area of the lodge and then introduced them to Melissa and Stephen, their assigned game guide and tracker. Richard was happy to see there were only two other people booked on the game drive, a Canadian couple. *The smaller the number the greater the experience,* he reminded himself.

It was Asami's first game drive so she listened closely to the briefing from Melissa, which covered all the dos and don'ts and all the need-to-knows. The guide's bullish prediction about spotting at least four of the Big Five lifted the excitement of the guests. She also said that although a leopard sighting would not be easy, with patience and perseverance during their stay they might get lucky.

Soon they meandered deep into the bushveld of the reserve. Except for some running commentary from Melissa, absolute silence and deep concentration prevailed amongst the group—each guest intent on making the first spot.

Stephen's skills as a tracker soon bore fruit. Within two hours they had excellent sightings of elephant, rhino, giraffe, herds of impala, kudu, warthog, zebra, bushbuck, tsessebe, waterbuck and wildebeest, as well as a large variety of birds.

"These wonderful sightings are so much more meaningful and memorable because we're experiencing them in the natural habitat of the animals," whispered Asami.

The long shadows and sharp silhouettes shaped by the setting sun, together with the distinctive smell of the bush and the dust kicked up by animals on the move, created a unique and special blend which touched the senses, not only for Asami, but also for Richard.

So far, the big cats evaded them—no lion, leopard or cheetah. Melissa pulled off the dirt track into an open clearing on high ground, maximising their 360-degree view.

"Okay, folks, at last our comfort break and the traditional bushveld sundowners and snacks," said Melissa.

Extra precautions were called for given the time of day and the fact that the group would be getting off the vehicle. Melissa encouraged them not to give up on the cats as ample opportunities lay in wait, if not that evening on the way back to the lodge, then in the following days. The sun hovered ever so slightly above the horizon, about to dip out of sight. The quiet noises of the evening started coming into their own. Suddenly, without warning, an echoing bark pierced the relative quietness.

Melissa calmed everyone's nerves. "No need to be scared, that's a frightened baboon sensing danger."

The group huddled closer to one another, experiencing the evening chill. In any event, they felt safer that way. A succession of distant, deep-throated lion roars following the bark of the baboon were enough to persuade Asami to put up with the discomfort of a full bladder. An offer by Melissa (who happened to be armed) to accompany Asami made no difference.

They had been forewarned about the evening chill and were therefore well prepared with blankets supplied on the vehicle, supplementing their own warm gear to give them cover against the biting wind. Hopefully the nocturnal creatures would now show themselves.

The lions and other cats continued to be evasive on the return trip and although the group was rewarded with some night sightings in Stephen's spotlight, Asami and Richard were keen to get back to a hot tub, followed by dinner and some good wine. After a long bumpy ride (a particularly uncomfortable one for Asami), the lights of the lodge filtered through the bush and soon they were met at reception by welcoming staff, offering steaming face towels and some refreshments.

Richard was touched by the unexpected, considerate and romantic welcome to his suite. A trail of red petals led invitingly from the front door of his dimly lit suite, past the king-size bed covered by a mosquito net, and into the candlelit bathroom. Steam floated from the ample bathtub, which overlooked the river below through a floor-to-roof window. The ambience was enhanced, not only by the full moon peering inquisitively through the window, but also by the scented bubble bath and enticing bottle of champagne resting in an ice bucket on the edge of the bath.

Richard popped the champagne, stepping into the bath. As he slid down into a comfortable lying position he looked out at the moon and thought about Asami, wondering when they would become lovers.

He closed his eyes, visualising her beauty, and recalled once again her striking image when they first met—a moment he would never forget. A breeze, as if someone had opened the door to his suite, disturbed his dreamy recollection. He sat upright, looking around expectantly, hoping that it might be Asami coming to join him, but then he felt the breeze again and realised his hope was nothing more than wishful thinking.

Later he met Asami outside her suite, ready to stroll to dinner, escorted by an armed ranger in case they unexpectedly ran into a wild animal. As always, she looked radiantly beautiful. She hooked onto his arm.

"You won't believe the fantastic welcome waiting for me at my suite," she said. "A path of red petals led from my front door, past the bed and into a candlelit bathroom."

"And I bet," said Richard, "a scented foam bath awaited you, with a bottle of champagne in an ice bucket on the edge of the bath."

"How do you know that? Did you spy on me?" she asked jokingly.

"I had the same, Asami. Perhaps they were unsure about which suite we would be bathing in. I found it rather romantic and so wished we were together," he said. "Did you think about me while soaking?"

"I did, but perhaps not in the way you hope. The turmoil of these last two days has thrown me and unsettled my feelings. We have much to talk about and much to decide, but please, let's not spoil this lovely safari experience you've so generously arranged."

He tried unsuccessfully to hide his disappointment. "I understand where you're coming from. I also agree we should put this aside for the time being and enjoy all this trip promises."

Andrew showed them to their dimly lit table, tucked away for maximum privacy near the glowing log fire at the far end of the dining room. They were true to their word, avoiding any discussion or comment about Martin, Mel or Simon (or his sexual orientation) or, indeed, about their own relationship.

The game drives over the next couple of days did not disappoint. They managed to also see buffalo, hyena, wild dog, lion, cheetah and leopard. Witnessing a lion kill was the highlight for Richard, but for Asami, the close encounter with a large male leopard took top honours. They followed the leopard for more than an hour, their vehicle getting as close as fifteen metres on occasions.

On their journey back to Johannesburg, Asami wondered, privately and worryingly, whether this was the end of their personal relationship, which, not so long ago, seemed gloriously promising. Not surprisingly, Richard's intermittent thoughts were no different.

21

Perched on the highest point of the rocky promontory, Asami relaxed into the rhythmic motion of the rolling waves beneath and around her. The sea gave off a crimson hue, reflecting the cheeriness of the sun creeping up from behind the Western Head, one of two prominent cliffs flanking the entrance to Knysna Lagoon. The tide receded slowly and the ocean remained relatively calm. Intermittent gusts of gentle early morning breeze blew Asami's hair across her face. She hugged her knees, pulling them up to her chest, and let the side of her face rest on her arms.

The peace, tranquillity and warmth ushering in the new day resonated with her pensive mood. She welcomed the 'me time', it afforded her an opportunity to reflect while Richard played golf. In two days' time she would be saying goodbye to him, something she didn't want to dwell on. Rather, she reminisced about the last few weeks. It had, despite the faltering start, been one of her best holidays ever. Each place they visited had been special in its unique way and all of them left her with happy memories that she would treasure for years to come, regardless of what may happen to her relationship with Richard. She couldn't think of any other place in the world that could offer the experiences she had enjoyed: open spaces, blue skies, green hills, magical bushveld sunsets, game reserves teeming with wild animals, warm seas, cold seas, pristine beaches, majestic mountains, clear lakes, world class vineyards, gourmet food, friendly people and so much more.

Richard remained true to his word. At no time did he again exhibit any anger, moroseness or other unpleasantness—quite the contrary. He hadn't again talked about Simon and nor had he again broached the subject of homosexuality. But Asami knew that at some point before returning home she would have to approach the issue, given her brother's position and, indeed, her own views about bigotry.

A sudden movement caught her eye. Two oystercatchers busied themselves prising mussels off the rocks immediately below her. She felt privileged to see them so close because they were an endangered species. For fifteen minutes or more the two birds held her undivided attention as she watched every little action.

More than an hour passed, and she was grateful to still be alone. She again looked at the empty, unspoilt beach which stretched for hundreds of metres to the west, its golden fine sand glistening in the early morning. The two beaches to the east, secluded amongst sandstone rock formations, were equally beautiful and quiet. She resisted the temptation to follow the tricky and sometimes treacherous path down to the beaches that spread below a high cliff.

She scrambled down to within a few metres of the water. Even the calmness of the sea didn't stop her getting showered by the surf breaking on the rocks around her. Just then she witnessed one of the most wonderful spectacles that anyone could ever wish to see—a large pod of dolphins, probably a hundred or more, surfaced in front of her, frolicking in the waves. They enthralled her, seemingly putting on a special show only for her. They propelled themselves out of the water, surfed on the incoming waves and raced each other, cavorting and carrying on for at least half an hour. Asami, taken by the exhibition, found herself applauding enthusiastically. They then left, not all at once, but in small groups, as if bidding her goodbye.

She thought about Richard and their relationship. That, after all, was the main purpose of her seeking the solitude she found in this place, to get away from Richard and other people—just her, the oystercatchers and the dolphins. She needed to think. She felt uneasy about falling in love. Although shocked by his homophobic reaction, she didn't think this was the sole cause of her unease. Something else niggled her, but she couldn't put her finger on it. She became misty-eyed, flitting from one memory to another of their time together.

Winding her way back to the house, she felt a sense of contentment. The three hours of solitude and introspection afforded her an opportunity to work through her feelings and concerns. She had made up her mind to engage seriously with him about his attitude towards gays. Their relationship couldn't possibly grow into something deeper, or even survive, unless he jettisoned his prejudices.

Sitting on the balcony, feet up on the table, she sipped the cold rock shandy, made as Richard had shown her. Looking out to sea, she could see the dolphin- and whale-watching boat, packed with tourists, moving slowly in a large circle. They had, she assumed, spotted some dolphins. Suddenly, Asami began to giggle, at first quietly and then louder, as she noticed the hairy growth on her legs. *It's been a good holiday.* Indeed, and a relaxed one too, most of the time. She shook her head in disbelief at how casual she had become these last few weeks. She needed to do something about those legs and wondered whether Richard had any spare batteries in his briefcase that would fit her shaver.

She wandered through to the study, not thinking he would mind her ferreting around. She scratched through his things but with no luck. As she closed the briefcase, she saw a letter which, quite uncharacteristically, she began to read. After the first few paragraphs she realised the letter had been written to Richard by Martin as he lay dying. She hesitated, feeling guilty. She wanted to read on but stopped herself. She closed the case, chiding herself for looking at the letter. *What's wrong with you, Asami, this isn't you.* She left the study feeling rather ashamed.

Her restlessness drove her, over the next few hours, to do menial tasks such as her washing and ironing and some of her packing, and even shaving her legs. In anticipation of Richard's return, she prepared a mouth-watering tuna salad with chilled fruit to follow. A bottle of crisp sauvignon blanc waited on ice.

"I hope you don't mind, I scratched around in your briefcase this morning looking for batteries for my shaver and—"

Before she could admit to seeing Martin's letter Richard put his arms around her, spilling some of his wine as he did so, and said he didn't mind at all.

"I don't recall having any batteries."

"No, I couldn't find any, but in the end, it didn't matter because I managed to find a razor." She decided against telling him about the letter.

They took their lunch and the bottle of wine onto the balcony to further embrace the glorious day: the skies were clear and a light breeze drifted in from the south-east.

Despite being in a frivolous mood and full of banter, Richard noticed Asami wasn't quite herself. "Are you all right, Asami? You're quieter than usual."

"The day after tomorrow I leave for home with great memories of a wonderful holiday, and I'm sad. Not only am I sad, but I'm also concerned, for you, for me, for us."

"I'm not sure I'm following you."

She walked to the edge of the balcony, sceptical of his feigned ignorance. She hung over the safety rail and stared at the waves crashing on the rocks in the distance. Richard soon joined her and she took hold of his left arm and leaned her head on his shoulder. They stood like that for a while, neither of them saying anything.

Gently he began to stroke her soft, shiny hair. "I'm also sad, my dear Asami, very, very sad."

"Have you given further thought to your feelings on gay relationships?" she asked, looking into his eyes.

"Much thought, Asami."

"And?"

"I'm sorry, but I have a problem with them. They're unnatural and biblically wrong. My conscience won't allow me to accept or condone homosexuality."

Although not expecting a different answer, Asami refused to leave the matter there. She drew away and sat down. He turned around to face her and leant against the balcony railing. She sipped her wine, pushing lunch aside.

"What does that mean in terms of the way you'll react to or treat gays? Will you try to avoid them or reject them? If they need your help will you shun them? Will you let a gay couple sleep in your home?"

He didn't want to be drawn into a discussion on the matter, but he knew it couldn't be avoided. "Asami, there are no easy answers and it's not a case of one answer covers all. It depends on the circumstances."

Before he could continue, she interrupted him. "But Richard, the Bible also encourages slavery, commands that women shouldn't speak in church and forbids remarriage after divorce except where the divorce comes about because of unfaithfulness."

He didn't respond.

"You see, Richard, you and others who oppose faithful same-sex partnerships rely on the literal meaning of isolated biblical texts dealing with homosexuality, in support of your views. However, you seem to accept that the literal meaning of the scriptures should be abandoned when it comes to slavery, the role of women in the church and divorce because, so you would argue, they were written for their times and are no longer applicable."

Richard disengaged from her, and fidgeted with his watch. She could see he didn't know how to counter her argument. Asami had no desire to embarrass him or to make him feel awkward, but she needed to follow through. She had witnessed first-hand how her brother and countless others, who weren't promiscuous, suffered vilification and humiliation because of their sexual orientation.

"Biblical interpretation is complicated and difficult," he said, "and it's not something you can deal with in the way you've tried to do. Many fine and learned biblical scholars and theologians have over the centuries interpreted the word of God with the guidance of the Holy Spirit and who am I to disagree with their view that the literal meaning of the homosexuality scriptures still holds good. I'm sorry, Asami, but that's my conviction and I must stand by it.

Besides, homosexuality is unnatural. It's against the laws of nature."

"Have you ever asked a gay person how he or she feels?" she questioned in a raised voice, not giving him a chance to answer. "Well, I have, many times, and I can assure you their sexual desire is natural and not contrived."

She poured herself another glass of wine, topping up his at the same time. "If our relationship goes further, how will you interact with my brother? Will you ignore or reject or admonish him? Will you not let him and his partner share a room in our home?"

He knew an immediate response would offend Asami, and probably cause the immediate collapse of their relationship. That was something he desperately wanted to avoid. "Asami, please, I beg you, can we put this on hold? Right now we're so far apart on this that I fear that to take positions will result in something neither of us wants."

Her feelings for him ran deep and she wanted to save their relationship, but not at the cost of embracing bigotry. She stood up and moved next to him, her dark eyes locking onto his face.

"Oh, Richard, I don't want this issue to tear us apart. I'm willing to give you time. I know it's not easy to change one's views on something like this, but to do that I need to know you are at least trying. That you are at least open to that possibility. So far, you have only insisted that you are not. If you are not open to change, then there is no hope. And without hope, there is no future for us."

He leaned in, hugging her and kissing her softly on the cheek, tasting the saltiness of her anxiety.

22

August 1997

"It's damn freezing," said Mel, through chattering teeth.

She sat curled up in a tight ball under a threadbare duvet on the uncomfortable two-seater couch which she picked up cheaply at a secondhand furniture shop. Their constrained finances precluded her and Simon having any artificial heating in the home. The midwinter evening temperature had plummeted inhospitably to about three degrees Celsius.

Simon knew their impecunious state could easily and swiftly be a thing of the past and wondered whether the time had not come to break free from the shackles that kept them painfully bound to an impoverished lifestyle. He tried to capture some warmth by cupping both hands firmly round his mug of coffee, unsweetened because of the sparse sugar stock in the house.

He looked across at his mother. "Can I get you another cup, Mum? It will help to keep you warm."

She stopped herself just in time from snapping at his silly statement. *I mustn't deflect my anger and frustration to my son because we're still on the bones of our arses,* she chided herself.

"No thanks, my son, I'm coffeed out," she replied gratefully, appreciating Simon's empathy.

Mel's financial position hadn't improved since the inception of Simon's so-called bursary, but he was reticent to ask for more, not because Richard would turn him down, quite the contrary, but because the extra free cash would almost certainly heighten his mother's suspicions. He didn't know for how much longer she could keep at it, working two jobs and having nothing to show for it. At least her medical insurance covered her anti-depressant medication.

"Mum ..." he hesitated nervously.

"Yes, Simon, I'm listening," she said, teeth still chattering.

"Mum, I know how we both feel about what happened and I do not for one minute want to underplay the damage and pain it has caused us."

Mel looked at him quizzically.

"What I'm trying to say is, should we not be looking to Martin Simmons' estate for some financial support? We, and you in particular, are in dire financial straits and they will get worse, a lot worse."

"Don't go there, Simon, please forget that now. What has happened to you? How can you even think of taking any help from him? That monster shattered our lives! Look at me, I look like a middle-aged cigarette-smoking soak and until recently you were an absolute wreck, about to lose the opportunity of a decent education."

"Mum, you don't look like a soak, you're still beautiful. I know he shattered our lives but why should that stop us investigating whether we are legally entitled to support. You see—"

Mel cut him off. "On what possible basis could we have a legal entitlement? You're losing your marbles, Si."

"I have gathered from my lectures that there are apparently some common law rules concerning support for family, even from a deceased estate, and I think it might be worth our while to look into this more closely."

"You're missing the point here, Simon." He looked perplexed. "As far as I am concerned, any family connection disappeared when Martin cut us loose."

"Mum, I don't mean to be disrespectful, but isn't that an emotional view birthed by pride? Whether we care to admit it or not, we are family, at least in the technical, legal sense. I know that you and I want nothing to do with him but that does not alter the familial tie and if, legally speaking, we are family and if, legally speaking, we are entitled to some sort of support, why the hang should we not grab that support with both hands?"

She jumped up from the couch and walked briskly to the middle of the room, facing away from her son. Slowly she turned, hands on hips. "I thought you and I were on the same page when it comes to that bastard. Why the sudden change, Simon?"

Besides Mel's confrontational body language, the bitterness and anger were evident from her raised voice and rapidly reddening cheeks. Simon knew to tread carefully, for fear of feeding any suspicions she might be harbouring. He put his arm around her. She tried pulling away, but he held her tight.

"Mum, let's not turn this into a fight. We need each other. It's just the two of us. We're drowning in an ocean of despair, with no life raft—and no, I haven't changed my feelings. As far as my emotions go, I hope that bastard is burning in hell for what he did. You know that. But why should we live like this when nothing but pride stands between us and accepting enough money to set us to rights? He owes us, Mum. And hang it all, why should he get to be warm in hell while we're freezing our arses off?"

Simon wasn't entirely convinced by his own reaction. He had recently done a lot of thinking about whether he and his mother had not been unfair in rejecting Martin's efforts at reconciliation.

"Although my emotions remain the same, I am, because of our desperate situation, trying to take the emotion out of it. I am trying to be more rational. We are, to put it crudely, in shit street with nowhere to go, and now there might be a glimmer of hope. If we let our pride get in the way, we will regret it, and probably suffer for the rest of our lives."

Mel wriggled free and moved back to the couch. "I don't want to fight with you either, and I know it's only the two of us and that we need each other, but I cannot understand why this change. Don't give me that crap about rational thinking and having nowhere to turn. Yes I do have my pride and yes it will not allow me to relent. I would rather walk the damn streets at night to survive than take charity from the coffers of Mr High-and-Mighty! You do what you have to Simon, but I am not asking for or accepting a single cent from the estate of the late Martin Simmons."

She stood, huffing, and stormed to her bedroom, slamming the door with such force that the thin walls shuddered.

He shouted after her, "It's not fucking charity, Mum, it's our right."

Simon knocked softly at her door. "Mum, Mum, please let's talk. We cannot, must not, allow this to come between us. I want us to work through the issues to make sure we are doing the right thing."

She didn't respond. He knocked again. "Please, Mum, I love you. Open the door so we can talk. We can't go to bed angry or upset."

He waited expectantly. Again no response. He knocked yet again.

"Leave me alone, Simon. I'm tired and upset," she said, choked-up.

*****

His mother left for work before Simon surfaced from a few hours of disturbed sleep. He struggled to get shut-eye, tossing and turning restlessly and anxiously for most of the night, stressing about his mother's deteriorating health, not only physically but also at the emotional and mental levels. He had wrestled into the small hours with possible solutions which, at the time, seemed workable but now in the cold light of day made no sense. He could feel panic setting in.

The phone rang. It was Richard. "Prof Markowitz tells me you're doing well and seem to be less stressed."

"Oh, hi, Richard," said Simon flatly.

"What's up, Simon? You sound awful."

"A bad, very bad night, and I don't know where I'm going from here."

Richard listened carefully, responding caringly. Simon relayed the events of the previous evening, including his mother's worsening situation.

"Oh dear, Simon, I am sorry. Don't you think it's time for me to speak to your mum? Also, I can easily arrange an increase in your monthly bursary payments."

After a lengthy, and at times intense discussion, they agreed such action would be counterproductive.

Richard would have preferred not to pre-empt the outcome of the Mantis Logistics project but felt he had to hold out some hope for Simon, particularly to limit the distractions from his studies.

"Listen, Simon, I have for a while now been working on a solution to your mum's situation and I am hopeful—more than hopeful—that it will come off, but only in a few months' time. You'll need to keep a close eye on her while I try and sort things out."

In Richard's mind, the Mantis project took on an almost desperate level of urgency that demanded a done deal outcome very soon, even on slightly unfavourable terms if need be.

"Do you think your mum can hold out for a while longer?"

"We'll try, what choice is there, given Mum's stubbornness."

"You're a champ, Simon," said Richard, with increased admiration. "Let's keep in touch and be sure to let me know immediately if things worsen."

Richard wasn't sure what he would be able to do if matters deteriorated further. *I hope they can hang in there. I must make Mantis happen.*

* * * * *

Richard swept into the meeting room like a gust of wind and plonked himself down across from John.

"What's the urgency, Richard, something new and interesting?" asked the ever hopeful John.

"It's the Mantis project. This deal needs to be put to bed fast and as a matter of considerable urgency, and when I say considerable, I mean as urgent as anything could possibly get."

He explained Mel's situation, emphasising its importance, certainly one of the two main objectives of the Candlewood Investments Trust.

"Let's summarise where we are with De Wet," said John. "You will remember that since the big negotiation at the end of June I've had some ongoing meetings with him, mainly around price and the basis for price adjustment if problems come to light during the due diligence investigation. You will also remember the confirmations from Piet about Mel."

"John, correct me if I am wrong. I think you and I were comfortable with the limited reps and warranties offered by De Wet. We were also happy with no due diligence walk-away rights provided a downward price adjustment is available if we discover material problems."

"Spot on."

"What then remains outstanding?"

"Not many issues, but they are crucial—the pre-adjustment price, the disclosure of Martin Simmons as the founder of Candlewood Investments and the disclosure that it is the party behind Three Rivers Trust, the period after which no claims may be instituted against the De Wet family in respect of the acquisition, and the limitation of the remedies available to the trust for breach."

"I think we accept De Wet's proposals on the last two points provided he drops his pre-adjustment price to the 250 million-rand level you've suggested. Are you sure that you and the valuers are comfortable with that number as representative of value in the company?" asked Richard. "I must be able to justify the price to the other trustees, based on value."

"We are. There's good sustainable value in the company having regard to its earnings over many years. That price includes a decent but justifiable premium in all circumstances, given that Mantis is a perfect vehicle for the trust's black empowerment objectives, including a stock exchange listing down the road."

"What about the third point?" asked John. "Piet wants to know who ultimately calls the shots at Three Rivers."

"Why do you think he's after that information? It can't surely be curiosity only?"

"I believe Piet wants to be sure he is dealing with someone reputable."

"I am willing to make a confidential disclosure to a mutually acceptable independent firm of auditors with a view to them making a high-level investigation and expressing an opinion as to whether reputational risk is likely. That's it, nothing more."

"Understood."

"How are your negotiations progressing with the new executive team and will they be on board in time, ready for the transition from closing?"

"We are almost there, Richard. I don't anticipate any insurmountable hurdles. It's understood that the new team will call the shots from day one and that Piet's team will stay on and co-operate with them for the transition period of six months."

"Excellent. I like our new CEO and CFO. They'll be a great loss to Framptons, but hey, that's not our problem. I'm also pleased they understand and respect the plans of Three Rivers concerning Mel's future and the need for strict confidentiality about this."

"Agreed, I don't think you need fear anything in that regard."

More than a week had dragged by since Simon last spoke to Richard. Despite Richard's reassurance and hope, Simon's anxiety continued unabated. Things were tense at home. He and Mel didn't talk about Martin Simmons again, nor did they dwell on Mel's financial struggles.

He tried his best to be kind and attentive without approaching any subject that could spark a row or foster tension. He found this frustrating as he was in a good place outside of the home. The bursary arrangement worked efficiently and effectively, and he continued to make noticeable progress in his studies, so much so that Professor Markowitz complimented him more than once. He resented his home environment because of the negative, sombre and oppressive atmosphere.

This cannot carry on. Richard said I could call him any time. I must do that, if for no reason other than to get a reality check.

They agreed to meet at Richard's home. "I've taken the afternoon off, Simon, so take your time. I know from what you said yesterday that you're struggling on the home front. Is it only your mum's financial position that is the problem or is there more?"

"It's kind of you to be so concerned and so willing to devote time to our problems. I feel like I'm becoming a pest."

"You're not a pest, far from it. I wish you would talk to me more often. As I've explained before, Martin and I were close, and I want to do whatever it takes to honour his last wishes."

"The financial problems continue to grow and Mum's health has worsened since we last met. It seems she is on the edge of a nervous breakdown—the creditors are hounding her, her car is unreliable because there has been no maintenance, her clothes are old and worn, and so on and so on. The broken relationship with my grandfather lies at the root of this," Simon said in a monotone, his shoulders slumped.

The reference to his grandfather came like a bolt out of the blue. Richard never expected to hear Simon acknowledge Martin as his grandfather. He didn't interrupt, allowing Simon to unburden himself.

"She is obsessed by her hate for him. This bitterness is eating her up and destroying her piece by piece. I've tried to reason with her. I've tried to open the door, but she remains adamant."

"What do you mean you've tried to open the door?"

"I've suggested that under common law there might be a possibility of qualifying for financial support from my grandfather's estate because we're family." There it was again: 'my grandfather'.

He then said something which nearly caused Richard to choke on his carrot cake.

"I'm feeling guilty about my grandfather dying without us putting things right. I feel guilty that we didn't respond positively to his many and, without a doubt, sincere approaches to reconcile. He so badly wanted to fix things, to make amends, to make right, but we wouldn't let him, and now it's too late."

The colour had drained from Simon's face and he looked crestfallen.

"I've been wanting Mum to accept again the reality of our familial tie with my grandfather so that at some point we can forgive and forget and move on with our lives, but she won't. She shows no interest in accepting it even if only to justify taking help from his estate."

"It's not too late, Simon. It's never too late. Your grandfather's spirit will know of your change of heart and forgiveness. More than anything else, even as he became debilitatingly weak in those last days, he craved your forgiveness, and now you have fulfilled his wish."

Simon turned his face away, not wanting Richard to see the rivulets of painful regret and shame trickling down his cheeks.

"What caused all this pain, Simon?"

Simon shuffled uncomfortably, taking a deep breath as he looked up, closing his eyes for a moment. Richard waited patiently, wondering what he was about to learn, remembering vividly the day he saw Simon and his friend cosying up to each other at the Ferns during Asami's visit.

"I'm ready to tell you, Richard, you need to know. Where shall I begin? It's so damn hard. The memories are sore, like a bogey man lurking in the dark, waiting to pounce."

Simon strolled across to the large window facing a colourful, picturesque winter garden. The sun streamed in. For a while, he stood there contemplating in a visibly melancholic mood, and then he began to speak.

"Not long after my fifteenth birthday we were on holiday with my grandparents, Martin and Emily, at their holiday home in the Drakensberg. Their many guests included Mum, her friends Denise and Julie, both members of my school's PTA committee, Denise's two teenage daughters and three other families—close friends of my grandparents—and Markus, a school friend and classmate of mine, and myself."

Simon remained at the window, gazing at the garden, as he continued to reveal details. Richard stayed seated, giving Simon the space he obviously needed at that moment.

"It all happened on a cool overcast day. Everyone, except for Markus and me, decided to take a long walk. We didn't join the others because of a blister on Markus's foot from a long hike a couple of days before. I took a bottle of vodka and some lemonades from the bar. My grandfather didn't mind if I or my friends had the occasional drink. The guest wing in which Markus and I were staying was away from the main part of the house and more than comfortable, with its own television and video set-up and top-of-the-range music centre. We talked about all sorts of arbitrary things, listened to some music and drank two or three vodkas each."

Simon stopped, turned away from the window and walked towards the chair less than two metres across from Richard. He sat down.

"Markus pulled a gay porn video out of his backpack."

Although Richard had anticipated something like this, he was a little taken aback at the calmness and quiet confidence with which Simon spoke.

"I guess the video, the effect of the vodka and the romantic setting in the Drakensberg freed up—at last—my inner self, that important part of me I had been suppressing for years." Simon's speech became laboured. "Girls never appealed to me. It's not something I manufactured or made up. Believe me, in this homophobic world I would have given anything to be straight." He paused. "There and then, Markus and I became lovers."

He hesitated, as if he wanted to be sure that Richard grasped his revelation. Richard remained silent and waited for the story to unfold.

"We fell asleep naked on the rug and the next thing I knew, or should I say, felt, was a painful winding kick to my ribs. My grandfather towered over me like a colossus, bellowing in his booming voice, 'You fucking little poofters, you despicable little faggots, what the fuck are you doing under my roof?' I had never seen him so angry and certainly had never heard such profanity from him. We tried to scramble to our feet, grabbing whatever clothing we could to cover our embarrassment. Whilst struggling to pull up my shorts, he slapped me with such force that he sent me careering to the floor with an almighty thud. Then, with an equally forceful backhand delivered with a resounding crack to the face, he sent Markus hurtling to the floor. In my confused and disorientated state, I felt the room spinning and became paralysed with fear. His huge, bulky frame hovered over us as we cowered on the floor. He shouted at the top of his voice, 'How the fuck could you do this to me, to us. You bring shame on this family, you horrible, horrible piece of shit. You're a fucked-up fairy.' I tried to say something, only to be drowned out by a thundering tirade of humiliating and degrading abuse exploding from his mouth. He bent over me and with one hand plucked me up roughly by the hair to almost waist level and then he punched me with sledgehammer force (at least that's what it felt like) to the mouth and nose. For a moment I blacked out. When I regained consciousness I could hear my mother's frenzied screaming. She grabbed onto my grandfather, struggling to hold him back. By this time Emily had also arrived, trying to help Mum restrain him. He was like a raging bull. The profanities continued unabated, drawing in some of the other guests to the commotion, including Mum's two friends and the teenage girls. Although his physical assault stopped, my grandfather's ranting about my sexuality and immoral ways raced on. Blood poured from my mouth and nose and a cut to my right eye. I remember vividly his last words: 'You are no longer part of this family, get out of my sight, leave this house now, I never ever want to see you again!'"

Richard was shocked and confused. He'd expected something like this, ever since he'd seen Simon whispering into that other fellow's ear. He had expected to be repulsed by Simon's story, by his behaviour. *And yet I'm not,* Richard realised. *I'm repulsed by Martin's behaviour.*

It didn't make any sense. Homosexuality was wrong, wasn't it? Isn't that what he'd always believed? What he'd always been taught? What it says right there in Leviticus? Yes. Yes it was. *So why am I mad at Martin instead of Simon?*

Simon was waiting for Richard to respond. *He's just as God made him,* Richard realised. *And nobody deserves to be treated the way Martin treated him.*

"I'm horrified, Simon, I don't know what to say, other than I'm so, so very sorry for the way your grandfather treated you. I can't even begin to imagine how humiliated and rejected you and your dear mother must have felt."

"This wasn't the first humiliation or rejection and certainly not the last. There have been many of those over the years, but none as gross, as painful and as lasting as his onslaught on that awful day."

"How far back do these go, Simon?"

"I can't remember exactly, but probably to my early teens when I was branded with epithets such as 'queer', 'poofter', 'moffie', 'faggot', 'fairy', 'pansy' and the like."

"Was this by boys at school?"

"Not only boys, but also by girls and even sometimes teachers and parents."

"You poor chap, Simon, how on earth did you cope?"

"It was exceptionally tough, especially as I was made to feel abnormal and a freak. Some even called me the personification of evil and sin. For many years, because I believed I was a freak and some form of abnormal being, I voluntarily committed to all sorts of therapies and programmes supposedly designed to 'make me normal'. Of course, none of them worked. You can't change a person's DNA. I isolated myself as much as possible, avoiding, where I could, things like Sunday school and church and participation in team sports, even my circle of friends at school was modest. On one occasion I was forced to undergo counselling with the school counsellor, not to help me cope, but to help me change my 'queerness'. I can't remember how many times I came close, dangerously close, to killing myself. But for the support of my loving and understanding mother, I would probably have succeeded. It was only after I came to know Markus that I realised I wasn't abnormal or broken or the personification of evil or some other dreadful societal misfit and that I was a perfectly normal human being, created in the same way as everyone else. It was then that I got shot of my demons."

"It's a dreadfully bigoted world in which we live, Simon, and an ugly stain on creation," offered Richard meekly, not knowing what else to do or say.

"I guess it is, but we, those not part of the mainstream, need to take a stand and show the world we belong as much as anyone else. I do, though, deeply regret that my mum and I turned against my grandfather. Things could have been very different. He begged, he pleaded, and he often camped outside our front door, sometimes late into the night and at the mercy of the elements, wanting to say sorry and to reconcile. We rejected him and chased him away, treating him like the scum of the earth. All his efforts, including his attempts through intermediaries, came to nothing. Sadly, Mum's heart is still as hard as stone and I don't see her relenting any time soon."

The afternoon morphed into evening and a relaxing dinner, giving Simon and Richard further time to become better acquainted. Each of them liked what they saw in the other. Richard again mentioned in passing his keenness to meet Mel as soon as the right opportunity came along. This appealed to Simon as he wanted his mother to see there were good men out there and that she had every chance of finding her soul mate, if only she would look at the world differently.

23

August 1997

The ringing on his private line jerked Richard away from his concentrated focus. He pushed the voluminous investment report to one side and lifted the phone from its cradle. The caller was either Asami or one of and his immediate family; no one else knew the number.

"How's that man from the foot of Africa?" came the friendly greeting.

"The African man is okay. And how's the gorgeous, beautiful, endearing and lovely girl from the land of the Rising Sun?"

"Oh, kind sir, pray, do continue. A girl could get used to such flattery."

"It's not hard, Asami, you know I adore you and that I mean all those things. You are truly the best thing that's happened to me and I miss you terribly. I long for you and must see you, soon."

"Ah, you're so sweet," she said sincerely, but ever conscious of the massive obstacle between them.

He and Asami had maintained contact regularly since she left South Africa, either by email or telephone. He missed her desperately, not forgetting the ultimatum hanging over his head. He knew she missed him. But he was also aware that their relationship caused each of them concern, perhaps for different reasons. They often wondered whether this could lead anywhere concrete, given not only their dramatically different cultures and backgrounds, but also the vast distance which separated them geographically. Then, of course, there lurked Richard's homophobia. It bothered them both. Their brains whispered to them to put the brakes on, but their hearts and burning desire for one another screamed otherwise.

"I have a bit of disappointing news I'm afraid, but it's not conclusive by any stretch of the imagination," said Asami. "The feedback from my network confirms that Hashimoto Katsu died in battle in Burma in early March 1943 but, and here is the disappointing bit, we have not been able to confirm whether he served in the 55th Infantry Regiment. Apparently the relevant records are either in a mess or incomplete or missing."

His lingering silence spoke volumes. Because of the information in the notebook, particularly the regiment number, and because an Englishman purchased the notebook from someone in South Africa, Richard convinced himself that Hashimoto's connection to the 55th would be confirmed.

"I share your disappointment, dear Richard but, as I said, this is by no means conclusive. All it means is that we must follow through and visit the address in Oseto. Every now and then we are tested in our resilience, fortitude and drive and I for one am not giving up now. We are well down the road and must push on. Our efforts must shift into overdrive. Are we in this together or am I losing my knight along the way?" she asked encouragingly.

His enthusiasm lifted again. He needed this project to succeed, at least for Martin's sake. "Not at all, your knight is right beside you. I am with you all the way. We have to find this family, we *will* find the family."

"Yes, we will," she replied confidently.

"What are your travel plans and commitments in a week's time? I would like to come over to Japan if it's not inconvenient for you. I can't bear not seeing you. Besides, I want to be there when we visit Oseto and I also want to follow through on the shrine initiative."

"That's wonderful, what a lovely surprise. I don't have any plans or commitments that will get in the way. Please do, Richard. You must stay at my place. I'll take some leave due to me and show you some of my world and, importantly, we'll carry on the search. I'm so happy."

* * * * *

He valued the recovery time in Tokyo where he spent a couple of days on some other business. The approach to Nagasaki Airport over Omura Bay filled Richard with nervous excitement. In thirty minutes he would be reunited with Asami. He had so longed for her. He again wondered how they would feel on seeing each other.

Asami eased her way through the crowds to the arrivals hall where she waited anxiously. She also wondered how the two of them would feel on meeting again. Suddenly her train of thought was broken, seeing Richard pushing his luggage trolley towards her. Their eyes locked and her heartbeat quickened in response to his flashing smile, a smile that made her feel uniquely special. She ran to meet him. As she neared, he pushed his trolley to the side and embraced her, picking her up off the ground and turning a full circle. Richard set her down gently and then they kissed, first fleetingly, and then long and tenderly.

They babbled and made small talk on the way to her apartment, often touching each other affectionately, exchanging romantic epithets. Occasionally Richard leaned into Asami, nibbling her ear and kissing her on the cheek. Although concentrating on her driving, she couldn't resist reciprocating.

Asami's lovely apartment on the second floor of a small apartment block in a well-appointed neighbourhood, although compact, exuded a welcoming homeliness.

"I've put you in my room, Richard. I'll sleep in my friend's apartment across the corridor, she's away on a business trip."

"I don't mind us sharing," said Richard hopefully.

"You know I can't, Richard, and you know why," she replied, gripping his upper arm.

"I think you'll change your mind, as soon as you hear what I have to tell you," he said, with an air of cautious optimism.

"Why don't you tell me over lunch, I'm ravenous. There's an excellent little Italian restaurant within walking distance."

She defended her choice, confirming there would be ample opportunity for Japanese cuisine later but that right then, she craved pasta. He didn't mind.

They lifted their wine glasses, toasting each other and their project, as well as their time together.

They talked about their budding relationship and how they had missed each other, but neither of them raised, for fear of spoiling their time together, their significantly different backgrounds and the huge geographical divide. She also had uppermost in her mind the one thing that came between them during her South African visit.

She walked Richard through her planned holiday itinerary, sharing information about some of the destinations.

"I am excited, Asami, and cannot wait to see more of your beautiful country, especially with my lovely and well-informed guide."

Feeling mellow and quite liberated from the constraints of a normal working day, they ordered a second bottle of wine.

"Asami, I have something serious and important to tell you."

"Oh, okay," she said, giving Richard a quizzical look.

"I am deeply ashamed of my past bigotry about gay relationships and I'm sorry you had to see that in me."

His unexpected confession and apology staggered her, leaving her to wonder whether this was another one of Richard's strategic ploys. She didn't react and waited for him to continue.

"Simon told me about the harrowing incident which led to the break-up. It distressed me enormously to hear about Martin's disturbing and disgusting assault on Simon and his public humiliation of him." Richard then revealed in graphic detail the events of that terrible day.

"I am horrified! How could he, I am horrified," she said.

"I've come to know Simon and to understand him," said Richard, struggling to maintain eye contact and fidgeting in a way she had not seen before. "I confess, I do not know any other gay person, but I now realise that Simon's not abnormal simply because he has a different sexual orientation. He has feelings and emotions just like you and me, except he is not attracted to the opposite sex. I feel terrible."

He paused for what seemed like a long time. Asami remained silent.

"I am, or should I say, I was, a victim of my upbringing, there is no other excuse." He paused again and then continued in a stammering voice. "I have accepted many things in my life at face value, probably because of my upbringing, instead of thinking about them and challenging them. Simon has graciously forgiven Martin. I doubt if one will find a nicer young man. I'm also pleased that Martin came to his senses and, like me, later came to realise and acknowledge his prejudices. If only Mel could understand this."

Asami leaned over and gave Richard a heartfelt hug.

They whiled away the hours in a light-hearted and jovial mood, chatting, laughing, touching, drinking and eating.

"I think we need to wend our way home, Richard," she said in a slow and deliberate tone, "before they throw us out and before we forget the way back."

They walked slowly, occasionally weaving arm in arm, enjoying continuous laughter, frivolity and slurred conversation, replete with double entendres. As soon as Richard opened the front door of Asami's apartment she pushed through, pulling him in.

"I'm coming back to my room," she said with a giggle.

"Where must I go?" he enquired, shrugging his shoulders and turning the palms of his hands upwards.

Asami jumped on her bed, giggling again. "You're going nowhere, handsome."

When they woke, Richard spoke first. "Asami, my love, you can't begin to imagine how anxious I've been about seeing you again, wondering whether our differences could be resolved."

She nuzzled into his neck, and whispered, "That's normal my darling. I too had anxious times, but I think today is a new beginning for us. I do love you."

At last John managed to set up an appointment with Piet De Wet who had recently returned from a trip to Australia.

"You were meant to get back to me within a week of our last meeting John," said Piet, off-handedly.

"Well, if you hadn't buggered off to Australia I would have been in touch," said John aggressively, having had enough of De Wet's rudeness.

John couldn't help smiling as Piet puckered his mouth like the contracted rear end of a terrified duck waddling away from a ravenous badger in hot pursuit. "Don't be a prick, John, why didn't you phone? I told you I wanted an acceptance of my last proposals within a week, otherwise there would be no deal."

"Do I take it then that you want me to leave?"

"Oh, for goodness sake, get on with it."

"Good, Piet, I think we can do business but not quite as you want." He slid over a typed sheet with bullet points, and said matter-of-factly, "I believe you'll find this counterproposal acceptable. It comes as a package, Piet, no more chipping away. I think both of us are close to deal fatigue."

John didn't let the puce look of apparent rage on Piet's face throw him off his stride. Without giving Piet an opportunity to say something, John pushed on. "My client will agree to everything you last proposed except price and disclosure of the people behind Three Rivers. Your concern on the last point can be adequately addressed in another way." Piet tried to interject, but John would have none of it. "All this is subject to you reducing the price to 250 million which, I might add, still gives you a premium over market value, and subject to the deal being structured in a way that ensures funds are available to meet any claim my client may have for breach."

"And how do you or your client think my concern about the identity of Three Rivers can be addressed?" asked Piet sarcastically.

"My client will agree to an advance confidential investigation by an independent firm of auditors, chosen from the four largest global auditing firms, on the question of reputational risk. You and my client must agree to abide by the outcome of the investigation."

"And, what else?" asked Piet scornfully.

"You are not serious, Piet. That's it. Take it or leave it. I am not bluffing, I will leave in ten minutes. I think my client has been more than generous and, might I add, more than reasonable at all times, unlike you."

Piet pushed back his chair, readying himself to storm out of the boardroom. "I leave in ten minutes, Piet, your call," said John, with considerable satisfaction.

He knew this was a make or break moment but felt confident of De Wet succumbing. The wind had been taken out of his sails on the Three Rivers identity question, and the need to have any claim of the buyer covered was commercially reasonable and justifiable. That left price, and on that Richard had made his position clear.

The ten minutes were about up, and John walked to the door, ready to leave. At that moment, Miss Prissy made an entrance in her usual haughty fashion, announcing arrogantly, "Mr De Wet says you have a deal and he would like to see first drafts of the agreements within five days."

John restrained himself from delivering a victorious air punch before saying, "Good. Tell Mr De Wet it's been a pleasure and he can see the draft agreements now on the understanding that they are still subject to review by some of the Three Rivers people."

He enjoyed a deep sense of satisfaction on handing over a sealed envelope containing the draft agreements.

As soon as John stepped out of the building, he called Richard.

"Hey, Richie, where are you? It sounds like you're on the other side of the world."

"That's because I am. What's up? I'm in Japan."

"What's happening in Japan? Hopefully you're not doing a deal there without me."

"Like I mentioned before, nothing like that, just some other business I am sorting out. Where are you with Mantis? Do we have a deal yet? We are past the eleventh hour and the clock is about to strike midnight."

"Great news, Richard, it's a done deal subject to finalising the written contracts."

"Excellent, you've made my day. I'm dying to hear a blow by blow commentary of the meeting." When John was done, Richard said, "Well done, that's excellent work, you are earning that exorbitant fee. You took a bit of a risk on the draft agreements though.

Keep up the pressure; I want us to get this whole thing put to bed within six weeks. There are no regulatory hurdles here. I want Three Rivers to take control and Mel to be in her new position by the middle of October."

"That's a big ask, Richard."

"I know, but make it happen. I am depending on you and I will make sure our attorney understands the urgency. Email me the draft agreements and I'll send you my comments within a couple of days. I don't think I'll find any problems, given that Sonny prepared them. This has to happen quickly."

* * * * *

Asami waited for the news at the end of the call, but Richard kept her in suspense. "What's happened, Richard? Tell me."

He did a little jig around the room, like an overjoyed schoolboy learning for the first time that his proposal to go steady with the fairest of them all had been accepted. She watched in amusement, waiting for his prancing to come to an end. When it did, he said with considerable exuberance, "We did it, we damn well did it. Oh, my goodness, miracles still happen, how wonderful."

"I can't share your joy, Richard, unless I know why you are so excited."

"I have so much to tell you my sweet, sweet darling Asami, but first the latest news, and then something else I've been dying to share since my arrival, but which has proved impossible because of your exhausting demands on me," he said with a roguish grin.

"Really! It's you that hasn't been able to control your testosterone," she retorted playfully. "Come on, spit it out."

"You remember the whole saga of the break-up of Martin, Simon and Mel and Martin's dying wish that I find a way to share some of his wealth with his daughter-in-law and grandson, and the hoops I've had to jump through to channel some financial support to Simon, and Mel's continued refusal to accept any help from Martin's estate?"

"Yes, of course I remember your considerable anxiety. What's happened now?"

Richard reminded her about the strategy he had briefly mentioned previously of trying to acquire Mantis Logistics, not only for black economic empowerment purposes, but also for bringing about a substantial improvement in Mel's life without her knowing the source of the funding for the deal.

"And, what's happened?"

"We have a deal, subject to contract, and hopefully within six weeks Candlewood Investments will indirectly control and own Mantis, and Mel's world will change dramatically for the good."

"You mean Mel will still not know the truth?" she asked, seemingly surprised.

"If she knew, she will not accept financial support."

"But shouldn't that be her choice?"

"Under normal circumstances, yes, but in this instance, no. Mel must be protected against the obsessive and irrational hate which blinds her."

For a fleeting moment she became suspicious again. She wondered about the reasons behind the large donation made by Candlewood Investments to her and Mr Yoshida's repatriation program and the apology Martin wanted made on his behalf to the family of the Japanese soldier. She hadn't been convinced by the explanation given to her by Richard. *I need to get to the bottom of this.*

"Well done on the deal, Richard. I'm not sure I can agree that it's okay to hide the truth, even in Mel's circumstances. It's a difficult one though and I hope it pans out and doesn't implode down the road.

24

Asami rolled out of bed, taking a moment to stare at the sprawled figure beside her. Unable to resist the temptation, she lifted the blanket and slapped Richard's naked behind. "Come, come, come, up you get, there's work to be done, lazy bones."

"Hey, morning to you too. What's up? What's happening?" Richard murmured, wiping the sleep from his bleary eyes.

"First, a quick bite, and then you and I are paying a visit to the Oseto administrative offices to examine the *Juminhyo*."

"What is the *Juminhyo*?"

"It's a registry of current residential addresses maintained by local governments in Japan."

"Would the registry also show personal details of residents in relation to births, marriages and deaths?"

"Definitely not, Richard. Such personal details are recorded in a family register known as a *koseki.* Each Japanese citizen has a *koseki* which is held at the municipal office having jurisdiction over that citizen's *honseki-chi,* being generally the place of birth, but the contents of a *koseki* are considered private and protected by law."

"Will we be able to access the *Juminhyo*, though?"

"Yes, but not the *koseki*. I think it will be useful to examine the *Juminhyo* to know who the current residents are of Hashimoto Katsu's 1943 home. Forewarned is forearmed, as the old saying goes."

"That makes sense. I'll pop in the shower and be ready to leave in ten minutes."

Asami, with Richard in tow, navigated her way comfortably and quickly to the appropriate office where she requested sight of the *Juminhyo*. The official returned within a few minutes, dropping the heavy register on the solid wood counter with a loud thud. She thanked him before starting to turn the pages.

"Got it," she said, looking up at Richard. "I think we may just have found the family of Hashimoto Katsu. The registered residents at the address have the same family name."

"Great, let's go," said Richard, already halfway out the door.

"You do have the flag and copies of the notebook, in case we need them?" she asked on their approach to the Hashimoto home.

"Right here, in this packet. I wonder if this is it. Could this be the moment?"

Walking up the path that winded its way through the manicured garden towards the house, they observed an elderly gentleman painstakingly removing shrivelled up leaves from a bush. Asami greeted him and a lengthy conversation ensued before she and Richard were invited to follow him into the house.

Before entering, she spoke again to the gentleman and then to Richard. "I've told him briefly that you're from South Africa, and the reason for our visit. He has no objection to us asking him and his sister-in-law questions and he understands I need to translate for you."

After introducing himself as Hashimoto Akio, the only brother of Hashimoto Katsu, he introduced his sister-in-law as the soldier's widow. He didn't identify her by name, and nor did he indicate whether she had any children. Asami made a formal introduction of herself and Richard. Refreshments were served as the four of them sat on the floor at a low table.

Richard addressed the elderly couple and Asami translated. He explained, without delving into unnecessary detail, the purpose of his visit to Japan and how he had been led to their home. He removed copies of the notebook from the packet and handed them to Akio, saying, "I believe these are copies of the late Hashimoto Katsu's military notebook."

Adjusting his spectacles, Akio brought the pages up towards his eyes and examined them closely before passing them onto his sister-in-law. "I agree," he said, "it seems like it is. My brother is identified by name and the address of this home where he lived. Nothing of my brother came back from the war, none of his remains and none of his property. We don't even know where or how he died."

"I'm sorry," said Richard, "that is very sad."

Akio and his sister-in-law nodded, and then Akio said, "You say you have a prayer flag which might have belonged to my brother. May we see it please?"

"I'm not sure it did belong to your brother," said Richard. "Based on our investigations it seems likely but by no means certain. There is a message written on the flag which refers to the soldier's wife and daughter."

Akio's shoulders slumped and his eyes closed as he pursed his lips. A similar sadness swept over his sister-in-law's face. "My sister-in-law did not have any children."

Richard and Asami's confident expectations lay shattered; each of them stared into the sad eyes of the other, searching for moral support.

"Hashimoto-san, you and your sister-in-law have been most kind in meeting with us," said Richard. "I so wish the outcome could have been different. You are, of course, most welcome to see the prayer flag I have, if you wish to."

"Thank you, perhaps we should. You never know, maybe the writing on the flag has been misread."

Richard passed the flag to Akio who showed it to his sister-in-law. Without any hesitation she shook her head briskly from side to side.

"Thank you, Mr Low, as you have seen, this was not my brother's prayer flag. May I ask one favour please, I would like to contact the person from whom you received copies of my brother's military notebook. We would very much like to secure its return, if possible."

"It will be my privilege to put the two of you in touch with each other, Hashimoto-san."

Neither Richard nor Asami said a word as they walked dejectedly back down the path. Asami slipped her hand into Richard's, and said, "These disappointments happen, Richard, but they make us stronger and even more committed. I love you. Be strong."

He squeezed her hand.

* * * * *

They had, as planned, taken time out, visiting the places on Asami's itinerary and bonding as a couple. Richard particularly enjoyed Urakami Cathedral, Kofukuji and the 500-year old Thousand Lantern Festival. But now it was back to the work of finding the soldier's family.

"Today, Richard, we are visiting the shrine in Seihi. The visit will give you better perspective. You'll see firsthand the lay-out of a shrine, although not all of them are the same. You'll also become acquainted with the difficulties we are experiencing in trying to trace the family through the records."

"I'm pumped, Asami, and ready to go."

"I take it, 'pumped' means you're excited and motivated?" He smiled.

They approached the entrance of the shrine area which stretched away from them, up the gentle lush mountain slope. The quietness and absence of any motorised traffic engendered a sense of spiritual tranquillity.

"The grounds beyond this gate, known as the *Torii or* the Shinto gate, and within the wooden boundary fence are deeply sacred and to be respected with reverence," she said, guiding him by the arm. "Before we enter the *Torii* we bow slightly and be sure to walk on the side of the *Sando* (the path towards the shrine) rather than in the middle, which is reserved for the gods."

The two of them entered through the *Torii* and up some stone stairs before reaching the *Sando.* Richard followed Asami's example, keeping to the side of the path. They stopped at a small pavilion, housing a font.

"This is the *chozuya,* a place for purifying oneself before continuing to the shrine," she explained. Again, Richard followed her example, filling the ladle with water, pouring it first over his left hand and then his right hand and then some into his left hand with which to rinse his mouth. Finally, he held the ladle upright, allowing the water to flow down the handle.

They continued onward to the shrine, passing some *Toro* (decorative lanterns) on both sides of the path, and then the *Shamusho* (the shrine administrative office) on the right side and the *Ema* on the left side, a wooden structure in which wooden plaques bearing prayers or wishes hung. Asami said they would later visit the administrative building. Next they came across some *Sessha* (small auxiliary shrines) to the side of the path before arriving at the impressive *Komainu* (the lion dogs), guarding the shrine.

"Do what I do, Richard, when we enter," said Asami. She bowed slightly, unobtrusively tossed a coin into the coin box and then rang a bell a couple of times. "The ringing informs the gods of our arrival." Following her again, Richard bowed twice to ninety degrees, clapped twice and then, as instructed by her in advance, paid his respects to the gods.

On returning to the *Ema* structure, Richard asked Asami to help him. He wanted to write a prayer on a hanging plaque. "What do you want me to write, Richard?"

"Clear the way, oh Lord, so that we find the family of the soldier and bring to them the closure they surely long for."

She wrote in Japanese and he hung the plaque.

Asami took Richard's hand and led him into the administrative office. "This is where the shrine records are kept."

He peeked down rows of shelves holding numerous piles of documents, never anticipating such an enormous records section. Asami spoke to one of the priests who seemed, from all indications, to be expecting her. After she introduced Richard, the priest led them to a specific area housing the family registers for the years 1942 to 1945. Asami opened them up, revealing hundreds of names.

A lengthy conversation followed between her and the priest before she turned to Richard. "No separate register exists of those who died during the various conflicts, including World War Two. He also says we cannot assume that any of the registers are complete or accurate. The priests try their best to keep details of families visiting the shrine and for this they are dependent on their co-operation and the information they provide. He also mentioned that the latest register is about five years out of date."

"Is there any quick way of knowing which persons on, for example, the 1943 register, are no longer on another register, such as the latest one?" Richard asked hopefully.

She knew the answer but nevertheless asked the priest. He pointed out that as the registers were not electronic, the only way this could be done would be to search manually in the later register for the relevant name.

After leaving the administrative office, Asami sought clarity from Richard. "I'm not following your thinking, Richard. What would be the purpose of making a comparison between registers if we don't know the family name of the soldier?"

"Here's my thinking. If you could find out from the Defence Agency the names of all the soldiers from the 55th Infantry Regiment of the 18th Division who came from Seihi and who died in action in the first two weeks of March 1943 in Burma, that will give us a good starting point."

"I'm confident I can get those names but as you know, residential addresses are no longer available. How will the names help?"

"It is highly likely that one of those named soldiers will be the one from whom the prayer flag came. We then search the 1942 and 1943 shrine registers and identify all the families with the same family names as those soldiers. There is then a possibility, a reasonable one I would guess, that our soldier came from one of those families."

Richard smiled and gave her a quick, angled nod.

"You are rather pleased with yourself, but that's more than fifty years ago. How does that help us in the search? Much happens in fifty years. Many of the 1942 and 1943 families may no longer live in this area."

"You're absolutely right, but if the family we are looking for still lives in this area, our chances of finding them improve dramatically if we extract from the *Juminhyo* the residential details of all families with the same names as those families we identify in the 1942 and 1943 registers. In other words, we should search for a commonality of family names from the three groupings, the soldiers in question, the 1942 and 1943 registered families, and those on the current *Juminhyo* register. Once we identify the families from the *Juminhyo,* we contact them and make enquiries."

"Okay, now I understand what you're getting at. Not just a pretty face, hey? What if none of the families from the compiled list can identify the flag?"

"That could mean so many different things. We know the family of the soldier probably came from this area in 1942 or 1943, if not, why would the flag show the official stamp of this shrine? It's highly unlikely that a family from another area brought their prayer flag to the shrine. Of course, it's possible that the family may, in the last fifty years, have relocated. It's also possible that they are still here but with no recollection or knowledge of the flag. If it's the latter, we will never find them. If it's the former, the search area then becomes the whole country, and possibly beyond."

*****

For the remainder of his visit, Richard and Asami spent focussed time discussing how best to progress the search for the soldier's family, which came to be known as 'the common name strategy'. After finding out the names of the soldiers who died, Asami would hire some students from the university to search the 1942 and the 1943 shrine registers as well as the *Juminhyo* for the purpose of compiling the list Richard had in mind.

"Once we have that list, Asami, I'll be back to visit all the families. All I need is a strong pair of walking shoes and a fit interpreter who knows his or her way around Seihi."

Sadly, the time had come for Richard to return to South Africa.

"I don't want you to leave, Richard," Asami said in a broken voice, hugging him tightly and unmindful of the many travellers and others milling around in airport departures.

"I love you, Asami," he whispered in her ear. "You know I love you, but I must go. There's other work calling for my attention back home."

"I know," she said, now sobbing quietly into his neck. "I love you too, but I'm not sure I can endure this pain too long."

"We've achieved much this trip, my dear Asami. I feel our goal is in reach, let's push on. I know it's not the same, but we'll talk every day."

"Promise?"

"I promise and thank you for an unforgettable trip. You mean so much to me. I'll be back as soon as that list of names is ready."

Richard kissed her goodbye and left hurriedly, not daring to pinch a last glance.

25

September 1997

Although an expensive exercise, one of the trustees of Three Rivers Trust flew out from Lichtenstein to sign the Mantis agreements. Because of the delicate position with Mel, Richard did not want his name, or the name of anyone associated with him, to be on any of the documents.

Richard took a call from John Matthews.

"I'm pleased with progress, John, that's excellent. I take it the auditing firm is ready to start investigating the reputations of those behind Three Rivers?" asked Richard, sitting back in his chair, with his feet on the desk.

"They are, and they understand this has to be completed within seven days. The due diligence team is assembled and also ready to jump in. We've worked through the more significant areas that are to be reviewed. You do understand, there are some areas we will not investigate at all because of time constraints but I believe the risks in those areas are, in the greater scheme of things, relatively immaterial."

"Understood and happy with that. Remember, in terms of the agreements, the sellers are committed to full co-operation for an accelerated DD and they know full well that Three Rivers wants closing in the middle of October."

"They are, and with a bit of luck we'll make your deadline. I'm not anticipating anything untoward. Piet has a reputation as a smart businessman who runs a top-rate operation."

"Great. And what's the progress with the attorneys and tax advisors on the structuring of the intended BEE leg? I'm keen to bring in a suitable black community grouping as stakeholders in Mantis as soon as possible after closing with the De Wet family."

"That's a work in progress, Richard, but we are far down the line. I also identified three black communities for you to consider as potential stakeholders. I'll get my report across to you tomorrow, if that's okay?"

As Richard finished his call he noticed out of the corner of his eye Olivia in the doorway, seemingly anxious. "What's up, Olivia? You're looking worried, and that makes me worried."

"It's Simon, he's in reception and worryingly agitated, wanting to see you. I must warn you, he looks terrible."

"Oh dear. Bring him to my office."

"Come in, Simon," said Richard, shaking Simon's clammy hand. His clothes were washbasket creased, his hair dishevelled, and his prominent jaw covered in stubbly growth. "You look terrible. What's the problem? How can I help? Did Olivia offer you some refreshment?"

"She did, thank you, but nothing for me now," he stammered.

"It's my mum. She's going to pieces. No, that's an understatement, she's already gone to pieces."

"Go on," said Richard empathetically.

"I fear she may be suicidal. It all started a few days ago when her car conked out yet again. She's now dependent on buses and the goodwill of the few friends she has left to get around, and you know how unreliable the buses are. Her money has run out and she is flat broke and desperate. She comes home after work and goes straight to her room where she curls up on the bed. She won't talk, and hardly eats. Richard, I'm scared, very scared."

As he said this, Simon put his face down into his hands, his shoulders shaking and then he wept uncontrollably. Richard shifted his chair closer to Simon, patting his back. "We'll fix this now, today, and that's a promise."

Richard picked up the office phone and spoke to Olivia. "Hey, Liv, please reschedule all today's appointments and order in a finger lunch for Simon and me. We'll be tied up for the next few hours. And some coffee would be great. Thanks."

Simon composed himself, looking embarrassed. He apologised.

"No need to apologise, Simon. You care deeply for your mum, and so you should, and quite clearly you feel her pain. Are you okay time-wise to stay here for the next couple of hours while we sort things out?"

"Of course, whatever it takes."

"We now have to intervene," Richard said firmly. "I know your mum won't like it, but we must assert ourselves and I'm counting on you to help me." After informing Simon of his immediate plans to help Mel, Richard said, "I'll be at your place in the morning to explain things to your mum. As it's Saturday tomorrow, I assume she won't be working."

"She's waiting tables at lunchtime. Oh boy, are you sure, Richard? The paw paw's going to hit the fan."

"Then so be it, the splatter will not kill us. We must intervene, for her sake and for yours. Leave it to me, I'll handle it. How far behind is she on payments to her creditors?"

"It's a lot, about R15,000. You're not intending to let on about the help from my grandfather, are you?" asked Simon, nervously.

"No, at least not yet."

"You don't know my mum. She can be feisty and stroppy, as well as stubborn."

"Well, let's see who wins this little battle. I can also be stroppy, and when I am I tend to get my way. Now, that will take care of the immediate stress. Do you remember I told you a while ago about a potential solution to take care of your mum's situation?"

"Yes, I do. I've been holding onto that with great hopes."

"Well, the solution has not yet been finalised but it's about done. I am more confident than ever that by the middle of October her position will change dramatically. I'll let you in on the solution, but you must keep this to yourself, for reasons you'll hear in a moment."

Richard spent the next hour telling Simon about the Mantis deal and his plans for Mel.

"Won't my mum know about Martin's involvement when all this happens?" asked Simon.

"No, if the purchase of Mantis comes off, it won't be capable of being traced back to Martin or anyone associated with him. Despite this, I am hopeful that one of these days we'll be able to put all this smoke and mirrors stuff behind us so that you and your mum can take up your rightful inheritance."

"I don't know how to thank you, Richard, or my grandfather, other than to say that I'll not disappoint. I'm committed to making a difference in this world and helping others who are less fortunate than me. Thank you, thank you. I will forever be grateful."

Richard handed Simon the keys for the pool car and they agreed to meet at Mel and Simon's house at ten o'clock the following morning. Richard pushed a wad of R100 notes into Simon's top pocket, saying, "Here, take this and stock up the food cupboard."

The crashing and banging from the front door suddenly disrupted Simon's concentration in front of the stove.

"Simon, Simon, where the hell is my car?" Mel screeched at the top of her voice.

"Hey, Mum, cool it. Your car's at the garage."

"My car's not in the garage, there's a strange car in my garage."

Here we go. "Mum, Mum, everything's under control. Repairs are being done on your car and the car here belongs to a friend who has lent it to us."

"You know there is no money to pay for the damn repairs? And where have all these groceries come from? Who is paying for this stuff?"

"Listen, Mum, we're not fighting tonight and you're not going to throw a little hissy fit. I won't put up with it, enough is enough," said Simon in a forceful, commanding voice. She had never been spoken to her in such a way by her son. "All will be revealed in the morning, but be assured, nothing illegal or improper is happening here. At ten tomorrow morning we are meeting with a very special visitor, and I mean a very special visitor. Then, and only then will you be brought into the picture. You are tired and terribly stressed, so I want you to enjoy a glass of wine with your son and try to unwind and relax."

"How can I?" she croaked tearfully. "The world is closing in on me and I don't know where to turn. Things are totally fucked up!"

"You can turn to me, Mum. I've got this."

She sagged down on the old green couch, looking more haggard than ever. She had no more fight in her and wished she could fall asleep and not wake up. Simon hardly ever heard his mum swear. He needed to calm her down. He placed a glass of red wine in her hand and sat next to her.

"My dearest, dearest Mum. Please, for a change, listen to me. Tomorrow you will see light at the end of the tunnel, I promise you. Our visitor will explain everything."

"I don't understand, my son. What do you mean there's light at the end of the tunnel? How can there be? Please tell me you haven't been chasing the Simmons' estate."

"No, and I refuse to answer any more questions. Take my word as your son, as your only family, that things are about to change."

He clinked his glass against hers. "To us, Mum, to us."

"To us," she said robotically, in a broken and defeated tone.

She knew they needed help; they were on the cliff edge staring into the abyss. She struggled to eat Simon's dinner, forcing the food down to avoid offending him. She fought the overwhelming urge to retch, feeling the knot tighten in her stomach. He could see his mother's discomfort but let her be.

Overcome by exhaustion and the couple of glasses of wine, she headed for bed. "Thank you for being there for us, my son. I love you. For the first time in my life I feel you are our anchor. It's not fair, I'm meant to be the stable one, the rock and the support."

Next morning Simon woke early, extremely apprehensive about Richard's visit. He consoled himself with the thought that he had to trust Richard; no other option was available for them to get out of their mess. He knocked quietly on her bedroom door. "Can I come in, Mum? I have some coffee for you."

Even though his mother didn't respond, he walked in anyway. To his surprise, he found her at the dressing table, drying her hair. "I must look respectable for our visitor. Tell me about him, Simon, please tell me."

"Richard Low, the guy who helped me get the bursary from the law firm. Remember, we've spoken about him a few times?"

"I do remember, but why so special and how come he's involved in our situation? I don't understand."

"It's hard to explain. Richard has taken on a sort of mentoring role for me and has become involved in ensuring my well being and development. I guess he feels he should keep an eye on me as he persuaded his former firm to give me a bursary."

"I can understand that as far as you are concerned, but how is it that he's involved in bringing about a change in my situation?" she asked suspiciously.

"Mum, why don't we let Richard explain. You'll see what I mean after you've heard him out."

"But why can't you tell me?"

Simon replied decisively and matter-of-factly, "Mum, this conversation is not getting us anywhere. I'm saying no more on the subject. It's early yet, why don't you finish beautifying yourself for our visitor and I'll take you out for breakfast," he said with a cheeky grin.

"Oh, stop it, you know I'm not interested in any sort of relationship, I have far too many things on my plate," she said in a lighter voice. Simon thought he even noticed a slight smile.

* * * * *

As they left for breakfast, Simon couldn't help noticing the extra effort on Mel's part. She wore a light, simple, colourful cotton frock, which showed off her petite, perfectly proportioned figure in a stylishly elegant but frivolous way. He was astonished that his mother could look as attractive as she did, given the tough times confronting her. *Perhaps this is the turning point,* he thought. He hoped so.

"Mum, I want you to know that you look stunningly beautiful. I'm proud to be your son," he said. She flashed a beautiful broad smile, giving his upper arm a squeeze.

They enjoyed their time together at breakfast, with no apparent mood swings, bitterness, acrimony or resentment. The Highveld spring morning brought its own joy: the blossoms were out, the heady, sweet smell of jasmine permeated the air, the birds twittered and chirped noisily, and the breakfast crowd streamed into the restaurant-lined street. Some were eating breakfast *al fresco,* others waited for tables and some simply wandered down the street, socialising and taking in the freshness of the new day.

They arrived home shortly before ten o'clock, feeling nervous—Simon, because he didn't know how Richard intended to handle the issues and how his mother would react, and Mel, because she had not met Richard before, and because of her concern about his helping Simon with the grant of the bursary.

"Come on in, Richard, and meet my mum, Mel. Mum, this is Richard."

Richard, dressed informally in shorts, T-shirt and sneakers, took Mel's extended hand and returned her firm handshake. "I am truly pleased to meet you at last, Mel. I've got to know Simon very well over these last five months and he's told me so much about you. I've been wanting to meet you for some time, but your son has been quite protective."

"Thank you, Richard," she said. "I can now thank you in person for arranging Simon's bursary. Without that help, he would now be stuck goodness knows where, trying to make his way. Thanks to you, he can now follow his dream." She looked up at Richard and said, most earnestly, "Thank you, thank you, we are truly indebted, much more than you will ever know."

Richard was touched by her sincerity, feeling a little guilty about his and Simon's charade.

Mel's appearance surprised Richard. She looked much younger and better presented than he expected, given her impecunious situation and unrelenting stress.

After Simon served the coffee, Richard spoke first.

"Mel, I take it you know why I'm here?"

"I don't want to be presumptuous, Richard, so I think it would be better if you tell me," she said quite formally.

Richard hoped this was not an early indication of her resistance to the anticipated change.

"Okay, fair enough," said Richard in an accommodating response. "Simon and I have spent many hours together over many occasions and he has told me, in detail, the history of your family, as well as the events leading to the fallout with his grandfather and—"

Mel cut in sharply. "Sorry for the interruption, Richard, but I'm sure Simon told you that he has no grandfather and that as far as we are concerned, Martin Simmons has no connection with our lives."

Although Richard had half expected Mel's bristling reaction, he nevertheless wanted to test the water.

"So sorry, no offence intended, Mel," said Richard with apparent contrition. "I know about the fallout with Martin and I'm also aware of the tragedies in your and Simon's lives and the fact that you are struggling financially."

Mel seemed embarrassed, but Richard kept going with a clipped, matter-of-fact cadence.

"I'm here to help and I can only do so if we are open and frank with each other and if you are willing to accept help. You can be immensely proud of your son, a wonderfully talented young man. I've become his mentor and his confidant and, in case you are wondering, I'm not gay. My only agenda is to see

Simon succeed. Life has dealt him a cruel blow and I am, fortunately, able to give him the help and find the support he needs to fulfil his dreams."

Simon sat quietly. Mel wanted to ask Richard why he became involved at all, but before she could, Richard continued. "It's been obvious to me for some time, from what Simon told me and from the fear, stress, anxiety and pain I've seen in him on more than a few occasions, that your lives are on the point of imploding unless some meaningful intervention happens. He feels the same way but has been reluctant to get the message across to you—after all, you are his mother and he has considerable respect, and may I say, love and adoration for you."

Simon had not expected Richard to be so forthright, so soon into the meeting. Still, he did not say anything. He trusted Richard and hoped he knew what he was doing.

Mel felt vulnerable and boxed in and was not sure how to take Richard. Her shoulders slumped forward, her eyes appeared dull and lifeless and she kept fidgeting nervously. "Things are indeed tough," she said in a whispered monotone, "in fact, more than tough, and it's been like this for a long time. Simon has told me that we could probably claim support from Martin's estate, and I know this could ease our burden, but I cannot bring myself to do it, it would be hypocritical in the extreme."

Although convinced he could persuade her to change her mind, Richard sensed the timing was not right to argue with her on such an emotive issue.

"I started at Mantis Logistics many years ago and I am in a relatively senior and responsible job. I've been hoping for a promotion and salary increase but regrettably the leadership in the company lacks generosity, although I don't think I need generosity, just fair recognition for my efforts. I had to beg and plead a while back to borrow some money which I am still repaying, with interest. I have thought of looking for another job, and on a couple of occasions I've submitted my CV to prospective employers, only to withdraw it. I don't know why I haven't followed through. Maybe I've lost confidence in myself or maybe it's a case of better the devil I know. I'm not sure. I am at the end. I don't know what to do and I feel humiliated and embarrassed that my son has to involve a stranger to give a helping hand."

"You and I may be strangers at this point, Mel, but Simon and I certainly are not. I could not possibly turn my back on him when, out of absolute desperation and love for you, he sought my help. Don't look on me as a stranger but rather as someone already inextricably involved in your son's life and someone who wants to help."

She remained sceptical. "Please, Richard, for my own peace of mind, I need to know how you became involved in Simon's life, the obtaining of the bursary, the mentoring and becoming his confidant."

He repeated the story scripted by himself and Simon and which he knew Simon had already passed on to his mother.

"But why Simon? Please don't think I'm ungrateful, quite the contrary, I'm trying to understand why him, and not another struggling student," said Mel with an innocence designed to mask her scepticism.

Richard saw through her probing.

"Prof Markowitz pleaded Simon's cause, and not someone else's. I respect the prof and we interact regularly on many things. When asking for my help, he emphasised that Simon's considerable potential shouldn't be lost because of the financial predicament in which he found himself. He knows my former firm well and asked whether it might be possible for them to step in."

Richard's response was given confidently, in the hope that no occasion would arise in which Mel could thank the good professor for helping her son.

"Prof Markowitz has time and time again shown himself to be a good man but also a humble man. Although known for helping students who find themselves in various kinds of difficulties, the good professor shies away from public recognition. He finds that sort of thing embarrassing."

"You don't think I could or should send him a thank you note?" she asked.

"It's entirely up to you, Mel, but be aware that, as the dean, Professor Markowitz's position could make things awkward. He wouldn't want to be seen, and can't be seen, as favouring any student when it comes to such matters. The student body is highly politicised and can quickly jump to unwarranted conclusions."

"Richard's right, Mum. The prof knows how grateful I am. A note from you will simply embarrass him."

"Okay, I hear where you're coming from," she said hesitatingly. "Richard, once again, thank you so much for opening this door."

"Be proud of your son, Mel, he has embraced the help and is, I believe, living up to his potential."

She seemed less agitated and calmer. Richard homed into the real purpose of the meeting. "I want to talk about the help you need and which I can give, Mel. My friendly garage is repairing your car and I'll pay for this. Simon has, at my insistence, given me your bank account details and I have transferred enough funds to pay your arrear accounts and to sustain you for a while longer, without incurring any further debt."

Mel began to sob. This time Simon put his arms around her and held her close. When she was ready to speak, she said, "I am overwhelmed, I don't know what to say. I feel ashamed and selfish that all this is because I won't go after Martin's money. He hurt Simon so terribly, he hurt both of us terribly and I told all and sundry I would never have anything to do with him."

"Let's take one step at a time," said Richard, with understanding. "You're going to be fine financially for the next couple of months, at least, and we can deal with the future at a later stage. The priority right now must be for you to get onto your feet, to give up waiting on tables, to enjoy life a bit and to regain your health."

"But, but I can't be a burden to you, Richard, especially as you've been so kind in helping Simon."

"You're not a burden to me, Mel. I want to help, and I can help. I am a bachelor with no dependents. There are no strings attached, but at some point, I would like to discuss with you some ideas about how you and Simon may be able to change your lives, but let's leave that for another day."

"I am humbled by your kindness and by your extreme generosity. You are an absolute saviour, a Good Samaritan. I will pay back every cent as soon as I can afford to, and yes, I would welcome the opportunity of hearing your ideas. I need to get these creditors off my back soon."

Richard decided against saying anything about the Mantis takeover.

Mel's demeanour and outward appearance changed visibly over the course of the visit, understandably so. Instead of slumping over, she adopted a more confident posture, and her eyes seemed to sparkle a little. When Richard stood to leave, she said, "May I give you a hug?" Before Richard could answer, she put her arms around him. "You literally saved my life, I mean that."

Simon, too emotional to speak, shook Richard's hand, his bottom lip quivering, as the three of them walked to the door.

26

September/October 1997

Richard swept past Olivia's desk, muttering and grunting. She had never seen him with dishevelled hair or his shirt hanging out. She followed him calmly into his office.

"Hello, Richard, anything I can do to help?"

"I wish there was, Liv. It's a stuff up of a morning. The bank has at this eleventh hour suddenly reneged on its funding commitment to our black empowerment partner on the Northern Cape mine deal. I'm damn angry. They're placing the entire acquisition in jeopardy. As you know, we've been working on the matter for months and, suddenly, out of the blue, the bank does this. Sods! I have a meeting with them in half an hour to find out what the hell they're up to. I promise you, Candlewood Investments will not do business with this bank again, ever."

The timing wasn't right to let Richard know about Asami's call concerning some problem with a residents' register. She wouldn't go into detail. Olivia popped off a cryptic email to Asami, promising to pass on the message to Richard as soon as matters were back under control.

Olivia delivered the morning routine cup of coffee to Richard, and said, "Here, a bit of fortification, and good luck with the bank."

Two hours later Richard stormed in. "Bloody bankers. I've had enough of that lot. There's no credit rating problem here, all they're doing is angling for a bigger slice of the action. Well, I told them to shove their funding. There are other banks out there screaming to do business with us."

"I'm sorry, Richard. By the way, Asami called and asked for you to call back as soon as you have a moment."

"I'll call her now."

"Hi, Asami, you've been trying to contact me. Sorry I couldn't take your calls, we have a bit of a crisis this end. What's up?"

"Hello, Richard, if this is bad timing we can chat later."

"Please go ahead, I'm listening."

"Since chatting yesterday there's been a small hiccup my end. A fire broke out at the Seihi administrative offices last night. The *Juminhyo* and some other documents went up in flames. No one knows the cause."

A long silence followed.

"Are you still there, Richard?"

"Oh damn it. I suppose the students haven't yet managed to do a name comparison with the *Juminhyo*?" came Richard's response.

"Regrettably not. It's a real pity because the *Juminhyo* is accurate and reliable. They have though completed the other comparisons and all that remained was the comparison with the *Juminhyo*."

"This isn't one of my best days. Where to from here? Can we not instead use the current shrine register for the comparison?"

"That is our only default position. Unfortunately, it's not as reliable and, as mentioned by the priest, it's about five years out of date. It's also conceivable that the family still lives in the area but that they no longer visit this shrine or that their details do not for some reason appear in the shrine register."

"I meant to ask you before, Asami, what are the chances of families relocating from an area like Seihi to another area?"

"Not much. Just about this entire area comprises farms which mostly pass on from one generation to the next. Sometimes the young people migrate to the big cities or universities and don't come back, but that is more the exception than the rule."

"Well, as you said before, these things are sent to test us, and we must strengthen our resolve. I'll be ready to come over in ten days' time to undertake the door-to-door searches. Would it be possible to arrange a furnished short-term apartment for me, initially for two weeks, in the Seihi area, as well as an interpreter?"

"Of course. I would have offered for you to share my place but it's the start of the university's second semester so I'm going to be heavily tied up. I hope you understand."

"Thanks, Asami, and understood. Two or more weeks is too long to be cramped. Besides, as you can imagine, I'm also going to be hectic, coming and going, and having meetings with my interpreter at all sorts of hours as we debrief and plan."

* * * * *

After meeting Richard at the airport, following his weekend stopover in Tokyo, Asami drove him to the rental apartment so he could settle in.

"Are you okay, Asami? You seem distracted."

"What do you mean?" she challenged with a noticeable edge to her tone.

"It's hard to explain, you're not your usual bubbly or affectionate self."

She hesitated, seemingly marshalling her thoughts. "All is okay, it might just be the pressure of the new semester and lack of sleep," she said, giving his arm a gentle squeeze.

"Fair enough, understood. I'm sure your time commitment on our little project has added to the stress levels. Hopefully my visit will alleviate things a tad."

As they drove up to the apartment, she pointed out its convenient location within walking distance of the shrine. "I trust you'll be comfortable here, I tried to locate you in the most convenient area for your searches."

On the table in the apartment Richard noticed various documents. A closer inspection revealed copies of the prayer flag and of the translated text into modern Japanese, as well as some copies of the separate name lists.

"This is perfect, thank you, dear Asami. And thank you for all these copies and especially for the way you've arranged the separate lists of names. I'm excited and, at the same time, nervous about the rollercoaster ride ahead. If I can visit four families on average per day, I should be through the initial sweep in just over fourteen days, assuming I don't find the family before then."

"Ah, there's a knock, that must be Takanashi Hotaka, the interpreter I told you about." Approaching the door, she looked over her shoulder, and quietly said, "You'll be safe in his hands and, remember, Takanashi-san is exceptionally fluent in both languages."

"Greetings, Takanashi-san," said Richard, making the customary bow. "I am so pleased you'll be looking after me on this important mission."

Hotaka responded with a bow. "It is a pleasure to meet you, Mr Low, and it will indeed be my privilege to help where I am able to on this laudable search. Nakamura-san briefed me fully." He bowed again. "I am at your service."

"Thank you, Takanashi-san, I am grateful. Come, sit down and make yourself comfortable while I see Nakamura-san off."

Outside the door they hugged before Asami left. "I'll call you this evening, Richard. Good luck."

"Some refreshment for you, Takanashi-san, before we start?"

"Not now, thank you, Mr Low." He unfolded a large Seihi street map on the table. "If you show me the list of families we need to visit, I'll plot their locations on the map, and this will help us to plan the sequence of our visits in a co-ordinated fashion."

Richard and Hotaka worked through to lunchtime on the map-plotting exercise.

"After lunch, Mr Low, if it is in order with you, we can group the families appropriately, given their respective locations, and then decide on the sequence of the visits. This will ensure a methodical approach and avoid unnecessary time wastage."

"I am impressed, Takanashi-san. I can see you are well organised and a clear thinker. That is in order, but now, let's pop down the road for some lunch."

After their short break, Hotaka and Richard resumed work and by late afternoon the fifty-seven families had been divided into fourteen groups, and the groups arranged and numbered in the order in which they were to be visited. They sat back, admiring their day's handiwork.

"Well done, Takanashi-san, we've achieved much today and now we are properly set to go."

"I think so, Mr Low. Before I leave for the day, may I see the prayer flag, please."

"Certainly, Takanashi-san." Richard unfolded the flag on the table. Hotaka studied the flag, rubbing it between his fingers and then lifting it up to the light.

"If only this flag could talk, I'm sure it would have some interesting stories," said Hotaka. "I see you have copies of the flag and text translation."

"I do. Nakamura-san is as well organised as you are. Let's call it a day and start fresh tomorrow. In the morning I'll share with you my intended approach when we visit the families and would appreciate your thoughts, Takanashi-san."

"What happens if a family no longer lives at the given address?" asked Hotaka.

"I'm anticipating a few of those. In such a case, we'll enquire after the names and addresses of previous occupants so we can follow up in the hope of finding the family who lived at the address when the Seihi soldiers left for war."

Asami called that evening as promised and enquired about Richard's first day.

"I must compliment you on finding Takanashi-san, wow, he's incredibly well organised and extremely efficient, thank you, Asami. Tomorrow, we'll visit the first group."

"Well done, it sounds like your day has been productive," she said in a flat monotone.

"I'm worried about you, Asami. I haven't forgotten what you told me earlier today and I guess it's been another hard day at work for you, but there's something more going on. I just can't put my finger on it. Is it us?"

"Don't be silly. Look, I can't chat long, I've one of my PhD students arriving any minute now to talk about her thesis. All the best for tomorrow, I'll try and call you in the evening."

* * * * *

"Good morning, Takanashi-san. I trust you had a good sleep and are ready to start our adventure?"

"Good day to you, Mr Low. I hope you too had a good rest. I'm raring to go."

"Excellent, have a seat. Takanashi-san, given that we're going to be spending many hours and days together, if you don't mind, please call me by my first name."

"Okay, Mr Low, ugh, I mean Richard, and please call me Hotaka."

"Will do, Hotaka. Let me share my thinking and, please, if you don't like any aspect, speak up. I'm a visitor to your beautiful country and I don't want to offend anyone or do anything inappropriate. I appreciate we must be flexible and ready to adapt to each situation, but here is the general plan, as I see it. When we first engage with a family, you'll introduce us by saying that you're acting as my guide and my interpreter and that I have come specially to Japan from South Africa to search for a family who lived in Seihi during World War Two so I can restore to them a prayer flag belonging to the family's loved one who died in 1943 in Burma and that there is a possibility the residents at the address may be able to help. Assuming the family is willing to co-operate, I will then ask whether any of their family lived at the address during 1942 or 1943. If not, I'll ask a series of questions aimed at gathering information that might lead us to the family that did reside there during those years."

"Sounds good to me."

"Good. If any members of the family we visit did live at the address, I'll enquire whether they lost a loved one during the Burma Campaign and if the answer is no, I'll seek to elicit information to help identify any family they know of from Seihi who lost someone in Burma."

"And, if the answer is yes?"

"I'll ask if the soldier had a wife and daughter."

"And if he did, that takes us one step closer."

"Wouldn't that be wonderful! But if that's not so I'll try to obtain information that may lead to any family they know of from Seihi who lost a loved one in Burma."

It took Richard and Hotaka a while to find their rhythm on the first round of visits, prolonging the footslogging to more than six hours. Of the four families visited, three had lived at the addresses from a time prior to World War Two and only one of those suffered the loss of a loved one in Burma, but he wasn't married. The fourth took up residence only recently, having purchased the house from a family who had lived there for four generations. Although Osaka contact details for the previous owners were provided by the current residents, they did not know whether the seller's family had sustained a Burma loss. No other significant information was gleaned.

"Allow me to provide you with some refreshment, Hotaka, as we discuss the events of the day and plan for tomorrow. How about a cold beer?"

"Thank you, Richard, that'll go down a treat. We must have walked about fifteen kilometres today. Some of the addresses for tomorrow are further out so we'll use my car."

Not having heard from Asami by eight o'clock that evening, Richard phoned her.

"Hi, Richard, sorry I haven't called but I'm feeling dreadful. I think it's the flu doing the rounds," she croaked.

"Oh no, you poor girl. Can I bring some medicine and food for you? Have you visited the doctor?"

"That's so sweet of you, but I managed to pick up some stuff on the way home. It's probably going to take a few days to work out. How did your visits go today?"

"I'll spare you the detail. Logistically all went off swimmingly, but nothing positive or negative from the families. Please look after yourself, Asami, you mean so much to me. I wish I could be there to take care of you."

"Richard, I'm not on my last legs, it's just a bit of flu. Let's keep in touch and good luck tomorrow."

The following twelve days were frenetic, both for Richard and Asami. Succumbing to work pressure, she forced herself out of her sick bed on the third day, managing to see Richard only four times during this period. On the first two occasions her condition remained the same but she declined Richard's offer to take her to the doctor, reiterating that it was just a dose of flu. The last two visits were brief as both of them were exhausted, but they promised to make up for lost time on their upcoming date on Friday evening.

So far, Richard and Hotaka had visited twenty-nine homes. Seven families weren't in at the time of the visits and six listed families, counting the Osaka family, no longer resided at their listed addresses. Of those six, they managed to secure three alternate addresses, which they intended to follow up. The current whereabouts of the remaining three families remained unknown.

"Let's hope those ones turn out to be irrelevant, Hotaka," said Richard. "I'm sorry about us having to work this weekend, but it seems we must if we want to see the seven families that weren't in."

"That's okay. I don't mind, this is a worthy cause and a bit of weekend work won't kill us. I'll see you at ten tomorrow morning at Nakamura-san's house."

* * * * *

Hearing the knock at the front door, Richard peeked at his watch and knew it was Asami, on time as always. He snatched up his overnight bag and rushed out to meet her.

"Hello, I don't think we've met before, my name is Richard, what is yours?" he said playfully, extending his right hand.

"Good evening, sir, I am Miss Nakamura from the 'anti-pestering' police squad. I have reason to believe you have been making a nuisance of yourself with the good residents of Seihi. Please will you accompany me down to the police station or do I need to handcuff you?"

They burst out laughing at their frivolous game, at the same time hugging.

"You do look beautiful, Asami, quite ravishing, I have to say. And you're looking well. I'm so happy."

"And you, my dear knight, are as handsome as ever. Shall we go?"

"Where are you taking us for dinner?"

"Guess."

"By the way you're asking me to guess, I think I know."

"It's time for an authentic traditional Japanese meal back at our foreshore restaurant."

"Fantastic. I loved the experience last time."

Beautiful memories flooded back as the gentle lapping sound of water reached Richard's ears. He paused for a while, staring at the colourful light reflections off the bay. Asami snuck in next to him, unobtrusively taking hold of his left arm.

"It's such an enchanting full moon. Fancy a little stroll in the gardens to work up an appetite?" she whispered in his ear.

He turned and tenderly kissed her. "Great minds think alike."

Holding hands, they ambled until they reached a bench.

"Let's sit a moment, Asami. This is a special spot for me. I sat here last time, and remember vividly the mesmerising effect of the night sky. For more reasons than one, it's a night I will always remember." They leaned in and kissed passionately.

"We had better make a move to our dinner before you get carried away," he said mischievously, nuzzling into her neck.

Asami responded with her trademark giggle.

"I'm so relieved, Asami, my love. There were moments over the last few days where I sensed a withdrawing by you, and it troubled me painfully."

She stopped walking and looked up into Richard's eyes, holding both his hands.

"Richard, I love you, I have never felt this way before, but I worry where our relationship is heading. My heart says one thing but my brain another. We come from enormously different cultures and our countries are simply too far apart ..." She left the sentence hanging.

"I know these are challenges, Asami, but we'll find a way round them. Let's keep the momentum of this magnificently romantic night going, please?"

"Of course." She stood on her toes, planting an affectionate peck on his cheek.

The following morning, he sneaked out of bed, trying not to disturb Asami. When he returned with her breakfast tray she still lay in the same position as when he left, her glossy dark hair, free from restraint, partially framing her serene face against the pristine white pillow. He leaned over and kissed her softly on the tip of her nose, lingering until the words of her subdued morning greeting danced slowly across her rosy lips.

"Our time is so limited, Asami. I wish I could skip the family visits this weekend, but I can't."

"No, you can't. There will be more families who are home only after hours, I'm afraid."

"Sometimes I feel like giving up. The family we're looking for could easily be one of the missing relocated families or may not even be one of the families on our list. It's very much a hit or miss affair."

"I know, but the family could also just as easily be one you have yet to interview. You must persevere and only when all avenues are exhausted can we in good conscience stop the search. Hang in there, Richard, your efforts could bring that all-important closure that some family has longed for these last fifty years. And, think of Martin."

"You're right, Asami."

* * * * *

Richard and Hotaka managed to see the seven missing families over the course of the weekend and then pushed on with other visits to Wednesday of the following week. By and large, events followed the same pattern as before—a few absent residents, a couple of relocated families, three Burma deaths, but frustratingly no eureka moment.

"How many families have we managed to meet so far, Hotaka?" asked Richard, after another long and exhausting day.

Downing his beer, pulling sheets of paper towards himself, Hotaka peered closely at the street map. "Thirty-eight, but, as you know, some were new families."

"I don't follow, what do you mean, new families?" asked Richard, rubbing his eyes and then his temples.

"Families who came later, well after 1942, families not on our list."

"Okay, sorry, I'm not concentrating that well, a bit tired and frustrated, I guess. Well, if we count the homes not yet visited plus the absent families still to see plus all the follow-ups, there's a way to go!"

"No question about it, probably another three to four weeks."

"I'm not sure I can survive that long," said Richard with a sigh, walking over to the fridge to grab two more beers. "I need to shoot back to South Africa for about two weeks to attend to some pressing matters. Will you be available to join me again when I return?"

"Sure."

"Listen, Hotaka, I have an idea. Why don't we mount large copies of the prayer flag and text translations with an appropriate message and Nakamura-san's contact details on wooden posts in highly visible areas outside the shrine? Maybe, just maybe, someone visiting the shrine will recognise the flag. We could do this before I leave."

Hotaka contemplated the suggestion, slugging back the rest of his beer. "I think it's a clever idea, nothing to lose and everything to gain. But we'll need to clear our plan with the senior priest."

"Understood. I also want to run the idea by Nakamura-san this evening. Right, that's it, enough work for the day, see you tomorrow at about ten. If we secure the priest's approval early tomorrow, we could have the posts up and mounted by the end of the day."

When Asami called a short while later, Richard updated her. "As you can hear, there's a way to go, probably three to four weeks of work. I can't carry on for that long without a return trip to South Africa." He then told her about his idea.

"That's a brilliant idea, Richard. Why didn't we think of that before?"

"Because you distract me, my sweet," he said teasingly. "Hotaka and I'll resume our searches when I return and I'll then also follow up on the relocations."

27

October 1997

John Matthews and Richard were more than pleased with the smooth closing of the Mantis acquisition before the mid-October target date. The board of directors had been reconstituted under the control of Three Rivers, the new executives were in office and staff had been brought up to speed on a need-to-know basis.

Richard decided it would be inappropriate for him to be at the meeting about to take place to give Mel the good news about her promotion; he would arrange to see her within a few days.

Mel walked past the ever-haughty receptionist who inspected her up and down as she headed for the main boardroom, unaware of the purpose of the meeting. Her heart skipped a beat and she became even more anxious when she saw the new CEO, the new CFO and Willem De Wet, the current COO. *Oh no, this can't be good, I'm going to lose my job.*

"Hello, Mel, I am Jason Tomlinson, the new CEO of Mantis, and this is Nonhla Radebe our new CFO, and you know Willem, of course."

She shook hands with Jason and Nonhla and acknowledged Willem, before taking a seat in the chair pulled out by Jason. She quickly opened the bottle of still water to get rid of her dry mouth, wondering how she would ever be able to repay the money owed to Richard.

Jason noticed the blood draining from Mel's tense face. Her nervous hand rubbing didn't go unnoticed either. "Mel, please relax, as you are about to hear, we are meeting to bring you only good news, at least I hope you will see it as good news."

Her colour started to return, her hands now still.

Jason continued. "As you already know, Mantis has been bought by an overseas buyer. Nothing much will change operationally. As we mentioned at the staff briefing, the previous senior management team will stay on for a while to help the new team settle in and to get to know the business."

For a fleeting moment Mel focused on the new CFO, wondering about the company's motive in taking the unusual step of employing a woman, never mind a black woman, in such a senior role.

"I believe you started with the company a long time ago and by all accounts you have been a loyal, hard-working, reliable and efficient senior staff member," said Jason. Mel smiled tentatively. "Mantis needs someone to take over from Willem as COO when he leaves at the end of twelve months and he has recommended you for the role."

She bit down on her quivering bottom lip, her tear-filled eyes flicking hurriedly from person to person, as she scrunched up the tissue in her hands. She never expected such an opportunity and didn't know what to say, looking again in disbelief, first at Willem, then Nonhla and finally at Jason. Each of them smiled. Her heart started to race again as did the many thoughts speeding through her mind. *Am I dreaming? Why me? Am I up to it? What will Simon say? Is this a new beginning?*

"My experience has been back-office management, how am I possibly going to be able to take over from you, Willem?" she asked rhetorically. Suddenly, feelings of inadequacy and insecurity overwhelmed her, and the floodgates opened.

Willem rushed to her side reassuringly. "Mel, you have all the qualities and attributes for this position and, on top of that, you are intimately familiar with the inner workings of the company. That which you do not yet know will soon become old hat as you shadow me over these next twelve months. I strongly suspect we won't need as long as that."

"I don't quite understand, am I to carry on with my current job, learning from you at the same time?" she asked with some concern and trepidation.

"No, no, not at all. If you accept our offer, you will immediately be promoted to senior general manager level with the title of Chief Operations Officer Designate, and you will shortly thereafter transfer into my area and shadow me in all my work activities. You will periodically be called on to provide some guidance and direction to the person taking over your current job."

She shook her head. "I can't believe this. This sort of break has never, never, ever come my way."

Whilst both Jason and Nonhla were concerned at the apparent cronyism when first told about the plans for Mel, those fears were now allayed. They liked what they saw and heard, and no longer doubted the sincerity of Willem's assessment.

"Would you now like to hear the good news?" Nonhla asked with a warm smile.

"What! More to come?" asked Mel, not for a second thinking about improved benefits.

"Of course, we cannot expect you to step up to such a senior role without upping your salary and other benefits."

Mel's grin spanned from ear to ear, and suddenly her natural beauty shone through.

"We take it, Mel, you are keen to give this a go, provided of course you're happy with your new package?" asked Jason expectantly.

"Of course, without any doubt," said Mel excitedly. "Thank you for the opportunity and thank you for entrusting me with this important role. I'm a long-serving member of the Mantis family, looking forward to spending many more years here—I hope. And, Willem, thank you for the recommendation," thinking she may have misjudged him in the past.

"Wonderful," said Jason. "Willem and I will leave you with Nonhla so she can work through the proposed new package with you."

*****

The sounds of up-tempo music became louder as Simon approached the house. Intrigued, he cautiously and quietly opened the front door, only to see his mother swaying rhythmically in time to the music blaring from her old radio, and a near-empty wine glass in her hand as she prepared supper. Dressed in her favourite skimpy denim shorts (which she hadn't worn for a long time), a cute summer top and sneakers, Mel sipped at her wine before seemingly toasting the balmy evening. The last time Simon witnessed his mother in such a festive mood was before the dreadful Drakensberg assault.

She shrieked with fright when his voice boomed out immediately behind her.

"And why all this noise and frivolity?"

Mel put her glass down, throwing her arms around her son, saying joyfully, "Oh, my son, my world has changed, you cannot possibly imagine what happened to me today. I'm floating on top of the world." She stepped back and danced a jig around the kitchen. "I'm also a little drunk, justifiably so, I have to say." She radiated a beauty and *joie de vivre* that Simon hadn't seen for many years.

Although Simon suspected that Richard's Mantis plan had materialised, he did not let on; instead he embraced his mother's excitement with genuine and deep-felt happiness.

He teased her. "So, what's his name, mother dear? Where did you meet him? What's he like? Are the two of you lovers yet?"

She played along. "His name begins with M and he does business nationally and internationally… he is successful and quite wealthy… he has been the subject of my attention for a long time but never noticed me before—and now, suddenly out of the blue, he wants me, saying he needs me. Are we lovers yet? No, but I expect we soon will be and, who knows, he might just be a keeper."

The two of them laughed and laughed, Mel pouring some more wine for herself, as well as a glass for Simon. "Come on, Mum, tell me what's happened. I've not seen you this happy for a long time. I can't wait to hear your news."

"Sit down, Si, and brace yourself for the big reveal, but only if you're a good lad," she said mischievously between the hiccups.

Sparing no detail, Mel told him about her meeting, about how frightened she became when summoned and then about everything that followed.

"I can't believe that Willem recommended me for the position, I thought he disliked m—certainly, he never showed any sympathy in the past. I think I pissed him off when I rejected his advances at the office Christmas party some years ago." She giggled again. "A bit of a jerk is Willem but, hey, now things are different."

"What do you mean?" asked Simon. "Will you give in to him if he makes another pass?" Mel knew Simon wasn't serious, giving the question a flippant, dismissive answer.

"You, young man, are sitting next to the Chief Operating Officer Designate of Mantis!" She clinked her glass against his, letting out a tiny burp and saying playfully, "Do you know what a big deal that is? Henceforth you shall treat me with the respect that my title demands."

He played along. "Of course, ma'am, whatever you say."

"And here comes the good news. Jason, the new CEO and Willem departed, leaving me with Nonhla, the incoming CFO so she could tell me about my new package." Mel paused deliberately for maximum effect.

"Come on, Mum, stop playing silly buggers, what did she say?"

"Si, you won't believe it, they more than doubled my salary, brought me onto the executive bonus scheme with a guaranteed minimum bonus equal to a full month's salary. I will also enjoy all the other executive perks, such as free medical insurance, company car with insurance, fuel and maintenance, free cell phone, extra leave and an entertainment allowance. What the hang has just happened to me?" asked Mel, not expecting an answer.

Simon was gobsmacked. When he eventually managed to find his voice, he turned to his mother, gently placing his hands on her shoulders, and looked into her sparkling eyes. "You deserve every bit of it, it's long overdue. You are a real beacon of hope in this messed up world. You are a true champ and you're my mum and I am proud of you."

Allowing the validation from her son to sink in, she said, "There's more."

"What!" said Simon, genuinely surprised.

"I have been offered shares in Mantis which, if past growth continues, will pay for themselves and be worth a small fortune after five years if I'm still at the company. And—wait for it—there is also an upfront non-compete payment of eighty thousand rand in return for agreeing not to join any competitor for three years after my employment with Mantis comes to an end."

"As deserving as you are, Mum, that's out of this world. I hope you accepted."

"Of course I did, there and then. Simon, our problems are over. Here's to new beginnings." They toasted each other.

"And we don't need help from the estate of bloody high and mighty Martin Simmons." She spat out the last words with vicious disdain.

Disappointment flooded Simon's face. *If only she knew.* "Okay, Mum, not now please; let's not spoil this wonderful, meaningful evening."

About to react, Mel caught herself in time. *This evening is about celebration.*

"By the way, I've been in touch with Richard to arrange a meeting so that I can share the good news with him and make plans to repay my debt. He suggested that we meet for lunch at the Country Club in Auckland Park. He wanted to meet tomorrow, anticipating no doubt that I needed help, but I told him I only wanted to share some good news. I can't meet tomorrow because..." She let her statement hang in the air, jumping off the couch for another jig around the room, singing, "because I'll be busy getting my company car. We've agreed to meet on Sunday."

Oh boy, an interesting meeting lies ahead. I wonder how Richard intends playing this one. I wish I could be there, but I want Mum to meet with him alone. I think he could be good for her.

"Are you sure this is only a business lunch, Mother?" Simon asked cheekily.

"Oh, Simon, you should know better. He seems like a helluva nice guy, but I'm not interested in any romantic liaison," she said unconvincingly.

*****

Simon walked his mother to her new car; she needed to leave immediately for her meeting with Richard, otherwise she would be late. The stylish cut of her natural blond hair and new tasteful summer outfit complemented her striking looks. She looked elegant and sophisticated. As he opened the car door for her, Simon caught a hint of subtle perfume.

"Have fun, and enjoy your lunch. By the way, I don't believe you're not interested in any sort of romantic relationship. Your stunning look today very much suggests otherwise. I don't think Richard will be able to take his eyes off you."

She smiled and gave him a wave of the hand as if to dismiss his last statement.

Mel took a short cut through the suburbs, enjoying the blooming jacarandas. *A week ago, I would never have dreamed of doing this, driving in a new car through the northern suburbs to have lunch at the Country Club.*

She parked under a leafy tree behind the squash courts, shielding her car from the burning overhead sun. Richard, waiting at the main entrance of the clubhouse, noticed the approaching figure in the distance. At first he seemed unsure that it was Mel, then he waved, evidently recognising her. She looked different from when he met her some weeks ago; although back then he did observe that under all the angst and depression, a gorgeous young woman hid herself. *It's hard to imagine that not so long ago she was on the verge of a nervous breakdown, looking quite emaciated.*

Richard extended his hand in greeting, thinking that a hug or a peck on the cheek would be too familiar. Ignoring his hand, Mel presented first her one cheek and then the other. He obliged, with a fleeting kiss on each cheek.

"Hello, Mel, it's good to see you looking so well."

They ambled through the exquisitely decorated clubhouse to an outside table overlooking the vibrant blossoms and manicured lawns stretching towards and around the cricket field. He ordered a gin and tonic for himself. "Well, Sundays should be relaxing time, so why not; the same for me, thank you," said Mel.

They took their time over their prelunch drink, managing to navigate their way through some initial stilted conversation.

"Well, well, well, out with it, Mel, let's hear your good news."

She hesitated, unsure where to start. "I still can't believe what has happened. As you know, not long ago my world crumbled. I hit rock bottom and life was not worth living. You came along in the nick of time, saving me from a fate I cannot now bear to think about. Richard, I am eternally grateful for your help and, of course, I am so proud that Simon had the courage to knock on your door." She leaned over and squeezed his upper arm. "This week, Mantis announced a change of ownership, apparently the De Wet family sold out to some European consortium, and then, totally unexpectedly, the new owners offered me the opportunity to take over from Willem De Wet as the COO in twelve months' time. It doesn't stop there… I have with immediate effect been promoted to senior general manager level with the title of Chief Operations Officer Designate and an out-of-this-world package."

Richard smiled knowingly. It would have been foolish for him to feign ignorance, given his appointment to the board of Mantis as a nonexecutive director, something of which Mel would, sooner or later, become aware.

"Why are you smiling like that, Richard? Damn it, has Simon let the cat out of the bag? I'll kill him, I wanted to tell you."

"Hold on, let Simon live a while longer. He hasn't told me any of this. I do however know about it because I attended a Mantis board meeting where this was discussed in advance of the offer to you."

Her posture stiffened and she pushed her drink away. "I'm confused. How come you're a Mantis board member? And is that in any way connected to your involvement with Simon and then with me shortly before my promotion?"

"Let me explain. My previous law firm, the one from which Simon holds a bursary, was, without any involvement from me, engaged by the European consortium to represent it in the Mantis acquisition. I had no knowledge of this consortium or its interest in Mantis. There is nothing odd or unusual in the retaining of my old firm, it specialises in this type of work and often represents foreign investors."

"Then how come you're on the board?"

"It's also not unusual for foreign investors to appoint someone to a board with deep local knowledge, often legal knowledge, who can be trusted. When you think about it, it makes sense. This consortium asked my firm to recommend someone to play such a role, and they put my name forward. They couldn't pick someone from within their own ranks as that would have been a conflict of interest. Although I sat in when the board discussed your offer, I recused myself from the discussion because of my involvement with you and Simon."

His explanation, given with conviction and sincerity, came across as plausible, seemingly satisfying Mel.

"I don't know you, Mel, except through Simon and our brief interaction some weeks back, but I must say, I am thrilled for you both, and I know this is a hundred and eighty degree turn of your lives. Congratulations, from what I know and from talk amongst the Mantis executives, you deserve it. Now, let's celebrate, I am famished. You can tell me more over lunch."

"Thank you, I do believe we have been given a chance for new beginnings. Before we go, when we met last time you said you wanted to share some thoughts with me about Simon and me turning our lives around. Do you still want to share?"

"I do, very much so, but the urgency has gone for the moment. Perhaps we can leave that for another time."

"I am intrigued but, yes, that's fine, let's do that some other time." She handed Richard an envelope as they moved through for lunch. "That's the money I owe you, Richard, thank you, most appreciated."

"Are you sure you want to pay it all now?"

"Yes, because of the events of the last few days, I can manage now."

Under The Oaks was a hive of gastronomic activity, complemented by a contagiously festive mood. As always, the food was scrumptious, and the service slick. Johannesburgers enjoyed their weekend lunches, often lingering well into the afternoon and, on occasions, into the evening. It would have been all too easy to be overcome by the convivial and inebriating lunchtime atmosphere, but both Richard and Mel remained on guard. Although they enjoyed each other's company, they hardly knew each other. In any event, their meeting was semiformal and not a social get together. Despite this, Mel did, more than once, out of the corner of her eye, catch Richard staring at her.

They were amongst the first to leave.

Richard waited until Mel drove off, giving him a last cheery wave. *What a lovely woman.*

28

November 1997

Asami picked up on the third ring. "Hi, Richard, still so frenetic?"

"Hello, Asami dear, I'm afraid so, and how are things your end?"

Her time continued to be dominated by her supervision of some PhD students and ongoing teaching commitments. Richard could hear she was down, struggling to meet all the demands on her time. Her many emails over the last fortnight gave much the same impression.

"I won't keep you, Asami, I can hear you're swamped. I wanted to say a quick hello, emails are so impersonal, and I wanted to let you know it will be at least another two weeks before I can come over again. I have let Hotaka know. I assume you've not heard from anyone in response to our posters outside the shrine?"

"Unfortunately, not. It's a long shot, so I'm not holding my breath."

"Have you managed to contact your Office of Foreign Affairs again about the notebook?"

"I have, a few times, and nothing, I'm afraid. Look, I'm sorry I can't chat longer but I'm drowning. Let's catch up later."

Worryingly, Richard once more sensed a cooling off; the intimate interactions from her seemed to be waning. When he had raised his concerns previously, she always offered the same excuse, blaming tiredness and pressure.

He allowed himself a moment to take stock. Simon and Mel were doing well, bringing Richard great satisfaction. He remained unsure though how eventually to reveal the truth about Simon's bursary and the Mantis acquisition and, more importantly, how to overcome Mel's dogged resistance to inheriting from Martin. He kept in touch with them at least once a week and planned to meet Simon shortly for a follow-up. Simon's studies were on track and Professor Markowitz appeared satisfied with his progress. Mel had, by all accounts, risen to the challenges of her new role.

The more Richard got to know her the more impressed he became. Many think-tank sessions followed at Mantis to plan the way forward. These were attended by the board members and executives, affording Richard the opportunity to interact with her in different situations. Not only did she own a deep knowledge of the Mantis operations, but she also demonstrated strategic astuteness.

He had met socially with Mel and Simon on two or three occasions in the last few weeks, aiming to strengthen his relationship with them. He saw Simon as an ally, and knew that to succeed in changing Mel's mind about Martin, this relationship had to be robust and capable of surviving the many challenges lying in wait.

He was fully aware that he had been burning the candle at both ends. Besides his involvement in the prayer flag initiative, which brought its own stresses, and his ongoing Mantis board responsibilities, which he took seriously, particularly at this early stage of the acquisition, Richard was almost consumed by sensitive and complicated negotiations to bring into Mantis a black empowerment shareholder. Over and above these demands on his time, he worked closely with John Matthews in trying to acquire one of the coal mines. He needed help, at least long enough for his depleted energy levels to recover, but unfortunately these matters were far too important and too personal to be effectively delegated.

A myriad of thoughts gate-crashed his mind, ranging from the mundane to the significant. Some left as quickly as they came, others lingered a while longer, and the more serious ones embedded themselves. He anxiously debated and reasoned whether to tell Mel about his involvement with Martin and his last wishes concerning her and Simon, or whether to continue indefinitely with the subterfuge in the hope that somehow Mel would come to her senses and make a claim against Martin's estate. He decided to talk this through with Simon later in the morning at their meeting.

Today Richard did not wander into his garden. Peering through the large window, the bright summer blossoms seemed to have lost their vibrancy and the early morning song from his feathered friends sounded more like a discordant din.

Arriving at the office, he met Simon in reception, early for their nine o'clock meeting.

"Hey, Simon, how're things? Come through, something to drink?"

"Hi, Richard, I'm a bit early, hope you don't mind. Coffee would be great."

No sooner had they plonked themselves down in the informal seating area in the corner of Richard's office, when the welcoming aroma of brewed coffee wafted in, preceding Olivia's arrival. She placed the coffee and rusks on the small table, noticing with concern the darker rings around Richard's eyes.

"Thanks, Liv. Well, Simon, how were the exams this last week—still cracking them?"

"Hopefully I've done well, time will tell."

"And your mum, how's she doing and how are things at home?"

"Fantastically. She seems to be thriving in her new position and, as you can imagine, totally consumed by it. You cannot begin to know the joy and happiness you've brought into our home."

Richard smiled. "That's kind of you to say so, but in truth your dear grandfather brought all this about."

"That may be so, but without your perseverance, neither my mum nor I would be where we are today. I do however have this burning desire to bring my grandfather back into the family, if you know what I mean. It's been too long. It's time to heal."

"I know exactly what you mean. I know your grandfather behaved abominably towards you and your mum but in the time I knew him, I saw a good man. He came to realise his prejudices and on his deathbed he showed deep remorse and regret. It's time to let bygones be bygones and to embrace the legacy left for you both. Perhaps it's time to come clean with your mother. What do you think? A sizeable fund awaits the two of you."

"I think whatever risks there are in telling Mum the truth, they're not going to change, regardless of when she learns the truth. I'm not sure how she should be told; somehow, I think it might be better coming from me. I don't mean to come across as greedy, Richard, but how much are we talking about?"

"Huge, Simon, more than you or your mum could ever contemplate." For a moment, Richard wondered whether to reveal to Simon the amount involved, but then decided to do so anyway. "Slightly in excess of five hundred million rand at last week's values."

Simon gulped, spilling his coffee and turning pale at the same time. He couldn't say anything, looking aghast at Richard.

"You'll need time to digest that, Simon. With some wise counsel and direction the two of you could grow that inheritance, not only for your own well being but also for the well being of your future families and others that you may want to help."

"I had no idea, my goodness! As you say, I need time to take this in."

"I can only imagine how your mum will react when she finds out about my subterfuge, but what will be will be. I'm still thinking about how best to respond to her when she learns the truth, so let's keep things the way they are."

"You mean, *our* subterfuge."

29

Asami insisted that on Richard's return to Japan, he spend the first night at her place before moving back to the rental apartment.

At the airport, she embraced and kissed him, but not in the same way as before, but rather like old friends meeting after a short separation. He felt awkward walking out of airport arrivals to her car. Conversation was stilted. Holding open the driver's door for Asami, it appeared to him that she deliberately avoided eye contact. She scratched in her handbag seemingly unable to find the car keys. When she did find them, she struggled to start the car, sighing loudly.

"Just wait, Asami, we need to sort this out. What is going on?" he asked exasperatedly.

She turned to him with a sad, pained expression creasing her face. When she took hold of one of his hands, he braced himself for the Dear John let-down.

"There isn't someone else and nor are you in any way to blame, Richard. I have not loved anyone the way I love you and I doubt I ever will. I've told you that before."

She couldn't, as hard as she tried, retain her composure and broke down, sobbing. It unsettled him even more to see Asami this way. He put his arms around her, pulling her head gently onto his shoulder. Her body shook from the uncontrollable weeping. When the crying stopped, she tenderly took his face in her hands, looking him in the eyes.

"You dear, sweet, sweet man. I know both of us will feel this pain for a long, long time." He could see her trying to control the tears. "When we first fell in love, I tried to fight it, knowing, at least in my head, that this day would eventually come. Sometimes, when my heart took control, I thought, I guess naively, that we could manage around the difficulties, but I now know differently. You sensed my doubts when you were last over here, but I relented, still hoping we could find our way forward. For us to continue on this journey will make our inevitable parting even more painful."

Richard knew, at least at the intellectual level, what she was driving at, having himself on occasions questioned the sustainability of their relationship, mainly because of their respective locations, work situations and cultural backgrounds.

"If I am honest, as I must be, I cannot see myself leaving Japan permanently to live elsewhere and nor do I see any hope of you relocating permanently to this part of the world." She paused, and then said, "Notwithstanding my time in England and my open mind, our cultural backgrounds are too different. I can't see any realistic possibility of us ever bridging the cultural divide. I'm so, so very sorry, dearest Richard. I still love you and I have no idea how I will get over you, but I must."

She leaned in and let her quivering lips linger on his cheek before she withdrew slowly and retrieved a tissue from her bag, wiping her nose.

Although Richard had an inkling that it might eventually come to this, the break-up still came as a huge shock. He sat there, motionless, staring ahead. She waited, not saying a word.

After a protracted silence, he spoke, slowly, deliberately and softly. "I have often thought about our future and, yes, there have been times when I thought our bubble would one day burst, but I hoped and believed, as I tried to explain to you a while back, and still do for that matter, that somehow our love would overcome and prevail. Your breaking up with me is painful, and right now, unbearably so. Can't we try and find a way forward? Surely we can overcome the challenges. We are not the first couple from different cultures and different parts of the world to fall in love, there must be millions out there, like us, who have succeeded."

Richard looked at her imploringly. "Please, Asami, my love, let's not give up so soon. We are better than that, we are meant to be."

"Oh, Richard, I wish you were right. I have had similar thoughts and hopes, and I have spent many hours and many sleepless nights, especially in these last few weeks, challenging myself, but regrettably and sadly I have not been able to reach the point of believing that we can make it. I'm sorry, Richard, I must be honest with myself, as much as it pains me."

He wanted to fight back, he wanted to beg her, but he knew her mind was made up.

She started the car, driving off tentatively. "I do think it would be best all-round if I check into a hotel," he said.

"No, please don't, my neighbour is away again so I'll sleep there tonight and both of us will simply have to keep our front doors firmly locked," she said with a faint smile, seeking to lighten the moment. He smiled back weakly.

"Let's at least enjoy dinner out this evening, Richard, and talk about the good times. I know, and I am sure you do as well, that we have many good memories that will remain with us to the end of our days."

"Dinner would be nice, Asami."

* * * * *

Reminisce, they certainly did, and as the evening wore on, with generous quantities of wine being taken onboard, they did so in more and more detail. They laughed, they cried, they became serious and at times morose, and then they laughed some more. Despite the circumstances, it turned out to be an enjoyable evening and another memory for them to take away and look back on in years to come.

Back at the apartment block, they held onto each other, hesitatingly navigating the stairs to the first floor, trying to be as quiet as possible. They fell silent at the front door of Asami's neighbour and, as if rehearsed, turned to face each other. He pulled Asami towards him; she didn't resist. They kissed passionately, his hands sliding down and clasping her firm bottom. They pushed into each other, signalling their immediate desires.

"I want you, Asami, I need you," he whispered hopefully.

Her breathing was fast and gasping. "I know, Richard, and I want you too, but we dare not." She broke free. "I'm sorry, please understand, we cannot slip back to where we were. Believe me, it's taking all the willpower I can possibly muster not to let myself go."

She turned her back, retrieved keys from her bag and opened her neighbour's front door. She didn't turn around again or say anything further before closing the door.

The knocking on the front door brought him out of his deep slumber. He glanced at his watch, scrambling to slip on a pair of boxer shorts before opening the door.

Asami greeted him cheerily. "Late breakfast awaits, please follow me, kind sir."

"Kind sir will, as soon as he has put on some clothes, unless of course *madame* would like him to follow her as he is," he said with a hint of cheekiness. She smiled and waved her index finger at him. "Naughty, naughty!"

The spread on the small table beckoned him enticingly.

"You are a magician, Asami, what time did you surface to produce all this?"

"I hoped to sleep in after our late night, but no such luck. I woke up thirsty at about six o'clock and couldn't get back to sleep. You know what it's like when the mind goes into overdrive. And you, how did you sleep?"

"Dead to the world from the time my head hit the pillow until you started banging the door down," he lied. The airport scene had played painfully over and over in his mind, making it impossible to harness any decent sleep, despite his inebriated state.

"Come, sit down and eat. I'm famished," she said.

* * * * *

Hotaka was already waiting when Asami dropped Richard off at the rental apartment.

"Greetings, Hotaka, my friend, I have missed you. How are you?"

"Very well indeed, Richard. I trust all is well with you?"

"Life's been a bit hectic, but I am well, thank you and keen to push on with the rest of our visits. Come in for some coffee and a chat about our plans."

They decided to complete the visits to the addresses on the list before chasing the follow-ups, unless for some compelling reason an earlier visit became necessary.

Every day was a hard slog with Richard and Hotaka only taking a break on Sundays. The more they pushed on, the more disheartened Richard became. Other than reducing the size of their list, there were no positives or promising outcomes. Richard and Asami remained in contact by phone, she continuing to be engrossed in her work, probably because she figured it would be best for them to remain apart.

Twelve days on, as per their established routine, Hotaka arrived at the apartment at nine o'clock, ready for the day's visits.

"Morning, Hotaka, let's have a quick coffee, come in."

"Thank you. You'll be pleased to know that except for relocations, we have only seven families left from the original list to visit."

"I guess in a way that's progress, but is it really? We're no nearer our goal. I fear this is going to be a dead end. Damn it, how I wish I had the soldier's military notebook. I feel like giving up and forgetting about finding the family. I've tried my best, Martin can't expect more."

"I understand, Richard, but hang in there. I'll help you. Let's complete our list and then give ourselves ten days on the follow-ups. If by then we've not found the family, it's probably unlikely we ever will."

"Okay, let's push on."

Their first scheduled visit of the day was to the Hidaka family at the northern end of Seihi. Hidaka Arata invited them in. They declined refreshments, and then followed their usual routine of Richard expanding on Hotaka's introduction and asking questions and Hotaka doing the translating.

"Hidaka-san has this home been in your family or your wife's family for many years?" asked Richard.

"No, Mr Low, we moved in only last year, having bought the home from a Mrs Kobayashi. I believe it had been her family home for many generations."

"Do you know where Mrs Kobayashi lives now?"

"Yes, I have her address, it's not far from here. She's not young anymore and has therefore moved in with her son-in-law and daughter. Give me a moment to scratch around for the address. Feel free to walk in Mrs Kobayashi's exquisite garden, through that door," he said, pointing the way.

"Another follow-up, I'm afraid, Hotaka," exclaimed Richard.

Both Richard and Hotaka gasped as they entered the tranquil and no doubt lovingly developed garden. "Hidaka-san did not exaggerate when he proclaimed the garden as exquisite," said Richard. They were immediately drawn to the magnificent mature cherry tree on the far side of the garden. "How many follow-ups do we now have?"

"They are mounting up, but let's stick to the plan," replied Hotaka, bending down suddenly to examine something near the base of the tree, partially obscured by a smattering of soil. He carefully wiped away the soil, exposing a wooden sign with part of it apparently broken off and some Japanese writing engraved into the remaining piece. Hotaka looked up at Richard and before saying anything, he inspected the broken sign more closely, this time staring at it for a long time.

"What's going on, Hotaka, why are you staring at that broken sign?"

Hotaka stood up, grabbing Richard's arms, just as Hidaka-san joined them. "I see you're admiring my lovely cherry tree. It is a marvel of nature when the blossoms are out."

Hotaka, unable to contain himself, addressed Hidaka-san directly. After a prolonged animated exchange, Hidaka-san left. Hotaka turned to Richard, quickly grabbing his right hand with both his hands, and saying with a huge smile, "Hidaka-san confirms what I guessed; the writing on this broken piece reads 'of love'. Hidaka-san has gone to fetch the other piece of the sign. He says he broke it accidentally when digging with a shovel."

"I don't understand your excitement, what's going on?"

"I said—" but before he could complete his sentence, Richard interrupted.

"I know what you said, Hotaka, I'm just not following."

"The words 'of love', don't you remember?"

Richard frowned and then suddenly, as if a light had come on, it dawned on him. "The prayer flag wording, 'Remember always, as I will, our tree of love'."

At that moment, Hidaka-san returned, gesturing at Hotaka with a small piece of wood in his hand. Hotaka took it and held it next to the broken sign. It matched perfectly. He beamed, then stood up and a further animated exchange followed between him and Hidaka-san.

Hotaka knelt down again, holding the pieces of wood in place. "Look here, Richard, can you see the writing on the broken piece?"

"I do, translate all of it for me."

"Hidaka-san agrees with me, the completed writing reads 'Remember always, as I will, our tree of love'."

"I can't believe what I'm hearing," said Richard. "Those are the precise words from the prayer flag. Surely this cannot be a coincidence? Hidaka-san, who placed that sign at the foot of the tree?"

Hidaka Arata smiled. "Mrs Kobayashi did. She told me the tree meant something very special for her and her late husband, so she had the sign made to commemorate their twenty-fifth wedding anniversary. I've been meaning to repair the sign because it belongs. As you can see, I haven't managed to get around to it yet."

"Thank you, Hidaka-san, thank you, you've been most helpful," said Richard with a smile and a bow.

On returning to Hotaka's car, Hotaka said, "I agree, this cannot be a coincidence, the evidence is overwhelming. Would you like to visit Mrs Kobayashi now?"

"I'm very tempted, but think I would like to first bring Miss Nakamura up to speed. May I give you a call this evening or tomorrow morning on the way forward?"

"Of course, I understand."

Richard delayed his call to Asami until her lunch break.

"Asami, I think we've found the soldier's family, right here in Seihi. I am overcome with excitement."

"Are you sure? How, when and where?"

"I would prefer to tell you face to face. I want us to share the moment together. Will you be able to come around to my place after work?"

"Nothing will stop me. I can't wait to be there. My last teaching session finishes at three thirty, so I should be with you before four thirty."

To kill time, Richard donned his running kit and set off on a tough run, up and down the surrounding hills. By the time he returned home, soaked in his own perspiration, he had just enough time for a quick shower before Asami knocked on the front door. She threw her arms around Richard's neck, giving him a joyous hug before stepping back. Her beautiful smile seemed to say it all. She gently nudged Richard out of the way, saying, "Come on, my knight, you can't keep this maiden in suspense, tell all, please, pretty please."

"And hello to you to, Asami. What can I offer you to drink, a beer or some wine or perhaps a cup of tea?"

"A beer will be good."

"Okay, Richard, enough drama… you have a beer, I have a beer, we're both comfortably seated, now out with it."

Richard gave her a blow-by-blow commentary on the events at Hidaka Arata's home. When he told her about the discovery of the broken wooden sign and the wiping away of the soil, Asami jumped up, doing a little dance on the spot and laughing. "Oh wow," she said, "this is one of the most exciting stories I have heard! Quickly, tell me the rest."

"I will if you let me." Richard then slowly rolled out the rest of the drama. "And there suddenly, we had Mrs Kobayashi's tree of love."

"This has to be the family. I agree, it cannot possibly be a coincidence," said Asami. "Why did you not go on to Mrs Kobayashi's new home to confirm the position?"

"I was sorely tempted, but realised I need to prepare for the handing over of the flag. I need to marshal my thoughts so I can say the right thing. There are so many things I want to say. I know you're swamped at work, but would you mind visiting first to check we have the right family?"

"Happily. I'll pop around there this afternoon after I leave here. This cannot wait."

A few hours later, she phoned an anxious Richard, waiting for news. "Richard, I have confirmation—this is the right family. Kobayashi Akemi, the soldier's widow, lives at the home of Tanaka Akio who is married to her daughter, Miyuki. The soldier's name was Kobayashi Takumi."

"I knew it the minute we found the sign by the cherry tree. I am so relieved. Is Mrs Kobayashi frail?"

"Not at all, she is sprightly, and according to her daughter in excellent health. When I showed her a photograph of the flag, she became quite emotional, understandably so. She is anxious for details about the flag's retrieval and its return to her. I told them briefly about you, without mentioning any detail concerning Martin, and said you are already here, ready to restore the flag to its rightful place and to explain its homecoming history."

"You need to guide me, Asami, if there are any particular cultural or traditional dos and don'ts that I need to respect or observe. I don't want to offend anyone. You will remember though, I told you that Martin wanted me to apologise on his behalf to the family."

"I do remember you telling me that and I also remember not understanding, and I still do not understand the need for an apology if Martin did nothing wrong. Why apologise and create unnecessary suspicion?"

Richard felt extremely uncomfortable, appreciating the merit in her scepticism. For a moment, he was tempted to forget about the apology altogether, but how then did he explain the intended inheritance for the family. There had to be some reason, however flimsy, for someone to leave a huge fund for the benefit of strangers. He could, of course, tell the truth, but then there will not be a snowball's chance in hell of the family accepting the funds. *Damn it, damn it, Martin, what were you thinking!*

Should he at least take Asami into his confidence and tell her the truth, he wondered? Did she read Martin's letter when looking for batteries in his briefcase? If she did, she would already know the truth. In any event, even if she left the letter unread, it didn't feel right at this eleventh hour to keep her in the dark. Hiding the truth from her would be unwise and dangerous, he figured, because it would put their relationship, whatever it might be, at risk if she found out that he had lied to her. Did he care? Yes, he did. He cared very much about their relationship, even though it was now destined to be a different kind of relationship.

He looked at her remorsefully. "I have not been open with you, Asami, about Martin and the death of the soldier. When we talked about this before, in the early days of our relationship, I found myself, as I do now, in a terrible position." He handed her a copy of Martin's letter. She read it slowly and then read it again, grimacing and shaking her head.

"I didn't want to tell the Kobayashi family the truth, and I still don't. Martin was a good man. Yes, he had faults, like all of us, and yes, he made mistakes, like all of us, but he came to acknowledge these things and wanted to make good. I knew him for many years, and I knew him well. He and I were like family. There is no doubt in my mind about the genuineness of his contrition. He was an honourable man. He died exceptionally wealthy, leaving behind considerably more than many generations of his own family could ever use. Wanting to leave money to the Kobayashi family is not an attempt to buy his way out of his guilt or to buy forgiveness, but rather a genuine desire on his part to underpin his confession and his expression of sorrow with goodwill and something concrete and practical. He could easily have left the funds to any number of charitable causes or religious bodies. I don't want to tell the Kobayashi family the truth, even though Martin insisted that I do so. In my judgment, no good will come from such frankness and, I am sure, the Kobayashis will, if they know the truth, refuse to take the money."

"Should this not be their decision, on an informed basis, instead of yours, Richard? And why do you think Martin's wish that the truth be told should simply be ignored?"

"You don't understand, Asami, he was a good man and I want to protect and preserve his reputation and what he stood for. I want you to read something else."

He gave her a copy of Professor Johnson's opinion which attributed Martin's killing of the defenceless soldier to post-traumatic stress disorder.

"I don't doubt what you say about Martin or what Professor Johnson has said. Brutality and sheer barbarism during human conflicts are common and, I know, very often the product of post-traumatic disorder. I get all that, and I understand your feelings about hiding the truth, although I do not share them. I believe in telling the truth."

"Thank you, Asami, I needed you to understand why I delayed sharing the full story with you until now. I respect your contrary view, but all my instincts tell me that if I avoid the confession and the detail of how precisely Kobayashi Takumi died, the prospects of a good outcome with the Kobayashis are that much better."

"I can't tell you what to do or not to do, I can only give you advice and guidance. You must understand though, I cannot be a party to any deception. My conscience will not allow that."

She walked to the fridge and took out another beer for each of them.

"Thanks, Asami, I'm sorry that you have got caught up in my trustee problems. I think I need two meetings with the Kobayashi family, the first with you there for the handing over of the prayer flag, and the second without you present, so I can give some edited background about the flag's retrieval and offer a watered-down apology, as originally mentioned to you, and so I can tell them about the funds Martin has made available for them."

"Are you sure that's the way you want to handle this?"

"I am sure."

30

Richard and Asami were excited and nervous on their approach to Tanaka Akio's home for Richard's first meeting.

He hugged the masterfully crafted presentation box containing the flag, neatly folded in soft white paper.

Asami reached out and squeezed his upper arm gently. Richard acknowledged her kindness with a smile and slight nod of the head.

Tanaka Akio, Miyuki's husband, met them at the front door and invited them in. After removing their shoes, they were shown into a guest room where members of the family were already seated expectantly on *tatami* mats around a table almost at floor level. The tea and food laid out on the table were ready to be served. Tanaka Akio ushered Richard to a seat opposite and furthest from the entrance to the room, and then positioned Asami next to him.

Tanaka Akio introduced the family members: Kobayashi Akemi, the soldier's widow; Tanaka Miyuki, the daughter of the Kobayashi's and the wife of Tanaka Akio; the Tanaka's youngest daughter, Keiko and her husband Matsumoto Hitoshi; and the Tanaka's eldest daughter, Mizuki. Traditions and formalities were observed, so Richard didn't offer to shake hands with anyone; instead he bowed as coached by Asami before they came to the meeting.

After the serving of tea and refreshments, Asami spoke to the family in Japanese, apparently in a formal and solemn tone, and introduced Richard. He knew she intended a formal introduction to explain that he was a lawyer from South Africa, attending to the estate of a client and this involved giving effect to the client's will and other wishes concerning his estate, including the prayer flag. She also told him that she intended to inform the family that he had, on the directions of his late client, undertaken a lengthy, labyrinthine search for the family to whom the prayer flag belonged, and that after almost a year of intensive searching, he felt honoured to be in their home to return the flag.

During the introduction, Asami often mentioned Richard by name. When she did so, the family looked at him, nodding occasionally. She told them that he would not at this meeting detail the prayer flag's history since the death of the soldier, Takumi-sama, as Richard felt it would be more appropriate to do so at the separate meeting arranged for the following day.

A long pause followed Asami's introductory words which, judging by the reaction of the family, were appreciated.

"Over to you, Richard."

He spoke slowly and with reverence, allowing Asami time to translate. "Kobayashi-sama," he said, addressing the soldier's widow, "I am honoured and indeed privileged to meet with you and your family in this home on this deeply meaningful occasion. I know you have been hoping and waiting for this day for more than fifty-four years. I trust that I bring with me the closure and fulfilment you and your family have longed for." He paused and looked at each family member. "I have never been to war. I have often through the media come to know about human conflicts and the tragedies and pain they cause, not only for those directly involved, but also for many others, particularly family and friends. I can only imagine the pain, the emptiness and loss your family has suffered." Miyuki leaned over and placed a comforting arm around her mother who wiped the occasional tear from her cheek.

"As a fellow citizen of our world, I am sorry for all the loss, tragedy and pain caused by such conflicts, past and present, and I pray that one day everyone will live in peace and harmony."

He didn't know whether in Japanese culture it would be acceptable for him to get up from his seat and walk to Mrs Kobayashi, but at that moment it seemed the right thing to do. He sat down next to her, giving a deep and prolonged respectful bow, and said, "I am honoured to be able to return to you and your family, your late husband's prayer flag."

The soldier's widow took the box with shaking hands and when she made eye contact, Richard thought he could see a sparkle. She said, *"Osoreirimasu, osoreirimasu."*

Asami translated softly. "She says she is very grateful."

Akemi hugged the box against her chest, tilting her head down so that the side of her face rested on the box. Richard withdrew quietly, back to his seat next to Asami. Mrs Kobayashi took time to examine from different angles the craftsmanship of the box. There was silence in the room. Her watery eyes focused on Richard and then she spoke with obvious tenderness, allowing Asami to translate.

"How thoughtful of you to have this beautiful presentation box made. I am deeply touched by the intricate craftsmanship, and particularly by the scene of the couple embracing under a cherry tree. We know you did this freely and out of the goodness of your heart, and that's what makes it even more special." The occasional tear drop spilled from her eyes, rolling down her wrinkled cheeks. "You are the one who has honoured us. We will forever be grateful, and we will forever treasure this gift which I know houses and protects our prayer flag."

Struggling to her feet with help from her daughter, Mrs Kobayashi shuffled over to Richard. Asami nudged him gently with her elbow, whispering, "Stand up." Richard responded, waiting for Mrs Kobayashi to come to him. She bowed and he reciprocated in like fashion. Something then happened which took everyone by complete surprise. She stepped forward and hugged him, placing her head on his chest in an unprecedented display of public affection. She stepped back and looked at him again, repeating her profound thanks, *"Osoreirimasu, osoreirimasu,* Low-sama." She bowed and returned to her daughter who handed her the presentation box.

Asami said something to the family which Richard did not understand and then she began to leave, beckoning Richard to follow. When they were outside the house, she said, "I excused our further presence, making it known to the family that we did so out of respect for their privacy. I know they were grateful for our sensitivity."

Richard took her hand as they walked down the street to her car and then stopped to face her. "Asami, this has been one of the most touching and extraordinary and, may I say, meaningful experiences of my life. As I said in Tanaka Akio's home, I am truly honoured and privileged to have been part of this journey. I cannot thank you enough for your commitment, encouragement and hard work and I know, without you, this would not have been possible." Richard gave her a hug. "You're an amazing woman."

In the car Asami turned to Richard, with a deep frown. "That magnificent presentation box, with the cherry tree scene, must have taken even a skilled craftsman many weeks to make. How could you possibly have had it made so quickly, given that you found the family only a few days ago? I am perplexed."

"Sheer brilliance, Asami, sheer brilliance."

"Oh stop that nonsense, come, seriously now, how did you manage it?"

"I arranged for its crafting many months ago in anticipation of finding the family; some positive thinking, you might say."

"But how did you know to have the cherry tree scene depicted on the box?"

"I made an educated guess that the tree mentioned on the flag was a cherry tree."

* * * * *

"Goodbye, Richard, all the best for your meeting. I so wish you would tell the Kobayashi family the truth as Martin Simmons asked in his letter. You can still change your mind, you know."

"Believe me, Asami, I've wrestled with this for a long time, and again through the night, but I cannot do this to Martin. I'm going to follow my instincts."

He gave her an affectionate peck on the cheek and walked towards the house, dreading the time ahead. She shouted after him, "Remember, Keiko is fluent in English and will translate for you."

His arrival and welcome were much the same as the day before, except that Keiko not Asami sat next to him at the table. He also noticed a new face at the meeting, that of an elderly gentleman, of similar age as Akemi, seated next to her. Tanaka Akio introduced him. Keiko translated, as she did for the rest of the meeting.

"Mr Low, may I introduce Yamaguchi-sama, a close friend of the Kobayashi family and a compatriot of the late Kobayashi-sama. They were in the same military unit and he was badly wounded in the same firefight that resulted in the death of the late Kobayashi-sama."

This revelation came like a bolt out of the blue, requiring Richard to call on all his internal defence mechanisms built up over the years to remain calm and composed. *I am well and truly fucked!* He could not now possibly proceed with his planned narrative, not knowing whether Yamaguchi witnessed the killing of the soldier. Richard and Yamaguchi-sama bowed to each other in acknowledgement of their introduction.

Martin and Asami win. In a way, Richard felt a sense of relief, as if a heavy burden had been lifted from his shoulders.

"Kobayashi-sama, Yamaguchi-sama and other members of the Kobayashi family, I greet you with respect and I come in peace from the foot of the African continent. To the Kobayashi family, I say thank you for agreeing to this separate meeting. For me, and no doubt for all of you, the return of the prayer flag marked an exceptionally special occasion, an occasion that I did not want to detract from or spoil by talking about how the prayer flag came into my possession. I am sure you want to know the history of the flag since the passing of the late Kobayashi-sama. I am in a position to tell you."

No one except Richard and Keiko spoke. All eyes focused on him as he began to reveal what he knew.

"The prayer flag came to me from the late Martin Simmons. He served as a young soldier with the Allied Forces in Burma and took part in the battle where the late Kobayashi-sama sadly died, and it was he who took the prayer flag. On his deathbed Martin wrote me a letter, and I can do no better than to share with you relevant parts of it."

Still no one else spoke. All eyes were focused on him. He began to read the relevant extracts.

"My Dear Richard …

By the time you read this letter, I will have boarded my flight from the departure lounge of life and, hopefully, I will have landed in a good place. Thank you for all your support and encouragement and for your willingness to listen to my ramblings. I'm sure they must have been incoherent quite often.

We have said our goodbyes and all the good things that needed to be said, and so I will not dwell on these matters.

It's no secret that my estate is substantial … My earnest wish is that the trust I have created will be managed with the necessary passion, wisdom and shrewdness to ensure its objectives are met for generations to come. Sadly (very sadly) I no longer have a family for this legacy of mine.

You will know that you have impressed me enormously, not only in the way you handled the legal work for the Sangster Group, but also in all aspects of your life … I trust you absolutely … you have been like a son to me. I sincerely hope you will accept appointment as the lead trustee of my Trust. …

Besides trying to persuade you to give up your law firm interests, to take up the enormous and demanding trustee challenges, I also want to contextualise some aspects of my trust."

As Keiko continued to translate, Richard looked once again at the faces in the room and as far as he could tell, the Kobayashi family and Mr Yamaguchi were listening carefully. He didn't see any lack of interest; quite the contrary. He continued.

"Let me begin with the prayer flag. There are two areas in my life where I have been heavily burdened with regret and shame, and one of them relates to the prayer flag incident. In recent years the constant memory of this evil darkness in my life has all but driven me to suicide. It has haunted me day and night. The enormity of my disgrace made it impossible for me to seek counsel from anyone, even from you. I have tried repeatedly to put this behind me as one of those things that can and do happen in war, but to no avail.

I desperately want to make amends to the family of the Japanese soldier who owned this flag. I need to confess my guilt and say sorry. You see, I never did kill this man in the ordinary course of battle; I killed a defenceless man in cold blood. Not only did I brutally murder him, but as in victory I claimed the spoils—his prayer flag and his military notebook."

Richard interrupted his reading and said, "We have carried out extensive searches for Kobayashi-sama's military notebook and were, at one stage, hopeful of finding it, but it was not to be. I am sorry."

He resumed his reading.

"The battle (one of many) in the jungle was all but over. We had overwhelmed the enemy and mop-up operations were underway. I came across this badly wounded soldier, bleeding profusely. His rifle and grenades were lying a safe distance from him. I couldn't control myself and in a moment of inexplicable madness, I ran up to him

aggressively, not hiding my intent. He threw up his arms in obvious surrender; his eyes pleaded with me, and at that moment, instead of reaching out to him, I took my bayonet and butchered him. As if that was not enough, I then shot him many times. …

Please, please, Richard, I want you to trace the family of this soldier and to confess on my behalf. Return the prayer flag to them and tell them I am sorry. Tell them I carried this burden to my grave. Use whatever financial resources you need from my trust to provide for them and their families, so they will never want for anything. This must seem crass but believe me this is not conscience money or an attempt to buy my way out of perdition. No time remains for the easing of my guilt and this is the only practical thing I can do towards making amends."

No one stirred, no one said a word and Richard waited for them to take it in.

"Thank you for listening to me so patiently. I come, as you heard, as Martin Simmons' messenger, to tell all, to confess and to say sorry." As he said this, he bowed to each person in the room.

He didn't know what to make of the ominous silence. He waited worriedly for a horrified outburst, or even worse still, for the family to walk out.

"I know this must come as a shock to all of you. If you will excuse me, I'll leave to give you the privacy you no doubt need at this time and I'll return when convenient for you to talk about some other matters."

Eventually Akemi spoke. Keiko translated. "Thank you, Mr Low, perhaps you wouldn't mind returning at three o' clock this afternoon, that will give us time as a family to reflect."

Richard eased himself up off the floor, bowed respectfully to Mrs Kobayashi and left.

The hours dragged by. Richard expected the worst. The body language of the Kobayashi family had given nothing away. *How could they possibly accept Martin's apology? Maybe I should have been less explicit.*

After an uncomfortable few hours Richard returned to find that Mr Yamaguchi had left, but all the Kobayashi family members were still there. After he sat down in the same place as before, Mrs Kobayashi spoke. Richard expected an emotional and angry outburst.

Mrs Kobayashi made eye contact with Richard as she spoke, seemingly selecting her words carefully. Keiko translated once more. "Mr Low, you have spent considerable effort and time and money, no doubt, in finding us. My family and I are very, very grateful. We appreciate your openness in disclosing with honourable frankness the circumstances of my husband's death; circumstances which, if viewed in isolation, are horrific and unforgivable. This is the only account we have of how my husband died. Yamaguchi-sama couldn't tell us because he was not in the immediate vicinity and, as you heard, he too was wounded. Thank you for not attempting to hide the truth. We believe you when you say that Mr Simmons was a decent man, an honourable man, and a man who cared more about others than himself. We also believe you when you say war scarred him mentally. We know that war does terrible things to people regardless of whom they are or where they come from. War turns people into monsters and killing machines, capable of unimaginable atrocities. Those who are, or who are perceived to be, on the 'other side' are not seen as humans and become targets for abuse, torture, maiming and destruction. They are not seen as people but rather as the evil on the other side, to be subjected to the worst possible acts that humanity can conjure up. We understand."

Akemi bowed. After a short pause, she said, "We accept your friend's apology and we forgive him. I speak for everyone around this table."

Richard didn't bother wiping away the tears rolling down his cheeks. "Thank you, thank you very much, Kobayashi-sama. I believe that Mr Simmons' soul, wherever it may be, is now, at last, at peace."

Akemi spoke again. "We also do not see Mr Simmons' offer of financial support as some sort of attempt to ease or remove his guilt or to buy our forgiveness. We accept Mr Simmons made the offer with a pure motive."

For a moment, Richard doubted his hearing, but after digesting the good news, he became excited as it seemed that all Martin's wishes concerning the Kobayashi's were about to be realised.

Akemi carried on. "However, we cannot accept the financial support, it would not be the right thing to do."

Richard felt encouraged at the absence of an indignant rejection of Martin's offer and decided to leave the subject in abeyance. He would persevere over the weeks ahead, but first he wanted to take counsel from Asami.

* * * * *

He wandered up to the shrine after leaving the Kobayashi home, wanting to be somewhere spiritually sacred. He took his time, walking slowly through the holy grounds and visiting the shrine itself. He reflected on the meeting, almost disbelieving of the outcome. Akemi's words of understanding and forgiveness rang in his ears and the image of her serene face lingered before his eyes. He felt an overwhelming inner peace and immeasurable joy. *The truth has indeed set us free, Martin, you and me.*

Leaving through the *Torii,* he knew a return visit was unlikely, except perhaps to attend to formalities and legalities if the Kobayashis changed their mind about accepting Martin's financial offer. His memories of Asami and of the places she showed him would remain with him forever, but it would be painful to return. At an emotional level he couldn't understand the break-up, but knew he needed to find the strength to move on.

Asami left the office early, her teaching commitments over for the day. She rushed to his apartment, hoping to find him there. She knocked tentatively, expecting the worst. To her surprise, she could hear singing coming from inside. Richard opened the door, greeting her with a smile. Unsure of what to make of this, she asked, "And?"

"And what?" he responded playfully.

"Oh come on, Richard, I'm dying to know. How did it go?"

Suddenly he became serious. "Come in, Asami, sit down." He sat next to her on the two-seater. "I told the truth, the full story, no half-truths, no hidden information, every little bit, just as Martin wished. I read out all the pertinent parts of his letter, with no glossing or spinning."

She looked at him in astonishment. "You did what! You were adamant about sticking with your original narrative. Why? What happened? Why the change of mind?"

"I had no choice. If I carried on with my original approach, I risked exposing myself and Martin to shame, ridicule and dishonour."

"Richard, stop speaking in damn riddles."

He told her what transpired with the introduction of Mr Yamaguchi. "I thought he had witnessed Takumi Kobayashi's killing and only found out otherwise after I told the truth."

She sat back smiling, turning more towards him, and pulled her legs up for greater comfort. "And? What reaction from the family?"

"With the benefit of hindsight, I'm so happy I told the truth. You were absolutely right. Things could so easily have gone the wrong way, all because of my pig-headedness." Richard gave Asami an unabridged version of what followed. "The Kobayashi's were most gracious in their forgiveness."

"How did they respond to the offer of financial support?"

"They turned it down but Akemi, on behalf of the family, said they did not regard the offer as crass or an attempt by Martin to ease a guilty conscience or to buy the family's forgiveness. They saw the offer as sincere and one made with a pure motive, but felt it would not be the right thing to do to accept the offer. Do you think their rejection of the gift might have been good manners, and that I should persevere?"

"I'm not sure, Richard, it could well be. Given the family's response and Akemi's apparent demeanour, there is nothing to lose by approaching Akemi again, but perhaps only after a week or so."

"Would you mind if I do this through you? I'll be back in South Africa and feel it would be more respectful to address this face-to-face. You know the background, so you will, I am sure, be able to engage with Akemi better than I could."

"How much money are we talking about, and how would the support to the family be handled, given Martin's wish that it should also extend to future generations?"

"A lot of money, Asami, probably about thirty million US dollars. The funds will be placed in a trust, controlled by reputable, independent professional trustees. They would manage the investment and distribution of the funds. I would be involved at the beginning in the setting up of the trust."

She sat bolt upright, letting out a soft whistle. "I had no idea."

They talked well into the evening, mainly about the Kobayashis and Martin, but also about their respective futures. Although they avoided the painful subject of their break-up, they again reminisced about the past, remembering with fondness all the good times. She also agreed to represent Richard in trying to persuade the Kobayashi family to accept the offered financial support. The more they discussed this the more optimistic they became about succeeding.

Except for the painful, heart-rending loss of Asami, his trip achieved much more than he had hoped for. Richard was ready to return home.

31

The unusual noise at the front door startled Mel; it sounded like someone was trying to force the door open. Although she thought it might be Simon, back from celebrating the academic year end, she remained alert. She tiptoed nervously to the kitchen, placing her dinner plate on the counter and arming herself with a large carving knife. She peeked cautiously at the front door from behind the perceived safety of the wall separating the kitchen from the dining area.

Hearing a key rattling in the door, Mel relaxed a little, thinking it could only be Simon, probably a little worse for wear. He deserved some playtime after all his hard work. She waited, still clenching the knife. Suddenly the door flung open, creaking on its hinges, and Simon staggered through, walking hesitatingly like a bewildered chameleon, uncertain whether to step forwards or backwards. He had a silly grin plastered on his face, seemingly trying to focus.

"Good party, Si?"

"For sure, a wee bit too much to drink," he said, slurring. He shuffled unsteadily towards Mel. "Come here, Mumsy dear, give your son a hug." He tried to hug her, but his wobbly legs failed him, and he collapsed onto the new leather couch. Mel smiled, ruffling his hair before returning to the kitchen to turn on the kettle.

"You need some strong coffee, young man," she said in a cheery voice. "I'm so pleased you've let your hair down a little. I know you are driven by the need to succeed and prove yourself, especially to Professor Markowitz and Richard, and that is good, but you must also play a little."

Slurping the black coffee, he said, "Mum, I've been thinking…" He hesitated, apparently trying to remember what he had been thinking about.

"Careful with that coffee, Simon, you're about to spill it over yourself," she said, waiting at the ready to grab the cup.

"I've been thinking about this for a long time and we need to deal with it; we must stop trying to run away from it."

"What on earth are you prattling on about? I think you need to sleep it off."

"I'm not prattling, Mum, I'm serious. I don't want to sleep, I want to talk about this, right here, right now," he insisted with a noticeable change in his tone. "I am deeply bothered, and we need to get a grip. It's about my grandfather, it's time we—"

Swiftly she cut across him mid-sentence, raising her voice sharply, giving Simon a no-nonsense stare. "Not that bullshit again, Simon, please stop it. I'm tired of repeating myself—there is no grandfather and there's nothing to talk about, nothing, *nada, nada, nada*, do you hear me, *nada*."

"It's not bullshit or any of the other ugly or nasty epithets you may want to attribute to the issue," he said, getting louder and becoming more assertive in his demeanour, whilst maintaining eye contact with Mel. "There's a lot to talk about. We, you and I, have been ugly in the way we rejected his many attempts at reconciliation. Damn it, we didn't even attend grandmother's funeral. I'm ashamed and so should you be. I cannot let this drift on, I will not let it drift on, it's time to fix things."

"We have nothing to fix, can't you get that through your thick head," she shouted, fast losing her temper. "I don't know what's happened to you. You're drunk and talking nonsense. You can carry on sitting here in your *dronkverdriet* state, but I've had enough, I'm off to bed."

With surprising agility, Simon pushed himself up from the couch and grabbed his mother by the arm. "You're not walking away from this. We're staying here until we've talked it through like two mature adults."

"Let me go," she hissed through clenched teeth. "You're hurting me." She wriggled free, continuing to spit out the words. "That swine means nothing to me. He ruined us. He has done nothing for us, absolutely nothing."

No longer able to control himself, Simon blurted out, "What the fuck do you mean he has done nothing for us. Where do you think the money is coming from for my bursary? Who do you think bought Mantis, so you and I could survive and enjoy a better life?"

"What did you say?"

Realising his *faux pas*, he said, "Nothing, we're not getting anywhere, I'm going to my room."

"No, no, no you're not. You wanted to talk about it, quote 'right here, right now' unquote, so let's talk. What did you say?" she asked emphatically.

Knowing he had let the cat out of the bag, he knew there was no point trying to escape his ill-timed outburst. "I asked you where you thought the money was coming from for my bursary and who you thought had bought Mantis."

"Meaning what?"

"The money for these things has come from my grandfather."

"I thought that's what I heard. I'm more than shocked by what you say. You and your friend Richard lied to me. I cannot believe it. I want to know the truth and the whole truth."

"I can't deal with this on my own, it goes far beyond me. I think we should sit down with Richard and he can put all this in the right perspective."

"Stuff Richard's damn perspective, Simon, I want you to tell me the truth. I'm going to be a laughing stock."

"Richard will tell you the truth. You need to hear the truth and maybe then, just maybe, you'll stop your pig-headedness."

Simon expected Richard to be annoyed when he told him in the morning about the showdown with his mother the night before, but to his surprise Richard seemed rather pleased that things had come to a head.

"Look, Simon, I agree, the three of us should meet. I would prefer to deal with this away from the office, so check with your mum if she can come to my home at about twelve tomorrow. I'll be back from church by then. I'll rustle up some snacks for a light lunch."

"Of course. I'll check with Mum and let you know."

The atmosphere in Mel and Simon's home continued to be frosty, to say the least, with Mel still livid about the previous night's revelations and doing her best to avoid speaking to Simon. After some persistent pushing, she eventually agreed to the meeting at Richard's home, making it abundantly clear that he and Richard had a lot to answer for.

Her anger spilled over into Sunday and Simon's attempt to lighten the mood with some small talk failed dismally.

"Come on, Mum, stop sulking, we'll sort all this out when we get to Richard's place."

"I'm not sulking. I am damn angry, and I have every right to be and I intend letting your friend Richard know, in no uncertain terms." She avoided eye contact with him, ostensibly focusing all her attention on the road ahead, and turned up the music to drown out Simon's efforts at a conversation.

On any other occasion she would have commented on Richard's exquisitely laid out garden which, given the time of year, portrayed a picture of melding colours. Not even the sound of gently trickling water and accompanying summer birdsong seemed to affect her seething mood.

Richard directed Mel and Simon along a neatly paved footpath that wound its way through the garden to a table near the swimming pool. The tropical plants amongst which the pool nestled had been cleverly positioned so as not to cut off the warmth of the sun. The *al fresco* set-up was inviting, but not to Mel in her current mood. A freshly laundered red and white checked tablecloth covered the lunch table.

While Richard busied himself with the drinks, Mel and Simon followed his suggestion and helped themselves to food. After plating up, Richard proposed a toast.

"Here's to your good health, your happiness and your future."

He held Mel's stare as she hesitatingly shared the toast. Mellow music played quietly in the background.

"Mel, I know you are angry with me and with Simon for our lack of transparency."

"Lack of transparency? What a joke. That's a soft spin if ever I've heard one. The two of you blatantly misled me, knowing how I felt about Martin Simmons."

Her face reddened as she spat out her admonishment. She lifted her drink and slugged back two large gulps, staring angrily, first at Richard, then at Simon.

Richard remained calm. "Call it what you will, but you need to look at the context. I could try to explain it to you but think it would be better if you read it for yourself."

He handed Mel and Simon a copy of Martin's letter, except for the introductory portion relating to Richard's appointment as trustee. Mel resisted, but Richard would have none of it; he shoved it into her hand until she grasped it.

"Please read each word with an open mind and keep the contents of the letter confidential. I don't mean to be rude or appear to be inhospitable but feel it would be best if I leave you to get on with it. Please help yourselves to more food and drinks. There's a good bottle of chardonnay in the ice bucket. I'll be in my study, Simon."

Richard filled in the time by responding to Asami's message from earlier in the day. She mentioned she wanted to share some good news. He missed her but had come to accept that she was right about the unsustainability of their relationship.

"Hello, Asami, how are you?"

"Well, thank you, Richard, and you?"

"All good here, although too busy, which includes some heavy emotional issues. In fact, as we speak, Simon and his mother are here at my house. Mel found out the truth and has confronted me. I have come clean with her and hope that by the time she leaves today, she will see things differently."

"Oh boy. I told you so. Rather you, than me, but now that she knows the truth, I think it will be easier, although not too easy, for you to find a solution. I wish you luck. Hopefully my good news will brighten your day," she said enthusiastically, pausing for effect.

"Well, come on, Asami, don't keep me in suspense." He heard her giggle which, momentarily, triggered romantic memories to come flooding back.

"The Kobayashi family have agreed to accept Martin's generosity."

"That's absolutely damn fabulous! This has made my day. How did you manage that?"

"The Japanese way: slowly, patiently and with dignity. It has taken many meetings and discussions. This will change their lives, and the lives of those who come after them, forever. They are poor, and I have no doubt they will use the money, not only to improve their own lives, but also to help many others who need help. They asked me to convey their deepest and most sincere thanks. I know they will contact you."

"I am truly humbled. I have learnt so much about truth, dignity and honour. Thank you, thank you for all your efforts. You will never know how much you have contributed to the changes in my life. I do wish things could be different between us, but I do understand. You are a beautiful, unique and exceptional person. I will always, always remember you." Richard paused, not for effect, but because he could feel his emotions overwhelming him.

"I'll be in touch shortly, Asami, about setting up the trust for the Kobayashi family. I'm not sure yet in which jurisdiction to do this."

"You are a very special person, Richard, and never forget that. I too wish the relationship between us could have been different. Keep well, I look forward to hearing from you again."

He welcomed the intervening solitude after Asami's call; it allowed him time to compose himself. His sad reminiscing ended abruptly when Simon knocked on the study door.

"I am bowled over, Richard, I don't know what to say, except that I had no idea, and I am even more ashamed."

Richard placed a caring hand on Simon's shoulder. "Let's hear what your mum has to say."

Richard noticed the half-drunk bottle of chardonnay near Mel. He poured himself a glass of red wine after Simon declined a top-up.

"Have you found the family of the Japanese soldier, Richard?" she asked quietly.

"Yes, only recently."

"What happened?"

Richard summarised the events surrounding the search for the Kobayashi family, the return of the prayer flag, Martin's confession, their forgiveness and, eventually, the acceptance of the intended financial benefits. He spared no detail when telling them about the gracious forgiveness.

She sat quietly, mulling over the Kobayashi story. Neither Richard nor Simon said anything. She poured herself another glass of wine.

"Si, no more for you as you'll be driving us home," she said, with what appeared to them to be a resigned smile.

"If need be, I can arrange a taxi for you guys or, if you prefer, you are most welcome to stay here for the night."

"Thank you, Richard, let's see. Why did you not tell me the truth like you did for the Kobayashi family?" she asked with an expression of hurt.

"I thought the end justified the means. All the indications were that you would have frustrated help even for Simon, had you known the truth. I'm sure you will concede this. He needed help, otherwise it would have been the end of his university studies and you too needed help desperately. I always acted in what I perceived was best for the two of you, I did the decent and caring thing in all the circumstances."

"And what about my Mantis promotion? Was that also a mere subterfuge?" she asked with a slight sharpness.

"The Mantis acquisition served the dual purpose of acquiring a viable business for the black empowerment objectives of the trust and of creating an opportunity for your deserved advancement once the De Wets exited. By the way, Willem De Wet speaks highly of you and fully supports your promotion, as does the entire board of directors. You deserve it."

Another lingering silence. Richard and Simon waited for Mel to speak.

"I am overwhelmed… just so much to take in and process. I'm confused right now, but I do thank you for opening up. I need to take time to reflect on this."

At that moment Richard knew the battle with Mel was over. How could it not be, given Martin's sincere and carefully crafted letter and the unselfish forgiveness flowing from the Kobayashi family.

* * * * *

A week slipped by with no word from Mel, although Richard heard from Simon the following day before he left for an extended holiday with friends in Mozambique. He phoned to thank Richard for the positive outcome of the meeting, saying Mel had thought and talked a lot about all the issues and seemed to be coming around.

Although Richard wasn't too concerned about the lack of contact from Mel, he nevertheless decided to call her, thinking she might need further reassurance. He also wanted to follow through on building a good and trusting relationship with her.

Richard's call didn't come as a surprise. Mel responded courteously and pleasantly, even showing more than a formal interest in his invitation for lunch on Saturday at Sophia's in the Rosebank Mall, to have a catch-up, as he put it.

He left for lunch early, planning to find out whether Warwick Pinkstone was still running his war memorabilia shop in the Rosebank Mall. Surprisingly he found Pinkstone in his little shop. The bells and chimes hooked up to the front door noisily announced Richard's arrival.

"Hello, Mr Pinkstone, I see you're still doing business. How are you?"

"Who wants to know?" barked the little wizened old man in a raspy voice.

Richard extended his right hand. "Hello, I came in earlier this year, quite a few times in fact, looking for a Japanese military notebook."

The same old frayed scarf hung round Pinkstone's neck and he wore the same baggy trousers and patched jacket, despite the intense mid-summer heat. He dabbed at his snotty nose with a crumpled-up handkerchief as he approached Richard with a laboured shuffle.

"No, no, I haven't had anyone in here looking for a Japanese military notebook. No, no, that's nonsense. I would remember. But if you are interested, I happen to have one in stock. A bit on the expensive side, mind you, they are rare."

"What, what did you say?" Richard asked incredulously.

"Are you deaf, young man? I said I have a Japanese military notebook for sale. Are you interested in the notebook or not?"

"Where did you source it," asked Richard, disbelievingly.

"From a lady a few years ago. She said her boss had asked her to get rid of it. Apparently it came into his possession during the Burma Campaign."

"May I see it please?" asked Richard politely, struggling to curb his excitement.

Pinkstone retreated to the back of the store and rummaged through some boxes, stopping frequently to wipe his nose with the back of his hand. After ten minutes Richard started doubting the existence of the book.

As he headed to the door, a jubilant shout from Pinkstone stopped him dead in his tracks.

"Here it is, here it is! Oh boy, what a beauty, such good condition."

Richard rushed over, eagerly latching onto the book. He inspected it excitedly, wondering whether he had, almost by chance, found the late Mr Kobayashi's military notebook.

"Do you know how I could have the writing translated?" Richard asked. "I'm looking for a specific book and if I find it, I am willing to pay a good price."

"My dear sir, I can oblige. You see, I am fluent in Japanese. What in particular do you want translated?"

"At this point, only one thing," said Richard hurriedly. "I would like to know the name of the soldier to whom this book belonged."

Pinkstone looked at the book and without any hesitation said, "Kobayashi Takumi."

THE END

www.ingramcontent.com/pod-product-compliance
Ingram Content Group UK Ltd.
Pitfield, Milton Keynes, MK11 3LW, UK
UKHW041953190726
13854UKWH00005B/1940

9 781916 081932